Something inside Evee told her to move on. To go upstairs and shower as she'd proposed earlier.

Instead, she stood staring at him, neither saying a word.

Before she knew it, Evee sensed what almost felt like human hands push her closer to Lucien, seemingly without her consent. Suddenly, Evee found her lips on Lucien's, kissing him fiercely. His hands cupped the sides of her face and he returned the kiss, matching her ferocity.

The moment her lips touched Lucien's, Evee felt such a thirst overtake her, it was like every ounce of moisture in her body had been depleted, her body suddenly dehydrated. So much so she could have drunk the entire Mississippi River and would still be craving more.

His full lips, so delicious, succulent.

Lucien's mouth moved over her chin, down the side of her neck.

A moan escaped Evee's lips, and she whispered, "Don't let me go...don't."

Deborah LeBlanc is an award-winning, bestselling author and business owner from Lafayette, Louisiana. She is also a licensed death-scene investigator, a licensed private investigator and has been a paranormal investigator for over twenty years. Deborah is currently the house "clairsendium" for the upcoming paranormal-investigation television show *Through the Veil*.

She served four years as president of the Horror Writers Association, eight years as president of the Writers' Guild of Acadiana and two years as president of Mystery Writers of America's Southwest Chapter. In 2007, Deborah founded Literacy Inc., a nonprofit organization dedicated to fighting illiteracy in America's teens. Deborah also takes her passion for literacy and a powerful ability to motivate to high schools around the country.

For more information, visit deborahleblanc.com and literacyinc.com.

Books by Deborah LeBlanc

Harlequin Nocturne

The Wolven
The Fright Before Christmas
Witch's Hunger
The Witch's Thirst

THE WITCH'S THIRST

DEBORAH LEBLANC

Recycling programs
for this product may
not exist in your area.

ISBN-13: 978-0-373-14036-7

The Witch's Thirst

Copyright © 2017 by Deborah LeBlanc

Printed in U.S.A.

Dear Reader,

Thank you for choosing one of my books to add to your collection!

Ever since I was a little girl, I've been fascinated with witches, especially after watching *The Wizard of Oz*. The thought that there were actually good witches blew my mind. The idea for the Grimoire Trilogy came to me when I asked a what-if question... What if good and bad witches/sorcerers collide and the only one who can save both is human?

I hope you enjoy reading *The Witch's Thirst* as much as I enjoyed writing it! I'm working on the third novel in the Grimoire Trilogy, *Witch's Passion*, and man-oh-man, does all hell break loose!

Feel free to find out more at deborahleblanc.com.

Deborah

My heartfelt thanks to Rich, Meme and Roe—
you help make so much happen!

Chapter 1

Evette—Evee—François watched as black and pus-yellow liquid flowed from Bailey's arm when Daven clawed through it. Both were Nosferatu and hell-bent on destroying each other. Aside from Bailey and Daven, six more Nosferatu had paired off, each viciously attacking the other. Her head captain, Pierre, supposedly in charge of the two-hundred-plus Nosferatu they forced to remain in the catacombs and allowed out only for feedings, did his best to stop the fighting. He'd stretched his bulk of a body to its full eight feet, had morphed into his natural state—bald head with a large, throbbing vein that started at his forehead and then extended over the crown of his scalp like tree branches. His fangs, the longest and most lethal of all the teeth possessed by the Nosferatu within the catacombs, were bared. His hands had balled into fists. And when he shouted, the walls seemed to vibrate with the fierceness of his voice.

"Enough! As leader of this clan, I say enough! Return to your assigned spaces at once!"

Instead of listening to Pierre, more Nosferatu began to fight. They hissed and shrieked, and Evee let out a heavy sigh. She noticed that the Nosferatu who weren't fighting were either hiding behind a crypt or had rolled onto a grave shelf, seemingly content to watch, but not wanting to engage in any brawl.

"We've got to get them under control before they kill one another," Lucien Hyland said emphatically. He took hold of the two steel bars from a floor-to-ceiling gate that separated the outside world from the catacombs of St. John's Cathedral. He shook them, then pulled the thick chain and padlock that secured the gates. Neither gate nor padlock budged.

"Cousin, get your hands away from the bars—" Before Ronan Hyland could finish his warning, two Nosferatu slammed into the gate. Both reached for Lucien.

Lucien sprang backward, away from the gate, then looked from his cousin to Evee, who was leaning against a stone column, arms crossed over her chest.

"Why aren't you doing something?" Lucien asked Evee, his emerald green eyes ablaze with anger. "You're acting rather nonchalant over this ordeal. Why? Can't you see they're going to kill each other? Can't you see all the…blood?"

"No one's going to die—unless you stick your hands back there again," Evee said. "They're fighting, yes, but it's not to kill one another. It's out of boredom. They're not used to being cooped up at night."

Ronan, who Evee had learned was the more serious of the cousins who'd been assigned to her, shook his head. "I don't understand. The Nosferatu aren't senseless beings.

Don't they know that keeping them here is for their own protection?"

Evee tossed him an exhausted look. "Imagine a room full of children and a huge storm is blowing outside. The children know the storm is dangerous, but that doesn't stop them from getting antsy and squabbling with one another when they're forced to stay indoors."

Ronan cocked his head as if considering her words.

Lucien let out a huff of frustration.

Evee closed her eyes for a few seconds. She'd felt exhaustion before, but never to this degree. She wished she had the power to turn back time. Two weeks of time at least.

Two weeks ago, things had flowed normally in her life. Well, as normal as life went when you were the middle sister from a set of triplets, and the triplets happened to be witches. The fact that she and her sisters, Vivienne and Abigail, were responsible for the Originals, those being the Nosferatu, the Loup Garous and the Chenilles, twisted the definition of normal all the more. By human standards, of course.

Along with the Originals, throughout the centuries, sprouted their offshoots, like vampires, werewolves, and zombies, etc., each created from either crossbreeding, malicious intent by some sorcerer with a wicked streak, or possibly an off-the-radar, wayward coven. Fortunately, others were in charge of the netherworld offshoots.

Evee and her sisters only tended to the Originals. She and her sisters were known as a Triad, which were triplet witches born from a triplet witch. The first set had been born in the 1500s, somewhere in France. According to legend, the first Originals and the chaos that went with them occurred when the first set of triplets got pissed off at the men they were supposed to marry. Evidently, the night before the triplets were to wed, they found their betrothed fooling around with other women.

Women scorned, men be warned, Evee thought. She supposed that creed existed even back in the 1500s because the anger of the first Triad played a huge part in creating the Originals. This caused the Elders from their sect, known as the Circle of Sisters, to punish the first Triad and the punishment carried to each generation of Triads that followed.

Evee thought cursing whole generations of Triads for something someone had done long ago was bullshit. She and her sisters had nothing to do with what had happened in the past by the first Triad. To her, it was simple. If a puppy peed on its owner's carpet, the owner might bop the pup on the snout with a newspaper to teach him "no." However, that didn't give that owner the right to go popping every pup born thereafter because the first one tinkled on a carpet.

Regardless, the creation of the Originals by her ancestors way back when must have been equated with peeing an ocean on a Persian rug, because Triads were still paying for the deed to this day. And there wasn't a damn thing she or her sisters could do about it.

So they'd simply lived with it. The Originals were assigned—Vivienne, or Viv as everyone called her, and the oldest of the three by ten minutes, took care of the Loup Garous; she, or Evee as she preferred being called, handled the Nosferatu; and Abigail, whom everyone called Gilly, managed the Chenilles. Once their routines had been established, life hadn't been so bad. Complex at times. But not terrible.

Until now.

For the last couple of weeks, they'd been stuck in a

nightmare that wouldn't go away, that no one seemed capable of waking them up from.

It wasn't like they hadn't run into issues with their broods before. Odd incidents were the norm when dealing with those from the netherworld. But for some reason, when the cousins—Lucien, Ronan, Gavril and Nikoli Hyland—arrived, all hell seemed to break loose.

They'd appeared at the Triad's front door, four extraordinarily handsome men, claiming to be cousins—although only two were with her right now—and swearing to protect the sisters and the Originals with their lives. They called themselves Benders and claimed their purpose was to save the Originals from monstrous creatures that hid in dimensional folds. They called the creatures Cartesians and said these were bent on annihilating the entire netherworld, especially the Originals and the Triad. With each netherworld creature's death, a Cartesian absorbed the powers of the creature it destroyed, then brought the essence of the kill to its leader, allowing the leader to grow stronger, which empowered him to create more Cartesians.

According to the Benders, the Cartesian leader meant to be the sole power of the netherworld, and once he had completed the task of absorbing the powers of every netherworld creature, humans were the next target. In essence, the Cartesians—specifically their leader—meant to control the very universe.

When Evee first heard the Benders' claims, she thought all four of them were a few cards short of a full deck. But in the days that followed their arrival, she'd seen much more than she needed to for truth to set in. Cartesians and the danger they presented were very, very real. She'd yet to see one of the creatures for herself, but her sisters Viv and Gilly had, and their descriptions had been all too vivid. Huge beings that appeared to be at least ten feet tall and had the expanse of body to match their height. They were covered with matted brown, gray and black fur, which hid thick scales like armor beneath it. Their teeth were all needlepoint incisors, and their claws were none like they'd seen before on any creature. At least four inches in length and razor-sharp. And the worst part was that they seemingly appeared out of nowhere.

The Cartesians' entry into this world came from rifts in the sky. The initial rifts were caused by natural disasters, odd cosmic alliances or an erred declaration. Their first experience with the Cartesians came after Viv, responsible for the Loup Garous, had told her brood in frustration that "she quit." She hadn't meant what she'd said, but exasperation could cause a person to throw caution to the wind. Once she'd uttered those two words, a small rift had occurred, and the Cartesians had gnawed, clawed and forced their hideous bodies through the opening and into this dimension.

So far, Viv had lost many Loup Garous to the Cartesians, and Gilly, some Chenilles. As if that wasn't bad enough, even stranger occurrences added to the Triad's terror. Something they couldn't understand, much less keep from occurring. Some of the Originals had gone missing. Simply vanished from their safe zones, from places that she and her sisters had controlled with border spells for years with great success. To date, Viv had nearly one hundred and fifty Loup Garous dead or missing; Evee had ten Nosferatu on the loose; and Gilly, fifteen missing Chenilles, plus two dead.

The missing Originals planted their current situation in the dirt of dire straits. Humans were now in danger. If they couldn't find the missing Originals and bring them over to the feeding grounds located at the North Compound in Algiers at their regular feeding time, which occurred in the wee hours of morning, they'd be seeking food elsewhere. They'd be looking at humans to satiate their hunger.

Adding to the dilemma, the wayward Nosferatu, Chenilles and Loup Garous were now open targets for the Cartesians. Evee had to find her brood so they could be watched over and kept safe from the enemy.

You would think that she and her sisters being witches could easily defuse the situation. But such wasn't the case. Along with the mayhem and confusion they faced, their powers and natural abilities like clairvoyance, channeling and mirroring seemed to be diminishing or worked haphazardly. Even the Triad's Elders, Arabella, Taka and Vanessa, appeared to be at a loss and utterly useless in helping them through the situation.

The only people they had to count on now were each other and the Benders, whom they'd decided to pair off with in order to cover more territory. Viv with Nikoli, she with Lucien and Ronan, and Gilly with Gavril.

So far the misfit teams seemed to be barely holding their own. At last count, Viv had located one of Evee's Nosferatu, whom she had Pierre fetch and return to the catacombs. Viv had also located at least twenty of her Loup Garous, whom she'd teleported to the North Compound, where Viv had them encamped.

Without question, the François sisters were torn in far too many directions. The missing Originals had to be located before humans were attacked, and the Originals who were already confined needed protection from the Cartesians. It didn't take a world of common sense to realize they couldn't be everywhere at once.

To aid in the matter, the Benders had established a

plan and built an electric field charged by their scabiors, the weapons they carried. The field, which the Cartesians couldn't penetrate, canopied each location where the Originals were kept. The North Compound for the Loup Garous, the Louis I Cemetery for the Chenilles, and, of course, the catacombs beneath St. John's Cathedral for the Nosferatu. The idea was to keep the Originals they now had safe within these electric domes, which would give each team time to search for the Originals who'd gone MIA.

The first time Evee witnessed the Benders' scabiors in action, she'd been nothing short of amazed. Alone, a scabior appeared toylike. A steel rod approximately eight inches long, its circumference about a half inch. A quarter-size bloodstone capped one end. But handled by a Bender, that which initially appeared benign turned into a weapon like no other Evee had ever witnessed.

A quick flip of the Bender's wrist, and the steel rod twirled between their fingers with a speed that seemed to defy the laws of physics. Once the scabior was charged and aimed at a Cartesian, it shot a bolt of electricity that pushed the monstrosity back into the rift, out of one dimension and into the next. The Benders' goal was to push the Cartesian back to as many dimensions as possible. The farther the dimension, the longer it took the Cartesian to find its way back.

With the electric dome charged, they could search for missing Nosferatu again.

It was dark outside, but barely, which meant she, Lucien and Ronan had plenty of time to search for the missing Nosferatu before feeding time arrived.

Suddenly, someone took Evee by the shoulders and gave her a gentle shake, breaking her reverie. It was Lucien.

"Evee, you have to do something to get the Nosferatu

under control," Lucien said. "I realize they're impatient and want freedom, but keeping them under the scabior dome's protection is crucial. Do something. A calming spell, anything that will keep them from destroying one another."

Evee took her time responding. She was overtaken by the depth of Lucien's green eyes bearing into hers, his shoulder-length hair the color of a black stallion's mane, his neatly trimmed beard and mustache that barely hid two prominent dimples that appeared whenever he smiled, something he definitely was not doing now. Evee guessed Lucien to be in his midthirties. He stood about six foot three and weighed maybe one seventy-five. Since she was only five foot seven, Evee had to look up at him, which she did feeling hypnotized. She couldn't help it. It made her feel like a slug, ogling him despite the fighting going on inside the catacombs, but it seemed beyond her control. She wanted nothing more than to breathe in Lucien's scent, a mixture of earth and musk doused by a fresh summer shower.

She was about to answer Lucien when Ronan suddenly appeared at her side. Another over-the-top hunk of a man who made it hard to concentrate on the task at hand.

"Evee, whatever malaise has overtaken you, you really need to snap out of it," Ronan said. "I know things may seem hopeless to you right now, but if the Nosferatu continue fighting this way, I'm concerned it will weaken the electric dome over the catacombs again."

"What makes you think that?" Lucien asked.

Ronan pointed to the dome. "Look."

Sure enough, the sparks of electricity that came from the four bloodstone-attached steel rods in four different directions had begun to flicker.

"We must calm them down," Ronan said.

Evee studied him for a moment. His collar-length black hair combed just so, his five o'clock shadow that accented a square jaw. His black eyes held such an intensity in them he could have melted a gold bar simply by staring at it and concentrating. Although he appeared a few years younger than Lucien, his height and build were similar to his cousin's. The biggest difference between the two men was Ronan's serious nature and the ease with which Lucien smiled.

Because there had been four cousins and three of the Triad, Evee had been paired with two Benders. Although they were two of the most handsome men she'd ever had the pleasure to meet, her initial intention had been to not allow attraction to enter into the serious business at hand. She'd never wanted to be drawn to either of the two men, although their good looks were second to none and each possessed unique qualities. But slowly and surely something other than the electric dome they'd created with their scabiors had begun to pulsate. Every time she looked at Lucien, she felt a jolt of electricity flow through her. When she studied Ronan, she felt sparks flutter through her, but not with the same intensity as she felt with Lucien.

Not that either mattered. They were men. They were human. She had no choice but to stay at arm's length.

Lucien pulled Evee away from the pillar she'd been leaning against and stood her upright, facing him.

"Please do something now, Evee," Lucien said.

Evee shook her head slightly as if just waking from a deep sleep. "I don't even know if my spells will work. Even my sisters seem to have problems with theirs."

"You have to at least try," Ronan said. "It's the only thing I can think of that's causing the dome to fade."

"What thing are you talking about?" Evee asked.

"The energy coming from the fighting Nosferatu."

"That can affect the dome?" she asked.

Ronan pointed to the arcs over the catacombs. "What else could it be?"

With a sigh of resignation, Evee went to the gates of the catacombs, pressed her body against it and raised her arms up by her sides and began to chant.

"Quiet now, ye creatures' mind,
Let thy actions turn from rage to kind.
See thy angst, fear and pain in vain,
So it is said.
So shall it be."

No sooner had Evee finished speaking the words than the Nosferatu that had been ripping into one another broke apart. They looked about, seemingly confused, as if unable to comprehend what they had just been doing. Each shuffled off to a corner and sat licking wounds, which immediately healed. A quiet hum soon filled the catacombs, except for an occasional impatient grumble from one of the Nosferatu.

At least the fighting had stopped.

"Why didn't you do that earlier?" Lucien asked.

"I—I don't know," Evee said. "I guess I was afraid it wouldn't work. Just another failure."

Lucien took hold of her chin with a thumb and forefinger and turned her head so she faced him. She had no choice but to look into his eyes.

"None of this is your fault. Whatever is causing the sporadic instabilities of your spells is not your fault. The Cartesians are powerful creatures, and their intention is to create havoc, to destroy the Originals and the Triad. Don't give up on your powers. Don't let the Cartesians see or feel your weakness, because that's what they'll focus on. We need to make sure you and your sisters stay safe, and the way you can help make that happen is to remain strong."

Evee nodded, reprimanding herself silently for having succumbed to complacency. There was no room for it when it came to protecting her Nosferatu, for it was her job to keep them safe.

Ronan nudged Lucien. "We need to strengthen the canopy again, then go hunting for more Nosferatu before it gets any later. It'll be feeding time before we know it, and the ones that are missing are going to be looking for food. That could mean attacks on humans if we don't find them and bring them into the fold."

Without a word, Lucien pulled his scabior from its sheath, which was attached to his belt, and Ronan followed suit. Together they did a quick flick of their wrists, twirled their scabiors around their fingers with lightning speed, then aimed them at the opposing poles. From the bloodstones that sat atop their scabiors shot a fierce bolt of lightning into the poles. They did the same with the remaining two poles, setting them alight until the catacombs lit up like a football field at game time.

Nosferatu scattered from the brilliance of the light, hiding behind crypts or crawling onto death shelves.

"Looks like that should hold them for now," Lucien said.

Evee nodded and then motioned Pierre, her overseer, to the catacomb gates. She told him what they had in mind, and that he was to keep tabs on all the Nosferatu within the catacombs just as he had been doing prior to them getting out of control.

Although Evee trusted Pierre with her life, she feared that if they didn't hurry and collect the missing Nosferatu and get all of them to the North Compound for feeding time, more fights would break out. Then they might lose the protection of the scabior canopy, and the Cartesians would find her Originals and annihilate them. Then it wouldn't be long before humans throughout the city would die senseless, useless deaths.

Evee feared that might be going on even now with her Nosferatu. She felt in her gut that somewhere in the city more deaths had already taken place. She could only hope she and her sisters wouldn't be next.

The Benders seemed very confident in their abilities and seemed to have a solid plan in place, or as solid as one might have in such a situation.

Evee, on the other hand, had not known this much fear—ever.

Chapter 2

Lucien didn't like the idea of leaving the catacombs to hunt for the missing Nosferatu. Although he knew that finding them was a task that had to be taken care of, he worried about the scabior dome flickering out again. If it happened once, it might happen again. Despite what he had told Evee about the energy generated by the squabbling Nosferatu making the dome less effective, Lucien wasn't convinced of that. That was just an assumption. He had no idea what had really caused the dome to weaken. The truth was that no Bender ever before had created a large-scale electrical barrier that locked in any creature. Having run out of options when so many Originals went missing, the cousins had found their task upon arriving in New Orleans more than overwhelming, and had opted to give it a try.

The first attempt had been at the North Compound to protect Viv's Loup Garous. When that had proven successful, he and his cousins had used the same technique to protect the Chenilles in the Louis I Cemetery, then here in the catacombs under St. John's Cathedral. The waning of power here concerned him greatly. Whatever hunting was needed must be done quickly and with specific directives so they wouldn't be chasing their tails as he felt they had been doing for the last day or two.

As Lucien considered a game plan, he noticed that Evee had moved closer and was now standing between him and Ronan.

"I know we have to look for the missing," Evee said. "But I want to apologize for zeroing out on the two of you earlier. All of the Nosferatu are my charge. You are here to help, which is much appreciated, and I had no business zoning out on you the way I did."

Lucien put a hand on Evee's shoulder and felt his pulse quicken when he touched her. Although Evee was dressed casually in jeans and a light blue T-shirt, she might as well have been dressed in a ball gown and tiara for all he cared. She was astonishingly beautiful no matter what she wore, and the simple act of touching her made his insides quiver.

"Don't beat yourself up over that," he said to her. "With all that's going on, I think you're handling yourself quite well. We just need to keep our heads about us." He gave her a soft smile. "For all you know, I might be the next one to 'zero out,' like you said, so I'll have to count on you and Ronan reining me back in." He squeezed her shoulder gently. "Don't worry, if you go to la-la land again, I promise to be there to bring you back."

He saw a flash of gratitude in Evee's eyes, and he felt his smile broaden. He forced himself to look away from her and down at his watch. "Time's pushing. If we're going to do any hunting for missing Nosferatu before feeding time, we'd better get started."

Evee nodded, took a step back and squared her shoulders. "If we're going to get this done," she said, "we'll need to split up. I know the two of you are here to protect me and my Originals, but look at what we're dealing with now. Too many missing Nosferatu, and humans, innocent humans, unwittingly waiting to be an Original's next meal. The closer we get to feeding time, the hungrier the Nosferatu will become. Humans will definitely be their target. So splitting up and hitting different directions only makes sense."

Lucien held up a hand. "No way are we splitting up."

"That would put you in too much danger," Ronan said, the frown on his face deepening.

"That would make us utterly irresponsible in our task to protect and defend," Lucien said.

Evee's eyes narrowed. "So are you saying that going off on your own, knowing there are loose Nosferatu, Loup Garous and Chenilles, any of which could slaughter you within seconds, is irresponsible?" she asked Lucien.

"Yes," Lucien said defiantly. "The bottom line is splitting more than we already have is ludicrous. We'd be asking for disaster."

"Yes," Ronan said. "Like we don't have enough to deal with now. I think we should stick together."

"Of course," Evee said. "Any wuss would want to play the safe card. Look, if the two of you would just stop yammering and get to searching, we might actually get the job done."

Lucien had to bite the inside of his cheeks to keep from laughing. If anything, Evee was not short on piss and vinegar once she had her mind set on something.

Ronan, on the other hand, evidently felt different. Appearing dumbstruck, he looked away, his cheeks turning a shade of pink.

"Look," Evee said to Lucien and Ronan. "I didn't mean for that to come out so…bitchy. I apologize."

Lucien looked up at her with a stoic expression. "Apology accepted."

With a sigh of relief, Evee looked from Ronan to Lucien. "We have to be levelheaded about this. I know what to look for where my Nosferatu are concerned. And believe me, as far as rifts are concerned, if I see so much as a deformed cloud in the sky, I'll be running to find you guys quicker than you can blink."

Lucien blew out a breath and glanced from Evee to Ronan. In his mind, Lucien knew Evee was right. They'd be able to cover much more ground if they separated. But his heart refused to let the words out of his mouth. He feared for her life and couldn't stand the thought of Evee heading anywhere alone.

Finally, Ronan said, "I hate to admit it, but what she's saying makes sense. I can head north into the Quarter and search there." He looked at Evee. "You'll have to tell me what to look for, though. Since it's already dark out, the Originals will have taken human form to blend in. They certainly won't have bald heads with thick veins and sharp fangs like the ones here. How do I tell what human is truly Nosferatu?"

"Good question," Evee said. "You can typically spot them easily if you know what you're looking for. I can usually locate a Nosferatu by scent. In your and Lucien's case, look for anyone standing about simply watching people, either an individual or a small crowd. If interest sparks, the Nosferatu will start following that person or crowd, keeping tabs on their every move. Also their skin will be much paler than the average human's. Some have eyes that are extremely light-sensitive, so they'll be wearing sunglasses inside buildings, even at night."

"What about clothing?" Lucien asked.

"No different than anyone else around them. Remember, they're trying to fit in and go unnoticed so they can scout out their next victim. And remember, too, the both of you are in as much danger as any human out there. I'm the only one who can control the Nosferatu. Don't confront them head-on or you might wind up being a meal. Should you find one, you need to come and get me or call for me. You can't fight them alone. They're too strong."

"This is sounding worse by the moment," Ronan said, sweeping his hands through his hair. "I've changed my mind. I really don't like the idea about splitting up."

"I know," Evee said. "And I agree that this plan is putting us a bit out there, raising the stakes and ratcheting up the danger, but think of what might happen if we don't do it. Let's at least give it a try. We can go in separate directions, hunt for half an hour, then meet back here in front of St. John's. That way we can report on what we've seen, then go our own ways again, each of us taking a different direction. At least that way we won't be apart for hours at a time. Thirty minutes, not that long, and if one of us doesn't show up, the others will know the direction to head to look for him…or her."

Lucien bit his bottom lip, rubbed a hand across his chin. "I don't think what I have to say about the plan matters. You're going to do what you want to do, right?"

Evee gave him a lopsided grin. "Pretty much."

"I figured as much," Ronan said.

"Fine, Ms. François, we'll do it your way," Lucien said with a half smile, which was the best he had to offer. He still thought the entire plan was a mistake. "Let's get it done and over with, then. Ronan, you head north to the Quarter. I'll take the riverbank west."

"Guess that leaves me with the east riverbank," Evee said.

"All right," Lucien said. "But what if something comes up and one of us needs help? We don't carry cell phones because they interfere with your spells and our scabiors. We have no way of contacting one another. You may have telepathic abilities with your sisters, but I don't have that ability with Ronan, Gavril or Nikoli. We have to find a method to reach out for help if we need it."

"Can you whistle?" Evee asked.

Lucien looked at her quizzically.

"Simple question," Evee said. "Can you whistle?"

Lucien pressed his bottom lip against his bottom teeth and let out a loud, ear-piercing whistle.

Evee clamped her hands over her ears until he finished, then said, "Sounds good to me." She turned to Ronan. "How about you?"

Without preamble, Ronan pressed two fingers against his bottom lip and let out a whistle just as shrill as Lucien's, if not louder.

"Good," Evee said. "If either one of you gets into trouble, whistle long and loud, and I'll come for you right away."

"No matter where we are?" Lucien asked. "Your hearing's that good?"

"Better than a hound's," Evee said.

"What about you?" Lucien asked. "What if you get into trouble? You plan to whistle, as well?"

Evee gave him a small smile. "Nope, sorry. I can't whistle my way out of a bucket. If I find my Nosferatu, I'll take care of them myself. I know how to deal with them. And if I run into a Cartesian, trust me, I'll run like hell and find you."

"You can't outrun a Cartesian," Lucien said. "If you see a rift appear, the best thing for you to do is hightail it into the nearest building. Stay out of sight. When the half hour mark comes around, and you don't show, we'll at least know what direction to head to find you."

"What exactly does a rift look like?"

Lucien thought for a moment, stroked his beard. "Think of it as a black wound, one blacker than black. You can see it even on a moonless, starless night. When it first appears it's like a black strip, a stitched wound in the sky. Then, as the Cartesians work their way through it, it begins to widen, like the stitches are being ripped away from the wound."

Evee shivered at the thought. "Believe me," she said. "Any of those ugly mothers won't have a chance to get a hand out of a rift before I haul ass. Don't worry. I'll keep my eyes peeled for anything odd in the sky."

"Doesn't sound like much of a plan," Lucien said.

"I agree," Ronan said, shifting nervously from foot to foot.

"Suppose you're so focused on finding the Nosferatu that you don't notice a Cartesian until it's halfway through a rift and reaching for you?" Lucien asked.

Evee gave him a stern look. "I'm not stupid."

"I in no way assumed or meant to imply you were," Lucien said, and arched a brow.

"I'll be alert," Evee said.

"But how can you look for your Nosferatu *and* watch for rifts overhead?" Ronan asked.

Evee scrubbed a hand over her face as if to wipe away frustration. "Remember, I have a slight advantage over the two of you. I can sense my Nosferatu. I'll keep my Spidey senses tuned to them while watching overhead."

It took another fifteen minutes before the three of them finally agreed to the divide-and-conquer method Evee had proposed.

When they finally left the catacombs, Ronan immediately headed for the French Quarter and Lucien started walking west, down the riverwalk. He watched Evee take off for the east bank of the river, watched her long, lean body stride with confidence, her shoulder-length black hair blown back by the wind. He remembered how her copper-colored eyes glinted with determination as they'd discussed their search-and-rescue plan. Lucien worried about her, more so now than ever.

Although the Triad looked similar, they weren't identical. Their eyes told different stories, as did their personalities. Evee always seemed to be the peacemaker, the one to handle things more logically than her sisters. She was also more apt to follow than lead. At this point, Lucien feared Evee had reached the point of desperation. That was why she had suggested they split up to search for her Nosferatu. He still felt like it was a big mistake.

As Lucien watched Evee's body fade off into the distance, his pace slowed. He continued heading west but kept looking back for her every few seconds. She continued heading east, and when he could barely make out her silhouette, Lucien suddenly felt like he was trudging through knee-deep mud.

He wasn't as worried about Ronan. His cousin was sharp and knew how to fight no matter what he faced. Ronan could easily take care of himself. But if a Cartesian attacked Evee, she'd be helpless. All the bravado she'd displayed in their conversation in the catacombs was one thing, but Lucien feared that dealing with a

Cartesian, especially the unreliability of a Cartesian, would be far beyond her powers.

As crucial as it was to find the missing Nosferatu before any humans were attacked, he felt it was a greater priority to keep the Cartesians away from the Originals and especially the Triad he was responsible for. He would never be able to live with himself if something happened to Evee.

Lucien trudged another block west before suddenly doing an about-face and beginning to head east, in Evee's direction.

Something about the woman drew him, called to him. Lucien couldn't quite put his finger on it, but he just knew that he had to take care of her above all else.

He picked up his pace, almost to a run, wanting to at least catch sight of Evee as soon as possible. He heard the calliope of a steamboat in the distance as it chugged along the river. He smelled burgers and fries, pizza and pralines, all of which made his stomach rumble. He couldn't remember the last time he'd eaten.

The farther he headed east, the more the crowds began to dissipate, and the cacophony of music, talking and laughter muted to a distant hum.

It felt like he'd walked five miles before he finally spotted Evee walking along the river's edge, just as she had been before. He noticed her gaze shifting from left to right, then up, obviously trying to sense her Nosferatu and watching for Cartesians at the same time.

Suddenly Evee came to an abrupt stop, and even from where Lucien stood he saw a quizzical look cross her face. She looked up again, turned her head to one side, and Lucien saw her mouth drop open. He followed her gaze and saw it—a widening rift in the sky right above her. A Cartesian was hanging out from it at the waist.

"Run!" Lucien shouted to Evee, then yanked his scabior out of its sheath.

The Cartesian, evidently hearing Lucien's yell, threw Lucien a piercing, evil look, narrowing its monstrous eyes.

Obviously determined to complete the task before it, the Cartesian turned away from Lucien, stuck one of its long, furry arms tipped with four-inch razor-sharp talons out of the rift, then lifted its arm up and out, aiming for Evee.

It wasn't hard to determine that Evee had seen the same, for she let out a heart-stopping scream, then took off running—right into the river.

Lucien charged his scabior and shot a bolt of lightning at the Cartesian, hitting it square in the head. It shrieked and flew backward into the rift, and Lucien heard a distinct pop that indicated he'd shoved the monstrosity into the next dimension. The rift remained open, however, and Lucien kept his scabior aimed there, pushing the Cartesian farther and farther back.

By the time Lucien was able to sound off two more pops, a more crucial sound reached his ear. Evee screaming for help.

Like a wild man, Lucien spun about on his heels, tracking the sound of her voice. Evee was still in the river, her head bobbing up and then going under the murky water. Each time her head poked out of the water, less and less of it appeared. She flailed her arms frantically, coughed and sputtered whenever her mouth broke the surface of the water.

Lucien was now stuck between a rock and a hard place. It was obvious Evee needed to be pulled out of the river, but the rift overhead was still open. If he ignored it and went after Evee, another Cartesian could easily make its way through the rift and take her.

Praying Evee could at least dog-paddle, Lucien put all his energy into the open rift and held on to his scabior with two hands. Although only seconds passed before he heard yet another explosive sound, which meant the Cartesian had been pushed into another dimension and the rift was finally closed, it felt like hours.

For the entire time he fought the Cartesian, all Lucien heard was Evee sputtering and screaming, "H-help! I c-can't swim!"

Chapter 3

Evee knew she was about to die. Panic-stricken, she paddled with hands and feet as hard as she could to stay afloat in the water, but it was only enough to get her nose and mouth to break surface—every once in a while. Each time she got sucked down below the surface, her mouth and nose filled with muddy silt from the river. Bad enough she couldn't breathe, it made her want to throw up. The few seconds she broke the surface of the water she spent coughing, gagging, trying to cøapture as much oxygen as she could before slipping helplessly downward.

She tried moving her arms like she'd seen swimmers do, out and down, kicking furiously, desperate to move up and forward. But her body refused to stay horizontal. It felt weighted with stones and determined to pull her feetfirst down into the depths of the Mississippi.

Evee didn't know what scared her more: the realization that she was about to drown or having seen the Cartesian take aim for her. Either way, she didn't plan to go quietly into any dark night. All she knew to do was to keep fighting, struggling, hoping.

For the life of her, Evee had no idea why she'd run into the river instead of in the opposite direction toward land and buildings. Surely she would have found a safe, dry place to hide. But something seemed to overtake her logical brain as soon as she saw the Cartesian's arm cock and aim. Her brain immediately screamed, RUN! And in that horrifying moment, the only direction that made sense to her was away.

Even as she bobbed up and then underwater, fighting for air, for her life, she still saw the gruesome face of the Cartesian in her mind's eye. Monstrously huge head covered with scraggly fur. Long, pointed ears that flapped over at the tips. A flat nose with no bridge, and nostrils that looked canyon-size. Eyes solid black, without pupils, and the size of saucers. And its teeth, the most horrible of all—each tooth a thick pointed incisor, a mouth equipped to shred and masticate anything it got hold of. She shuddered, thinking about it.

Trying to keep her wits about her and forcing herself to think of the water, the enemy trying to destroy her now, Evee kicked harder, moved her arms and hands overhead, then down one at a time, hoping for progress. She heard herself crying out for help, but the voice sounded like it came from far away and from someone else. She didn't know which was worse: drowning or being chewed to death by a Cartesian. Both carried the same weight of fear in her heart.

Exhaustion sat atop her like concrete blocks, forcing her lower into the water. She barely had the energy to care anymore.

As she sank lower into the dark water, Evee suddenly felt an arm wrap around her waist. Freaked, she twisted and turned, trying to get away. Opened her mouth to scream, only to have it fill with silt. She only had a few seconds of breath left in her lungs, and she used it to struggle all the more. The more she fought, the tighter the grip grew on her waist.

Finally, after what seemed to take an eternity, her head surfaced above water. Evee coughed, spat and gasped. When her lungs filled with air, her brain suddenly went into overdrive. She screamed, looking left and right, then up, searching for the Cartesian. Then the pressure around her waist registered once again, and all she saw in her mind's eye were long black talons ready to gut her from stem to stern. She screamed, whirling about, shoving her elbows backward, trying to pummel whatever held her.

"Stop, it's me, Evee. It's me."

Evee heard the voice, but her fear overrode recognition. She tried frantically to get away. "Let go, you ugly son of a bitch! Let me go!"

Arms wrapped around her waist tighter, and she felt her back pressed against...a man?

"It's me, Evee. Lucien. You're safe. It's okay. You're okay."

Startled, Evee turned her head sharply to the left. Lucien's face loomed beside her. A whimper of gratitude escaped her.

"The C-Cartesian," Evee said. "I—I...it..." Before any more words could form, she burst into tears that quickly turned into sobs, her body shivering against Lucien.

"I know," he said softly against her ear. "But you're safe now. I've got you. The Cartesian is gone. You're safe."

Evee put her arms around his neck, and Lucien swam closer to shore. Before long, he stood upright, leaned over and scooped her into his arms.

Without another thought, she wrapped both of her arms around his neck as he walked onto shore, and buried her face in the crook of his neck. She shivered as if she'd just been dunked into a tub of ice water.

"I'm taking you home so you can get into some dry clothes," Lucien said matter-of-factly.

"I—I can walk from here," Evee said through chattering teeth. She removed her arms from around his neck, and Lucien set her tentatively, seemingly reluctantly, on her feet.

The minute her feet touched the ground, it felt like every muscle in Evee's body suddenly turned to mush. She felt her body go limp, but before she hit the ground, Lucien had her back in his arms again.

Neither of them spoke as Lucien walked the long distance to her home. She clung to him once more, buried her face against his chest. She felt safe in his arms, as if the bulging muscles in his arms and chest, his soft breath against her hair and face, was the safest place on earth. He never once broke stride or panted for breath as he cradled her.

It wasn't until they'd crossed the threshold of the three-story Victorian that Evee and her sisters called home, which they'd inherited from their mother, that Lucien set her feet back on the ground. He held on to her arm, as if making sure she'd stand steady before fully releasing her.

Evee had no sooner leaned against the kitchen table to catch her breath than Hoot, her horned owl familiar, came flying into the room at full speed. He flew straight toward Lucien, swooped down onto his left shoulder and dug his talons into him.

"Let go of him now!" Evee shouted hoarsely at Hoot, shooing him away.

"He has no business being here, Evette. Make him leave," Hoot demanded.

Evee was grateful that she was the only one, besides the Elders, who could understand her familiar. Everyone else, including Lucien, only heard squawks, squeals and chirps. She shooed at Hoot again. He remained on Lucien's shoulder, talons digging in deeper until Lucien grimaced.

"You had no business bringing him here alone," Hoot said. "And look at you. Just look at you. Soaking wet. What did he do to you? Did he hurt you? Are you bleeding anywhere? Have you been bruised? Damaged?"

Unable to answer Hoot's questions without sounding like a loon, Evee said sternly, "No! Let go of him right this minute or I'll put you in your cage."

With a shrill shriek of anger, Hoot finally released Lucien's shoulder and took flight, leaving the kitchen and heading for the foyer.

"That's some pet you have there," Lucien said, rubbing the shoulder that Hoot had dug into.

Evee sighed. "He's my familiar and overprotective."

"What exactly does a familiar do? Does every witch have one?"

"Most of the witches I know do. Familiars are supposed to be our eyes and ears when we're not around. Their purpose is mostly to warn us of pending danger. Hoot does that for me, but he's also bossy and gets carried away at times."

Lucien gave her a small smile. "It's nice to know you have someone looking after you."

Their eyes locked for a moment, and Evee felt her knees grow weak. Not from exhaustion this time, but from desire. It felt like desire, anyway, but could have been the aftermath of shock from the Cartesian attack and near drowning. She shook her head slightly, trying to clear her thoughts. It was then she noticed that she and Lucien were both soaking wet and dripping water all over the floor.

"There's a shower down here if you'd like to use it," Evee said. She pointed past the kitchen toward the front of the house. "Just past the foyer and living area is a hallway. Take a left there and you'll find a bathroom. Last door on the right. I'll use the one on the second floor." As an afterthought she put a finger to her lips, then said, "I'm sorry I don't have any dry clothes to offer you. House full of women, you know. But there's a robe hanging on the back of the bathroom door that you're welcome to use. And back here…" Evee led him to a small room located at the far end of the kitchen near the back door. The room held a washer and dryer, utility sink and folding table. "You can just toss your clothes in the dryer while you shower."

"Thanks," Lucien said. "Dry sounds like a great plan. I'll wait to shower when I go back to the hotel."

"Y-you're going back to the hotel?" Evee asked, then mentally admonished herself for sounding so needy.

They stood so close together in the small room that she felt Lucien's breath as he spoke. Just being this close to him calmed her. She forgot about the wet clothes on her own body and the chill that had her shaking since Lucien pulled her from the river. His presence sent heat radiating through her body, chasing away any semblance of cold.

"If you don't mind," Lucien said, "I'll dry my shirt first so you can direct me on the dryer settings." He grinned. "Too many buttons and gadgets on that machine. Left to myself, I'd probably shrink my shirt down two sizes or nuke it into ashes."

"No problem," Evee said, then held her breath as Lu-

cien reached behind his head with both hands, grabbed
the back of his T-shirt and pulled it over his head.

Seeing him bare-chested with rippled abs and sculpted,
muscular arms stole what little breath Evee had left. She
gasped to refill her lungs. An embarrassing sound at such
a wrong time.

"Are you okay?" Lucien asked, his brow knitting.

"Huh?" Evee had been so absorbed with the sight and
scent of Lucien so close to her, she hadn't heard what
he'd said.

He handed her his wet shirt. "I asked if you were okay.
You gasped. I was concerned it might have come from
residual water from the river in your lungs."

"No, no, I'm fine." She took his shirt, threw it into
the dryer and set the dryer on its gentle cycle so the T
wouldn't shrink, then pressed the start button.

Evee glanced back at Lucien, trying not to focus on
his chest. "Your jeans are heavier material, so set the
dryer on time-dry for them." She pointed to the appropriate knob. "Both shirt and jeans will be dry before
you know it." Evee didn't tell him what cycle would be
best for his underwear. For all she knew, Lucien might
be flying commando. Either way, she felt confident he'd
figure it out.

Since the incident with the Cartesians and the near
drowning, Evee felt out of sorts and confused. She found
herself wanting, aching to feel the safety of Lucien. Just
like when he'd carried her home.

She felt heat radiating from Lucien's chest, which
was lightly matted with dark brown and black hair that
formed a narrow path to the top of his jeans.

Evee felt awkward as she watched him remove his
watch and set it on the washer. She had no business stand-

ing here. She had to shower and dress, as well, yet felt glued to where she stood. Unable to take her eyes off him.

Lucien turned to her, and she studied his strong, chiseled face, his eyes greener than the depths of the Pacific Ocean. An unspoken question flickered across his face, and Evee fumbled for something to say.

As Lucien stared at her, his eyes soft yet piercing, she said, "I—I'm sorry about earlier."

"Sorry about what? You didn't do anything wrong."

Evee glanced down for a few seconds before looking back up at him. "I forgot to say thank-you."

"For?"

"Saving my life. You know, from the Cartesian, from drowning."

"My pleasure, I assure you." Lucien tilted his head slightly. "If you don't mind me asking, don't you control the element of water?"

Evee nodded.

"Yet it frightens you. Why is that?"

She shook her head. "To tell you the truth, I don't know what the water thing is all about. I never did get it. I'm supposed to control the element of water, and I can, but from a distance. I don't know why I have such a fear of it. All I think about is drowning. Maybe it's a former life thing. Maybe I drowned in some other life and hold repressed memories about it. Then again, it could just be a weird phobia." She shrugged, feeling all the more uncomfortable. She was rambling like an idiot. She felt her cheeks grow warm. "I think not understanding it frightens me most of all."

"Life has a lot of unanswered questions," Lucien said, his voice low and husky.

She nodded and watched as his amazing eyes turned to a smoldering forest green.

"Whatever the reason," Evee said, trying to get her wits about her, "please accept my gratitude for your help."

"Accepted," Lucien said with a soft smile.

Something inside Evee told her to move on. To go upstairs and shower as she'd proposed earlier. Instead, she stood staring at him. Neither of them said a word.

Before she knew it, Evee sensed what almost felt like human hands push her closer to Lucien, seemingly without her consent. Suddenly, she found her lips on Lucien's, kissing him fiercely. His hands cupped the sides of her face and he returned the kiss, matching her ferocity.

The moment her lips touched Lucien's, Evee felt such a thirst overtake her, it was like every ounce of moisture in her body had been depleted, her body suddenly dehydrated. So much so she could have drunk the entire Mississippi River and would still be craving more.

His full lips, so delicious, succulent.

Lucien's lips moved over her chin, down the side of her neck.

A moan escaped Evee's lips, and she whispered, "Don't let me go...don't." She tangled her fingers into his collar-length black hair and pulled him closer.

Without warning and in one fell swoop, Lucien dropped his hands to Evee's waist, then lifted her up onto the dryer. He cupped the back of her head and kissed her long and deep.

Evee wrapped her arms around his neck, tangled her fingers into his hair. Her hair and clothes were still soaked from the river, but neither seemed to notice or care.

Lucien's hands moved at what felt like an infinitesimally slow pace, from her waist to the top of her thighs.

She groaned reflexively, and Lucien broke their kiss, studied her face, his eyes smoldering green, hypnotic.

Their eyes remained locked, their faces only a few inches away from each other. Lucien's eyes seemed to call on something deep inside her.

Locked in that moment, Lucien moved his hands to rest near the top of her thighs. He placed his thumbs between her legs, and she felt heat roll from her with the fierceness of a bonfire. He pressed his thumbs down a bit harder and began to rub his right thumb left and his left thumb right in the center of her legs.

Evee gasped loudly. She heard a loud humming in her ears and suspected the sound to be her own blood rushing hot and fast through her body. She arched her back, pushed her hips toward him.

Evee's mouth found Lucien's again and she took his tongue into her mouth and sucked hard as his thumbs moved faster, pressed harder against her.

Fire roared through her until Evee broke their kiss and arched her back, crying out, "Yes! Lucien, yes!" And in that moment a tsunami of all orgasms overtook her, washing away the fear that had held her captive earlier, shoving away every insecure thought, every inhibition she'd ever known. Shaking, she clung to Lucien once more.

"I need you," she said unabashedly. "I need you inside me."

Lucien took her face into his hands. "There's nothing I want more. You're one of the most beautiful women I've ever known, Evee. But taking you now, after all you've just gone through, would make me feel…" He smoothed her hair with a hand. "Not now. Trust me. We'll have our time together. When and if it's right. I promise."

With that, Lucien gently moved his hands from between her legs, wrapped them around her waist and lifted her off the dryer and placed her on the floor.

Evee wobbled once, and he caught her. He held on to her arms until her feet felt steady beneath her.

"Go now," Lucien whispered in her ear. "Shower. Get into some dry clothes. I'll let Ronan know what happened— except for this part, of course. We'll regroup."

Evee nodded slowly, then made her way clumsily back into the kitchen and through the foyer. As she headed up the stairs, her body still humming from Lucien's touch, she was grateful Hoot had made himself scarce. The last thing she needed was her familiar giving her a morality lesson and killing her buzz.

Three steps up the stairway Evee suddenly realized she'd stepped into a huge pile of shit. For it was then that she felt just how badly she wanted Lucien.

She walked slowly. Each step brought different emotions. The need for Lucien. God, he must think her a slut. She'd all but attacked him. All but begged him to screw her right there on top of the dryer.

Evee started to feel ashamed of herself. She should have shown more restraint. She had no business wanting any of the Benders. They were human, and her body hungered for more than a one-time fuck. That Evee could make happen at any time. But the Benders were different. Not only were they handsome, intelligent and powerful, but any woman would be stupid not to desire their heart along with their body.

And there lay her downfall.

No Triad shall marry or live intimately with a human.

The curse of the ages. If it was broken, they were assured it would cause the destruction of the world. That was the purpose for the mirrors inside their Grimoires. They replayed each day since they were created, scenes of Armageddon.

Except as of late. Over the last week, the mirrors inside

their Grimoires had stopped replaying the destruction of the world. All three showed nothing but swirls of gray smoke. And no one, including their Elders, had any idea as to why. When Evee stared at the mirror in her Grimoire, she felt hopelessness, helplessness. As far as any of them knew, the end of the world might already have begun.

Heaven help her if she had had sex with Lucien. It might have been the match that lit the fuse to a bomb that would blow the hell out of everything.

Herself included.

Chapter 4

Once his clothes were dry enough for him not to look like a drenched rat, Lucien quickly dressed while Evee was in the shower. He felt guilty for leaving without saying goodbye, but after the incident on the dryer, he thought it best to be on his way—quickly.

Lucien couldn't quite wrap his brain around what exactly had happened on Evee's dryer. One moment they were staring at each other, and the next her lips were on his. Her body so close to his sent more messages than he'd been able to sort through. He sensed passion pent up like a pressure cooker without a release valve inside her. So he'd provided one. Anything beyond that, and he'd have forever considered himself a schmuck. It had taken what felt like superhuman strength to control the need he had for her. Sending her off to shower while he waited for his clothes to at least half-ass dry, then leave, made him feel like chicken shit. But he figured better chicken shit than regret.

Instead of going to the hotel to shower as he'd told Evee he would, Lucien decided to scout for Ronan first and give him a heads-up on the Cartesian attack. With that in mind and visions of Evee burned into his brain, Lucien automatically reached for his left wrist to initiate the locator implanted in his watch. It took a second for him to realize it wasn't on his wrist.

Lucien stopped abruptly. "What the hell...?" Then he remembered. He'd taken it off at Evee's, right before tugging his shirt off and tossing it into the dryer. Why the hell did he remove it in the first place? The only time Lucien ever removed his watch was before stepping into the shower, even though the watch was waterproof.

Habit, he assumed. Clothes came off to shower, thus off with the watch. But now his butt was in a sling. He couldn't just walk back to Evee's after what had happened a short time ago. She might view his return as an excuse, get the wrong message. Not that she'd have gotten the message wrong. Not completely anyway.

Hell, who was he kidding? He was the one who'd have the problem if he had her alone right now. How was he going to get his watch back without it being awkward for either of them?

Nikoli, the oldest of his cousins, always reminded them of the Benders' mantra whenever they headed out on a mission. *Keep your dick in your pants and your mind on the mission.*

Normally that wasn't an issue for Lucien. Women flirted certainly, and, occasionally, he'd reciprocate. But that was as far as it went until the mission was over and all they'd gone there to accomplish had been completed.

This was different, though. The mission wasn't "normal," as it involved the Triad, whom they'd never protected before. It slid off the normal scale with the number of Cartesians they'd encountered so far and the Originals they had to find and protect. All new challenges for them.

As Evee was for him. What he felt for her whenever he was near her was far from normal. She was an extraordinary woman who always smelled like gardenias and daffodils. Her smile melted his heart, and her copper-colored eyes grew so bright when she got excited they could've lit up a quarter of the universe. Evee might have come across as the gentlest and quietest of the Triad, but she carried an innate strength that was unmistakable.

"Hey, what're you doing here?" a man asked, yanking Lucien from his thoughts. The voice came from behind Lucien, which caused him to clap a hand on the sheath of his scabior and spin about.

It was Ronan.

"Aren't you supposed to be hunting the west side of the riverbank?" Ronan asked.

Lucien slapped a hand over his thudding heart. "Man, don't you know better than to sneak up on me like that? I could've fried you."

Ronan gave him a lopsided grin. "Nah, your reflexes are too sharp for you to make that kind of mistake. So, what are you doing here?" He took a step closer to Lucien and sniffed. "And why do you smell like…fish and dirty gym socks?"

Uncomfortable with the number of people milling about Toulouse Street, Lucien motioned for Ronan to follow him into an alley just off Dauphine.

"What's going on?" Ronan asked. "You're acting weird."

In the muted silence of the alley, Lucien relayed to Ronan what he and Evee had gone through on the east bank. As he wound down the telling of the incident, even in the faint glow of streetlamps, Lucien saw Ronan's face turn beet red.

"I told you!" Ronan said. "Didn't I tell you it was a bad idea to split up? Evee could have died. On our watch, she could have died!"

"Shh," Lucien warned. "If your voice gets any louder, we'll start attracting a crowd."

"Shh, my ass," Ronan said. "The Cartesian, the water…" He ran a hand through his charcoal-black hair and started pacing in a tight circle. He stopped abruptly. "Where is Evee now?"

"Still at her home, as far as I know," Lucien said, shoving his hands in his pockets.

Ronan stepped closer to Lucien. "Hang on a minute. What were you doing on the east bank when you were supposed to be scouting the west?"

Lucien lowered his eyes for a second, then shrugged. "Instinct more than anything. I just got a sudden urge to follow her. I'm glad I did."

Ronan's eyes narrowed. "So you saved her from the Cartesian?"

"Yes."

"And from drowning?"

"Yes."

"Then what?" Ronan asked.

"What do you mean?"

"What happened after you pulled her out of the river?"

Lucien glanced away for a millisecond. "I carried her home. She was in shock, shivering. Couldn't stand on her own two feet."

"Then what?" Ronan asked, taking another step closer to Lucien. "What did you do when you brought her home? Just drop her at the front door? Make her tea? Get her a warm, fuzzy blanket to wrap around her shoulders?"

Lucien stared at the fury evident on his cousin's face. "What's with the twenty questions and why are you so pissed?"

Ronan turned away, folding his arms across his chest. "You broke protocol. It's not like things aren't screwed up enough here. Breaking protocol confuses things all the more."

Lucien frowned. "Protocol for what? Rescuing a woman from a Cartesian and then from drowning?"

"Splitting up in the first place," Ronan said, pounding a fist into the palm of his hand. "I could have saved her from that Cartesian and from the water."

A neon light suddenly went off in Lucien's head. It answered a lot of questions and made him sick to his stomach at the same time.

"Ronan?" Lucien said.

"What?" Ronan turned to face him, his expression roiling with anger.

"You like her, don't you?"

"Who? What the shit are you talking about?"

"Evee. You like her, don't you?"

Lucien saw Ronan's shoulders slowly relax from their defense position. He unfolded his arms and shoved his hands into his pants pockets. "Keep your dick in your pants and your mind on the mission," Ronan said, his voice low, resigned as he stated the Benders' mantra.

Even in the darkness of the alley, Lucien saw defeat dull his cousin's large black eyes. In all the years they'd known each other, not once had Lucien ever seen Ronan make such a fuss over a woman.

It broke Lucien's heart to see his cousin look so dejected. The words that came out of his own mouth milliseconds later rattled him to his core.

"If—if you're interested in Evee," Lucien said, "you

should let her know. Eventually this mission will come to an end and so will the Benders' mantra. So, good, bad or indifferent, at least Evee will know how you feel."

Ronan blew out a breath. "I can't. I'm not good with women the way you are."

"Well," Lucien said, "you can either let your shyness rule your heart or take a chance and tell her how you feel."

Ronan looked him in the eye. "And what if she rejects me?"

"Then she rejects you, and you'll move on," Lucien said. "But you'll never know where you stand or *if* you can stand beside her unless you try."

Ronan slowly nodded, yet remained silent.

Now that he'd offered his heart up for slaughter, Lucien squared his shoulders and said, "Let's make another run through the Quarter, and then we'll go to the hotel so I can shower."

Ronan nodded again, still silent.

Although he hadn't uttered a word, Lucien knew his cousin well enough to know he was pondering what they'd discussed about Evee. Even now he was probably formulating a plan.

With a heavy heart, Lucien steeled his jaw and reminded himself that he was a Bender. He had to find the missing Originals, watch for Cartesians and take care of the Triad. That was his purpose, his innate ability.

And that's all there was to it.

Squaring his shoulders, he began walking again, and Ronan followed him. They moved along the streets of the Quarter, Lucien using hand signals to guide Ronan in one direction or another.

Lucien looked over the faces of the people on the streets. Surveyed those who stood or sat in the bars and restaurants he strolled into and out of. He tried to remember the things Evee told them to watch for. The whiteness of the Nosferatu's skin, sunglasses in the dark because some couldn't tolerate any form of light. The problem was, after much searching, everyone started to look the same. Men—women—drunk.

After an hour of looking, they still hadn't turned up anything. Lucien tried thinking like a Nosferatu, one hungry, away from its clan, not knowing where its next meal would come from or how it would get back to the catacombs. Maybe the missing Nosferatu didn't want to connect with its clan again. Maybe it wanted the newly found freedom.

Lucien clearly remembered what Evee had said about the lost Nosferatu. If they weren't reunited with their clan for feeding time at the compound, they'd find something or someone to drain of blood.

Once again, putting himself in the shoes of a Nosferatu, Lucien knew he'd go to a place with the most noise, the biggest cluster of people it could find. Once it defined its prey, it'd probably lead them down some dark alley.

The one place Lucien knew that fit this compilation, with many offshoots and empty, dark alleys, was Bourbon Street. First they had to study the street with the beat—Bourbon. A place whose streets and sidewalks held the footsteps, vomit or piss of some of the most rich and famous people from around the world.

Following that logic, Lucien signaled Ronan to his side, told him his game plan. Then they parted, each man taking a side of Bourbon.

Just as Lucien expected, as they walked the crowded street, glancing down one alley after another, they were faced with large groups of people laughing, talking, cramming the bars. How were he and Ronan supposed to identify a Nosferatu in this cluster? It felt like an impossibility.

An idea struck Lucien and gave him pause as he allowed himself back into the mind-set of a Nosferatu. He knew it would find an alley to make the kill. Its prey might be found in the crowded streets, but the kill would be done in seclusion. Not public.

So what made sense to Lucien was to walk Royal Street, which ran parallel to Bourbon, then straight ahead, checking out every alley between Iberville to Esplanade, which crossed the parallel streets. He signaled for Ronan, told him to focus on the alleys between the streets he felt were the likeliest place a Nosferatu would strike. They'd walk in tandem as much as possible.

It wasn't until Lucien reached Barracks Street that something caught his attention. Sucking sounds, mouth to flesh. He looked across the street for Ronan and saw he was ahead, near Esplanade, dodging into yet another alley. He didn't want to call out to him and warn whatever he'd have to face in his own alley.

Lucien removed his scabior from its sheath and made his way toward the sounds he'd heard.

The only streetlights he had to work with were the weak streaks shooting from pole lamps on Royal and Bourbon. So the farther he walked down Barracks, the darker it became.

He heard a woman moan. "Oh, baby, yes! Put it in now!"

Lucien walked faster, zeroing in on the woman's voice. As he made his way toward the voice, a skinny, haggard-faced woman approached him, a hooker looking for a john, wanting a good time, a night's wage. He ignored her and had walked another half block when a drunk stumbled out of a side alley and bumped into him. The drunk threw a punch at Lucien as if he was the reason he'd misstepped.

Lucien dodged the fist and quickened his pace, his ear still tuned to the woman's voice.

"Oh, yeah, baby. Give me more. I want more."

By the sound of her voice, Lucien suspected she was already copulating, or was about to, with whatever man she'd picked up on the street. From where he stood, Lucien noticed the woman had her back to him in an alley that grew darker with every step he took.

Even in the darkness, however, Lucien noticed something white just over the woman's left shoulder. No question, it was a Nosferatu in midtransformation.

"What the f-fuck?" the woman said.

There was no mistaking the balding white head, the large vein that bulged from its forehead. Quite noticeable even in the dark.

Despite her slurred speech, a testament to heavy alcohol consumption, the woman evidently didn't care for what she witnessed, either. That white bald head, the cauliflower ears, the pointed fangs that should have been front teeth. Her screams, when they came, told Lucien she had suddenly turned stone-cold sober. But her cries for help were drowned out by revelers shouting, laughing, talking up in the Quarter, where the action was at an all-time high.

Lucien remembered what Evee said he should do if he spotted a Nosferatu. Yet he stood mesmerized, watching the Nosferatu's clawlike hands wrap around the woman's arm, holding tight. Its head tilted back, fangs showing, ready to strike.

Suddenly snapping out of his stupor, Lucien placed

two fingers against his bottom lip and let out a loud, shrill whistle.

So far, the only thing his whistle did was create a diversion for the creature. It turned to Lucien, hissed, then sank its fangs into the woman's throat. Its eyes rolled back in its head as it drank, sucked, consumed the meal before him. As much as he wanted to do something to save her, Lucien knew he was no match for a Nosferatu. He didn't have the weapons or the magic to send it to its knees.

In what felt like the blink of an eye, he found Ronan at his side.

"Son of a bitch," Ronan said, looking at the Nosferatu feasting on the woman.

"No shit," Lucien said.

Evidently irritated by the sound of Lucien and Ronan's voice, the Nosferatu abruptly threw the woman it had been feeding on to one side. And a second later, it stood right in front of the Benders, a hand on each of their throats.

"You stupid, little men. What were you whistling for? Your dinner or mine?" the creature said.

Its grip on Lucien's neck felt like a band of steel. Its fangs were exposed, twisted and yellow, and dripping with blood.

In a flash, Lucien did the only thing he knew to do. He kneed the Nosferatu in the groin. He didn't know if it would have the same effect as it would've had on a human, but he didn't care. In that moment, he had to do something.

Fortunately, Lucien's effort threw the creature off balance, which caused it to release Ronan and Lucien, giving them time to unsheathe their scabiors.

Although he had his weapon in hand, Lucien wasn't

quite sure what to do with it. There'd be no pushing the creature back into another dimension, because it belonged in this one.

When the Nosferatu regained its balance, it grabbed for Lucien again. Instinct kicked in, and Lucien used the bottom, steel part of the scabior and quickly skewered the Nosferatu's right eye. Lightning fast, as if on the same brain frequency, Ronan jumped into the fray and jabbed the steel rod of his scabior into the creature's left eye.

The figure wailed and screeched, clawing at its own face. Lucien knew the Nosferatu would heal itself soon enough, and its eyes would be as good as new or better than before they'd been destroyed.

Although pus ran from its eye sockets, Lucien and Ronan witnessed the regeneration process firsthand. The Nosferatu's eyes grew larger. Empty sockets at first; then new orbs appeared, black pupils. As suspected, the creature was regaining its sight.

Not knowing what else to do, Lucien prepared to attack the eyes again, once it got a bead on him. He held his breath, waiting.

Suddenly, the Nosferatu jerked backward as if bashed with a two-by-four from behind. It fell on its side onto the ground, and Lucien saw a long, ornate silver dagger jammed into its back and extending out of its chest, right through the heart.

Shocked, Lucien looked about in the darkness and spotted Pierre, Evee's head Nosferatu. He stood beside his felled creature, brushed his hands together and shook his head.

"Such a waste," Pierre said. "He should have followed orders and stayed with the group in the catacombs."

As Pierre spoke, Lucien heard the voices of people gathering at the intersection of Barracks and Bourbon.

The sound of sirens wailed in the distance, and in a flash, Pierre disappeared into the night, leaving Lucien and Ronan to face the crowd, the dead woman, the dead Nosferatu who, in death, had reverted to human form, and the police, whose sirens Lucien heard in the distance.

Lucien felt like a mouse stuck in a trap. He heard chatter coming from the crowd, each telling a different story, yet carrying the same theme. Lucien and Ronan were going to be fingered as murderers.

How the hell was he supposed to explain this to the police? And where was Evee? She'd specifically said to whistle for her and she'd come. Pierre had shown up instead. And although Lucien was grateful that he'd arrived in time to save them from the Nosferatu, it infuriated him that they'd been left alone to face the consequences of something and the someones they'd been sent here to protect.

Chapter 5

After showering, Evee threw on a pair of jeans, a maroon scoop-neck sweater and work boots. The entire time she'd stood under the water, Lucien had been on her mind. Although she really didn't want him to leave when he did, Lucien had been strong enough to stop things before they'd gotten out of hand. He would probably have blamed himself for taking advantage of her under duress—and he wouldn't have been that far off the mark. She'd been so petrified, had felt so vulnerable that more than anything she'd needed to feel strength and a sense of someone being in control. Lucien provided both in spades.

Knowing that didn't keep Evee's body from shivering as she went to her closet for a light jacket. The cold didn't cause her shivering. The need for Lucien did.

A short, loud screech had Evee spinning about on the balls of her feet and her heart racing up to her throat.

It was Hoot, her familiar, who stood perched at the foot of her bed frame.

Evee slapped a hand to her chest. "Don't do that!" she said. "You scared the hell out of me."

The horned owl's large eyes blinked slowly. "Good," he said.

Evee scowled at him. "What do you mean good?"

"At least I have your attention now."

"What the hell is your problem?" Evee asked, slipping on her jacket.

"Problem? I'm not the one with the problem, Evette François. You are." He blinked, turned his head around at a ninety-degree angle, then whipped it back in her direction.

"I'm fine," Evee said. "So how about you mind your own business for once?"

"That's not my job, and you know it."

Evee sighed and glared at Hoot. "Then spit it out. I've got things to tend to."

"Spit it out? Have you no brains left in your head?" Hoot asked. "You damn near get killed by one of those hideous monster things, jump into the river when you can't swim for shit, then not only lead but encourage that Bender guy to put his hands on your privates."

"I don't need you riding my ass about any of it right now." The last thing Evee wanted or needed was Hoot giving her some type of moral-code lesson when all she wanted to think about was Lucien. The musky, wet smell of him. How his hands had felt on her body. How even through her wet clothes she'd felt their heat burst into a furnace so hot it would have melted an eighteen-wheeler loaded with rebar.

"As your familiar, I'm allowed to ride whatever the

hell I want to protect you," Hoot declared. "You had no business being with him in that intimate way."

"How do you know there was any intimate anything?" Evee asked. "You disappeared. If you were so against me being with him, why didn't you do what you always do—stick your beak in where it doesn't belong?"

The owl let out a short, angry screech. "Unlike you, I've been out searching for the Nosferatu."

Evee put a hand on her hip. "And what do you think I've been doing? Playing solitaire all this time? I've been looking for them, too."

"You weren't while you were playing touchy, feely with that Bender."

"How can you make that claim when you weren't even here?" Evee asked.

"Oh, I was here," Hoot said, whipping his head about as if checking for intruders behind him.

He turned back to her. "Here just in time to see the games you two were playing."

"Oh, shut up," Evee said. "Nothing happened."

"From the groaning and moaning you were doing, that sure was some kind of nothing." Hoot chirped.

"Enough," Evee warned.

"What're you going to do, tape my beak shut?" Hoot asked. "Look here, missy. You've got a lot on your plate right now. You may be paired with him, which is a ridiculous idea in my opinion, but that doesn't give you the right to act like a harlot."

"Stop," Evee warned again. "Or I'll not only tape your beak but clip your wings."

Hoot squawked. "Liar, liar, pants on fire."

"What good are you as a familiar if all you're going to do is chew me out for every little thing I do?" Evee said.

"My job is to help you see straight in case you go

crosswise, and you, Ms. François, have gone crosswise big time."

"What part of 'enough' don't you understand?" Evee said, heading for the foyer.

"The part where I tell you humans are dying," Hoot said, and blinked twice. "And one of your Nosferatu."

Evee froze in place, and her body temperature suddenly felt like it had dropped twenty degrees. She turned slowly to face Hoot, who was now roosting on the stairs' newel post.

"What humans? Where? Which Nosferatu?" Evee asked, her questions coming out rapid-fire.

Hoot fluttered his wings as if ready to take flight, then settled back into place. "Two humans in Chalmette. One in the Quarter."

Evee felt her mouth drop open. She snapped it shut and swiped a hand over her face. "Chalmette? You mean the Nosferatu have gone beyond the city proper?" She leaned against the front door for support.

The bird gave her an affirmative squawk. "Not only that, it seems like some of the missing Loups, Nosferatu and Chenilles are attempting to form their own feeding pattern."

Evee held her breath as he continued.

"Some of the Nosferatu, in human form, of course, lured a couple out to one of the abandoned areas in the ninth ward. Sucked them dry, then left. The Loup must have been hiding in wait. As soon as the Nosferatu left, two Loups ran in and devoured the corpses, leaving nothing but bone, which, of course, the Chenille finished off. Every drop of marrow."

"You're sure about this?" Evee asked.

Hoot blinked twice. "Witnessed it myself."

"Any other witnesses?"

"For the woman in the Quarter, yes. Chalmette, no. Sooner or later somebody is going to find those bodies back there, though. Police are going to get involved. There won't be much of the bodies left to identify, but still…"

Evee felt tears suddenly burn against her eyelids. The Triad's problems had just multiplied a hundredfold. If the Originals had trekked all the way to Chalmette, they could, for all intents and purposes, travel into another state. That wasn't something she and her sisters had considered. The Originals had been cared for and fed for years in the same way, the same place. Dealing with that, the Triad used logic and assumed they'd remain close.

So much for logic.

"What about the Nosferatu?" Evee asked.

"Which one?"

Evee let out an exasperated sigh. "The one you said was dead, damn it."

"Don't be snapping at me," Hoot warned. "I'm just the messenger. The Nosferatu was Chank. You know, the redhead when he's in human form. He lured a drunk woman into an alley in the Quarter. Two of those Benders and Pierre stopped it, but not before the kill. The drunk woman didn't stand a chance. And if those Benders keep sticking their noses where they don't belong, they'll wind up sucked dry and chewed through to their fingernails. Lucky for them, Pierre came around and rescued them. Had to run a silver dagger through Chank. From the looks of things, no other way to stop him."

"Which Benders were involved?" Evee asked, worry suddenly flooding over her. She thought of Lucien.

"What does it matter which? They're all nosy busybodies who have no business here."

"Which ones?" She all but yelled the question this time.

Hoot screeched loudly. "How the hell do I know? The one with the short black hair. The quiet one. And the one you were playing house with earlier."

Ronan, Lucien, Evee thought, grateful they were safe, but still feeling like she needed to throw up.

She felt her brow knit and glared at her familiar. "If you knew...saw all this going on, why didn't you summon me?"

Hoot screeched loudly. "Summon you? I tried when I saw what was happening in Chalmette! But you were obviously too busy playing hussy with one of the Benders to hear me. That's why I had to come back here, hoping to find you!"

Evee rubbed her forehead, left the foyer and went into the kitchen. Feeling lost, she shrugged off her jacket and tossed it over a kitchen chair. She grabbed the kettle from the stove and without thinking brought it over to the sink and filled it with water. She placed the kettle on the counter, not bothering to bring it back to the stove for heating. Instead, she sat at the kitchen table and placed her hands over her face. Shook her head. Her world had become an impossible place in which to function, to live, to think.

"Evette, you have to listen to me," Hoot said.

Evee lowered her hands and looked up. Saw her familiar perched on top of the kitchen chair opposite her.

"I think I've heard enough from you for one day," Evee said, forcing back tears, fury and uncertainty.

"Too bad," Hoot said. "You're going to listen."

"I don't have to listen to shit. You're not my boss or my father." Evee scowled.

"No, but I am your familiar. Same thing. And you're going to listen." Not waiting for Evee to respond, Hoot hurried through his words. "You're heading off a cliff with that Bender. And it has little to do with sex and you know it. What you have to guard is your heart. You have Nosferatu missing, others killed, and the rest locked in the catacombs. You keep hunting for your missing Nosferatu, just like your sisters are looking for their Originals, and none of you are being successful at it. I don't know why you can't hone in on your brood like you usually do."

Evee swiped a strand of hair out of her eyes. "You think I don't know that? I feel like I've been running in circles and don't know how to straighten any of this out. And for your information, you horny-eared copperhead, don't you think if I could hone in on my brood I'd have done it days ago?"

"Okay, given, but you have to admit, this has gotten way out of hand. Much bigger than anyone suspected." The bird blinked and bobbed his head. "You're going to have to devise some other system to feed your brood."

"Another system?" Evee looked at her familiar with incredulity. "It took years to set up the one we have now."

"Maybe so, but how are you going to get the Nosferatu out of the catacombs and safely to the North Compound with so much going awry? They'll be out in the open. Have you forgotten about the Cartesians? And now humans are being killed. Police are going to get involved soon. You and your sisters could be found out."

"No shit."

"Just saying."

"So what's the answer?" Evee asked, feeling her cheeks heat with anger. "You're sitting on top of that chair spouting all that verbiage like you're high and mighty. Do you have an answer for these problems?"

Hoot turned his head until he nearly faced backward, then turned back to Evee and blinked without saying a word.

"I didn't think so." Evee scowled. "Don't you think that if I knew how to stop all this crap, how to get my Nosferatu back and turn things back to normal, I wouldn't have done it by now? And as far as the Benders are concerned, forget it. We've got to worry about humans now. *Dead* humans."

"Have you considered that what you're doing with that Bender might have something to do with what's happening?" Hoot asked.

"I didn't *do* anything with the Bender," Evee said, knowing she was bordering on a technicality. "Look, give me time to think, will you? Go. Leave me."

Hoot squawked, and without another word, left his perch on the kitchen chair and flew out of the room.

Evee dropped her head back into her hands. She felt guilty about having been here, in this house with Lucien, experiencing his touch, her explosive orgasm. All the while humans died by the Originals, and one of her Nosferatu had to be taken down.

Wearily, she got out of her chair and was about to head to the bathroom to wash her face when the back kitchen door opened with a bang.

Elvis, Gilly's ferret familiar, scurried into the house followed by Socrates, Viv's Bombay cat and familiar. Both ran around the kitchen table, claws clicking on the wooden floor. As they skittered to a stop near Evee, Hoot evidently decided to join the party because he swooped into the kitchen from wherever he'd been roosting moments earlier. He settled onto the kitchen counter and eyed the other two familiars. Within seconds, Hoot started shrieking and squawking at the top of his lungs. Elvis responded with loud chitters and chirps, and Socrates began to caterwaul so loudly it hurt Evee's ears.

No sooner had Evee put her hands over her ears than

Gilly and Viv hurried into the house behind their familiars. Viv closed the door behind them, and both turned to Evee wide-eyed.

Evee felt her heart skip a beat, fearing by the look on her sisters' faces that something more had come to torture them.

Dropping her hands from her ears, Evee yelled over the brash symphony of animals, "What's wrong?"

"What?" Gilly shouted, obviously having a difficult time hearing over the noise.

"What's wrong?" Evee asked again over the cacophony of animal noises.

Gilly looked over at Viv questioningly.

Frustrated, Evee held both hands out, glared at the familiars and shouted, "Y'all shut the hell up now!"

Elvis gave one last titter, Hoot a short squawk, and Socrates let out one innocent meow.

When all was quiet, Evee asked once more, "What's wrong?" She swiped a strand of wet hair out of her face. She hadn't had time to dry it after her shower.

"You haven't heard?" Viv asked.

Evee frowned.

"About the humans," Gilly said, then stomped a foot. "The *dead* ones, Evee."

"Yeah," Evee said, looking away. "Hoot filled me in a few minutes ago. He saw the whole thing."

Viv did a double take. "What? He saw it? What about Pierre and Chank?"

Evee nodded. "That, too."

"You mean your familiar saw all this going on and didn't summon you?" Gilly asked, putting a hand on her hip.

"He claims he tried, but I didn't hear him, didn't feel

him," Evee said. "I didn't know about the humans or Chank until Hoot came here to tell me."

Gilly eyed her. "How can you not pick up an emergency summons from your familiar? What were you doing while all that was going on? And why is your hair wet?"

"Shower," Evee said, feeling her cheeks flush. "Didn't have time to dry it." Before her sisters pummeled her with more questions, she shot out her own. "Why are the two of you here?" Aren't you supposed to be looking for Chenilles and Loup Garous?"

"We were," Gilly snapped. "Found out about the humans and Chank and have been racing around like fools trying to find you. Wanted to make sure that you knew and that you were okay. Is that a crime?"

"I didn't say it was," Evee said. "Why are you being so bitchy?"

Gilly held her arms out. "This isn't bitchy. It's pissed. We've been out there busting our humps and you've been here taking a shower."

Evee turned away from her sisters and went to the counter, picked up the kettle she'd filled with water earlier and headed for the stove. She didn't want to explain to them that she'd needed a shower after the whole Cartesian and river ordeal. She feared if she did, she'd spill the beans about Lucien, as well. As upset as they appeared now, even dropping a hint about her sexual encounter with Lucien, albeit one-sided, would have thrown both of her sisters into cardiac arrest.

"Well?" Viv said. "Explanation please." She pursed her lips.

Ignoring her, Evee put the kettle on the stove and turned on the burner. She really didn't want tea, but at least this gave her something to do.

"Evee, you know the death of the humans and the witnessing of the Nosferatu takes our situation to a whole new level," Viv said. "The police will get involved, which is going to make this catastrophic. This situation is bigger than I think even the Benders realize. We need to figure out some kind of workable game plan. All we've been doing is chasing our tails, looking for Nosferatu, Chenilles and Loups."

Gilly nodded. "Agreed. Dead humans. We're way over our heads...wait a sec. What's up with that?" Gilly walked over to Evee and touched her right shoulder, just near the edge of her scoop-necked sweater, and tugged it down an inch.

"What?" Evee asked. She felt Gilly pull the back of her shirt lower.

"What the hell?" Viv said, and hurried over to Gilly's side.

Evee tried looking over her right shoulder to see what her sisters were gawking at. She couldn't see anything. "What? What, damn it?"

"Your *absolutus infinitus,*" Viv said quietly.

All Triads since the 1500s were born with a black *absolutus infinitus* birthmark on a certain part of their body. Evee's was on her right shoulder, Gilly's on her right ankle, and Viv's on her right hip. The mark was part of the curse carried by all Triads.

"What about it?" Evee asked, still trying to look over her shoulder.

"It...it's gray," Gilly said, her voice soft with astonishment.

"Get the hell out," Evee said, and took off to look in the foyer mirror.

When she reached the mirror, she turned sideways, reached back and tugged on her shirt. Her sisters stood beside her, silent. Frustrated, Evee yanked her sweater up and over her head, not caring that she stood only in her bra and jeans. She turned sideways again, and felt her mouth drop open. She saw it, plain as the nose on her face. Her once charcoal-black *absolutus infinitus* had faded to an ashen gray.

"What happened to it?" Viv asked.

"I don't know," Evee said, still staring at her shoulder in the mirror. "I never felt anything, never noticed any change to it until you mentioned a minute ago." She turned to Gilly. "What does it mean? The color change?"

Gilly glanced over at Viv and they both shrugged.

"It's gray, like the mirrors in our Grimoires," Gilly said. "Maybe they're tied together somehow."

The Grimoires were books of spells that had been handed down from one Triad generation to another. As part of their punishment, the first set of Triad had been forced to write every spell known to the Circle of Sisters and the Triad, along with the purpose of each spell, and the consequence of each spell once cast. The spells had been written on parchment paper and bound in elderwood. Inside the front cover of each Grimoire, a notch had been cut out of the elderwood, just big enough to hold a fist-size mirror. The mirror had been purposely set into each Grimoire so that whenever a Triad opened her book, the first thing she saw was the reflection of an apocalyptic destruction of the world. A reminder of what would happen should a Triad shirk her responsibilities and duties of the Originals assigned to her. It showed blood and gore, and the world as a wasteland. Viv, Gilly and Evee read their Grimoires daily, right before a feeding, noting new spells that might be needed should something go awry with their Originals.

Only a few days ago, when they opened their Grimoires, the sisters had been shocked to find that the mirrors no longer showed the apocalyptic vision. They only reflected gray swirls. Nothing more.

"When did your *absolutus* turn gray?" Gilly asked.

"I told you," Evee snapped. "I don't know. I'd probably still be oblivious of it if you hadn't noticed it. It's not like I check on it every day."

Gilly turned to Viv. "What about yours?"

Viv glanced around the foyer as if to confirm that no one was around but her sisters. Then she unbuttoned and unzipped her jeans. She wiggled her jeans down just enough to bare her right hip, where she carried her *absolutus infinitus.*

It, too, had turned gray. Viv's hands shook as she pulled up her pants, zipped and buttoned them back into place.

"What the fuck?" Gilly blurted. "It's gray, too."

"You think I didn't notice?" Viv snapped.

"You didn't notice the change before?" Gilly asked.

"No." Viv looked up at her sisters blankly.

"But you shower every day, right?" Gilly said. "Wouldn't you have seen it in the mirror?"

"Well, I didn't," Viv said. "This is the first I've seen it like this."

Evee and Viv looked at Gilly simultaneously. "What about yours?"

Gilly's eyes widened, and then she nodded. She leaned over and lifted the right leg of her linen pants and twisted her right foot slightly inward. Her *absolutus infinitus* sat right above her right ankle as usual, its color unchanged—charcoal black.

"I don't understand what's going on," Evee said. She shivered. "I'm freezing here. I've got to dry my hair before I get pneumonia. You two go back to the kitchen.

Get something to eat. I'll dry my hair and meet you back there in a few."

When Evee got to her bathroom, she saw Hoot perched on the counter near the bathroom sink.

"I told you," Hoot said.

Ignoring him, Evee opened a vanity drawer and pulled out her blow-dryer. She plugged it in, turned it on and aimed a blast of warm air at her familiar.

Hoot screeched and flew off the counter and out of the bathroom, all the while yelling, "Told you, told you. See what you get for being a hussy?"

"Shut up," Evee said, aiming the blow-dryer at her hair. If Hoot snapped back a reply, she didn't hear it. Blessed be the dryer.

By the time she finished with her hair and made it back into the kitchen, her sisters were seated around the small kitchen table, each with a steaming bowl of gumbo in front of her and a cup of tea.

Gilly motioned for Evee to sit next to her, where another bowl of gumbo and cup of tea had been set out for her.

Evee sat and picked up a spoon, ready to dig into her food. The first bite drew a sigh from her. "This is so good," she said, and quickly dug in for another spoonful.

"Thanks," Viv said. "Made it a couple weeks ago. Put it in the freezer for a rainy day. Or shitty day, whatever works." She shrugged.

"Uh, by the way," Gilly said to Evee. "Before I forget to tell you. We've been summoned by the Elders. I'm sure they've heard about the humans and want an update from us."

Evee felt her shoulders droop. "When?"

"This evening. Before the feeding."

"That late?" Evee said. "Don't they usually go to bed around seven or something ridiculously early like that?"

Viv shrugged. "It's not usual times right now."

"Oh, and something else," Gilly said. "We were wondering…" She looked at Viv.

Viv arched a brow at her sister while spooning more gumbo into her mouth.

"What were you doing here showering when you were supposed to be out looking for your Nosferatu earlier?" Gilly asked.

Evee stared down into the bowl in front of her. "I, uh… I had a situation with a Cartesian."

Viv and Gilly dropped their spoons into their bowls simultaneously.

"When? Where?" Viv asked.

"What did you do?" Gilly asked.

"Were you hurt?" Viv asked anxiously. "You don't look hurt."

Evee held up a hand to stave their questions. Ate one more bite of chicken and sausage gumbo, then readied herself for the inquisition.

Finally, she said, "We split up. Me, Ronan and Lucien each went separate ways to cover more ground and look for Nosferatu. I was headed downriver, Lucien upriver, and Ronan took the Quarter."

Her sisters stared at her bug-eyed.

"Anyway, I was walking riverside when a rift opened in the sky out of nowhere and a Cartesian hung out of it so low it could have scooped me up in one grasp. Luckily I caught him out of the corner of my eye and took off running. Only ran the wrong way. Right into the river until I couldn't feel the bottom anymore."

Gilly gasped. "You can't even swim."

Viv reached out and touched Evee's arm. "You must have been terrified."

Evee nodded, her eyes brimming with tears again as she recalled the event. "I didn't know what was going to happen first. The Cartesian attacking me, or me drowning."

"Obviously neither happened, since you're sitting right here," Gilly said, sounding grateful. "What did happen? The Cartesian, you stuck in the water...?"

"Lucien showed up," Evee said. "Must have doubled back, because the next thing I knew the Cartesian was gone, and Lucien was pulling me out of the water."

Gilly cocked her head. "And did he bring you back here to the house?"

Evee swirled bits of chicken and sausage around in her gumbo with a spoon, knew what was coming next. Finally, she said. "Yes, he brought me here."

"What about Ronan?" Viv asked. "Where was he during all this?"

"I told you," Evee said. "In the Quarter. He wasn't anywhere near the river."

"Where are they now?" Gilly asked.

"Who?"

Gilly rolled her eyes. "Lucien and Ronan."

"Far as I know, Ronan's still in the Quarter," Evee said. "Lucien may have gone after him, I'm not sure."

"In soaked clothes?" Viv asked.

"Yeah," Gilly chimed in. "You said he pulled you out of the river. Surely he'd have gotten soaked doing that, right?" Suddenly, Gilly's head popped up and she sniffed the air, turning her head slowly from left to right, sniffing the entire time, like a cat tracking a mouse. A few seconds later, she got up from her chair, following her nose into the utility room at the back of the kitchen.

"Well, I'll be damned," Gilly said, which caused Viv to jump up from her seat and head to the utility room.

Evee took off right behind them.

"What's wrong?" Evee asked when she finally caught up with her sisters.

Gilly twirled about and faced her. "You had sex in here, didn't you? I can smell it."

Evee felt her cheeks burn with embarrassment. "I did not have sex," she proclaimed.

"Oh, yeah?" Gilly said, then reached for an object on the washer and handed it to Evee. "Then what's this doing here?"

Evee turned Lucien's watch over in her hand, wondering how it had gotten there. Then suddenly remembering him taking it off before stripping out of his shirt.

"Fess up," Viv said. "What happened?"

There were too many other things going wrong now for Evee to start playing fifty questions with her sisters. "Okay, all right, but I didn't have, like, real sex with Lucien. He helped me home so I could shower and get into dry clothes. We happened to kiss. He sat me on top of the dryer, then put his hands…his thumbs between my legs, and before I knew it fireworks happened."

Gilly's mouth dropped open, as did Viv's.

"What were you thinking?" Gilly asked. "We barely know these men, and you let one of them touch you like that? You should know better—"

"I knew better," Viv interrupted. "But it still happened."

Now it was Evee and Gilly's turn to stare at their older sister.

"Except we went all the way. Nikoli didn't just touch me."

"You mean like the real deal?" Evee asked, feeling a bit envious.

"Yeah." Viv nodded, and a small grin spread across her face. "And more than one time."

Gilly placed a hand on her forehead and groaned.

"What?" Viv said to her. "You mean nothing's happened between you and Gavril?"

"No," Gilly said gruffly. "Nothing."

Viv looked over at Evee. "Why Lucien? Why not Ronan? Convenience?"

"Not really," Evee said, feeling slightly offended that her sister had made the question sound like she screwed everything in sight every chance she got. "I mean Ronan is a really nice guy. Good-looking, too. But there's something about Lucien that...well, draws me to him. I couldn't have stopped that first kiss even if I'd have wanted to. Couldn't have stopped him touching me."

Gilly slapped her hands on the table. "Maybe that's why your and Viv's *absolutus infinitus* turned gray. Because of what happened between you and Lucien, Viv and Nikoli. You know the curse says we can't marry or live intimately with any human."

Evee and Viv looked at Gilly simultaneously before Evee said, "I didn't marry Lucien."

"And I'm not living intimately with Nikoli," Viv shot back. "We simply had sex."

Gilly sat back in her chair. "I think the both of you are working with semantics here. It's all in the interpretation of what the curse actually meant. Do we know that for sure? I mean, we're talking the 1500s here, when the curse was cast. What if the original Elders considered living intimately together to mean just having plain old sex? Back in that day and age, the only women who screwed just to screw were harlots in bordellos. If that's the case, wouldn't that mean that just having sex without being married was part of the curse, as well? What if the two of you having sexual encounters with those Benders caused all this chaos to happen? The missing Originals, the attacks on humans?"

Viv scowled at her. "Man, oh, man, you really stretched that one out of your butt. Regardless, it's not like I can take it back now, right? We didn't oppose the curse. We didn't defy it by marrying those men, and we're not living intimately with them. Period."

"As I said," Gilly said. "Semantics."

Despite the reprimand coming out of Gilly's mouth, Evee could've sworn she saw envy and longing in her sister's eyes. Had she had the chance, she'd have slept with Gavril. Evee knew it as well as she knew her own name.

"Not," Viv retorted.

Evee put the tips of her fingers from her right hand against the palm of her left, calling for a time-out. Viv and Gilly stared at her, anger still popping in their eyes.

"Who did what, when and where is not what's important right now. Dying humans are. We've got to find our missing Originals and get them confined, and the ones who are confined need to be protected from the Cartesians."

"That's all we've been trying to do," Viv said. "With not much success, I might add."

"Maybe once we fill the Elders in, they'll have some ideas. Especially about why our spells are weakening. Hell, we can't track our own behinds, much less our own broods. We need backup. Serious backup."

"No way on the Elders," Evee said. "The sex part with the Benders will come out, and that's the last thing we need."

Elvis, Gilly's familiar, suddenly raced into the kitchen, tittered, then let out a short screech as if in agreement.

"Hush," Gilly told him, then turned to Viv. "I don't

think it's going to do us any good to go back to the Elders. They were supposed to contact the others from the Circle of Sisters to help with spells from different locations. If they did, I certainly haven't seen any evidence of it. Have you?"

Viv and Evee shook their heads.

"Look," Evee said, "we have to keep our heads and hands about us, and no more panty play with the Benders." Even to her own ear, the last part of what she'd just said sounded flat, unconvincing and regretful. "I think one of the biggest challenges we've got coming up is feeding time. It'll be here before we know it, and I have a feeling that the Cartesians are going to attempt a strike while we're transporting our broods to the North Compound." She turned to Viv. "Your Loup Garous are already there, but I don't know how we're going to get the Nosferatu and Chenilles out there without a Cartesian attack."

"Maybe there's a different way for us to set up the feedings," Viv said. "What if I had my ranch hands drain the cattle's blood and then we can pick it up and bring it to the Nosferatu instead of bringing the Nosferatu to the compound? The corpses will be there for the Loup Garous, who are already in the compound to eat. When they're done, I can have my ranch hands, Charlie, Bootstrap and Kale, gather up the bones...damn, never mind. I've never allowed the ranch hands to go into the North Compound, and I can't have them go there now. Too big a risk. Can't chance a Loup attacking any one of them."

"Seems like the only part we're short on," Gilly said, "is getting the bones collected and brought to the Chenilles in the Louis I Cemetery. And since Viv is the only one who can control the Loups, we'd have to count on her to collect the bones and transport them over here."

She shook her head. "No way I can see you doing that by yourself."

The three sisters looked down at the floor, then up at the dryer, all three sighing in unison.

Still holding Lucien's watch, Evee fingered it. The watch seemed so apropos. Their spells, ideas and time were running out.

As hard as she tried to stop the thought, it floated loud and strong in Evee's mind. Unbidden, unwanted.

Soon they could be facing the total destruction of the Originals and the Triad.

Chapter 6

The safest—and only place—Lucien and Ronan could think of to ride out the storm of the deaths in the Quarter was their hotel room.

Ronan turned on the television, watching for any updated news reports, and Lucien went straight for the shower that he'd been needing for some time.

After undressing, Lucien turned the shower on hot and the knobs to full jet. He stepped into the spray and leaned forward against the wall of the shower. He closed his eyes and let the jets of hot water soak his hair, pelt against his body.

He tried emptying his mind of the vision of the murdered woman, of the merciless Nosferatu, the gawkers and hecklers. It was then Lucien felt the weight of the entire mission abruptly settle on his shoulders. This was far bigger than anything they'd ever faced before. And with certainty, he knew it would get a lot worse before it got better.

Despite the weight and horrible images fleeting in and out of his mind, Lucien suddenly found himself thinking about Evee.

Evee's explosive reaction to his touch surprised him, and it had taken Lucien every molecule of will he possessed to send her off to shower and for him to leave her home.

Lucien was anything but a prude when it came to women. He'd known many of them over the years. but no one like Evee François. She was tall and slender, with black hair that fell soft and straight to her shoulders. Her eyes were the color of shiny copper pennies, her nose small and perfect. Her lips, so full, luscious, they held the power to drop any man to his knees to beg for one more kiss, one more touch. Her mouth had ravaged his as if she meant to pour the very essence of all she was into him. Oh, how she'd clung to him, kissed him, wanted him.

Although all the triplets were beautiful, there was something about Evee that stuck to Lucien like dried lavender. And he refused to let it fade away. Maybe it was the softness of her voice, the pureness of her heart, how easily she stood up for what was right. Evee took her responsibilities so seriously, yet, at the same time, she held the essence of a certain type of woman Lucien had always craved for and never found. Until now.

The problem was he'd not only found what seemed like the perfect woman, he'd wound up shooting himself in the foot at the same time. He'd all but offered Evee up to Ronan on a silver platter. But he hadn't been able to help himself. He'd never seen his cousin so enamored by a woman before. And despite what he felt, Lucien always had believed that blood was thicker than water. He'd suggested Ronan pursue Evee. And Lucien had no plans to counter or one-up anything his cousin did. In the end, the decision would be Evee's.

Once he finished showering, Lucien got out of the tub, dried off with a white, fluffy towel provided by the hotel, then tried to get dressed. The problem was his pants. All the thinking he'd done about Evee had left him with a hard-on. Even the idea of possibly losing her to Ronan had not squelched his desire for her.

Lucien had to wonder if something wasn't wrong with his own head. How could he feel such sexual desire right now? They'd just witnessed a woman's murder and blinded a Nosferatu.

Groaning, Lucien lightly slapped the front of his pants. It did nothing but bring Evee even closer to mind. How just the slightest touch of his thumbs between her thighs had sent her into an explosive orgasm that left her shaking. He had never known a woman to be so responsive to his touch, and he thirsted for more. What man in his right mind wouldn't?

With one last grunt, and envisioning an impossible geometrical equation that needed to be solved before the room exploded, Lucien was finally able to zip his pants. The bulge behind the zipper was still evident so he quickly threw on a black T long enough to cover it.

No sooner had he put himself in order and stepped out of the bathroom than the hotel room door burst open, and Nikoli and Gavril stormed in. Gavril gently kicked the door closed behind him.

Ronan, who'd already showered and dressed, lay across one of the beds with an arm over his eyes. The commotion with the door had him out of bed and standing military straight.

"Where have you been?" Nikoli demanded, glaring at Lucien.

Taken aback, Lucien glared at his cousin. "What the hell's wrong with you? I just finished showering."

"How convenient," Nikoli said, then turned on his heels and walked over to the window on the other side of the bed and stared out of it.

Lucien glanced from Ronan to Gavril, then aimed his chin at Nikoli. "What's with the attitude?"

"We've been summoning you by satellite for over an hour," Gavril said, pointing to the watch on his left wrist.

All the Benders wore the same gadget. It looked like a watch only with more buttons and tiny knobs along its perimeter than any NASA gismo. It operated as a watch, compass and homing device and emitted a red beacon in the center when one Bender summoned another. And that was only activated if one of them stood in deep shit.

Puzzled, Lucien shook his head. "If you summoned me, I never—" He looked down at his wrist, saw nothing and did a double take. He'd forgotten he'd left his watch at Evee's.

"Where's your locator?" Gavril asked, frowning. "You never take it off."

Lucien's mind went on pause for a moment. It was true. He never took it off, except to shower, which was something none of his cousins knew. The watch was waterproof, shatterproof, but obviously not dumb-ass proof, for he'd left it on Evee's washer. For some reason he couldn't explain at the moment, or possibly ever, he'd removed it in Evee's utility room and placed it on the washer before they'd…well, before.

"Yo, cuz, you've gone deaf, too?" Gavril asked, plopping down in an overstuffed chair. "Where is it? You get robbed?"

"No," Lucien said, feeling awkward. "I didn't get robbed. Must have left it at the François house."

At the mention of the Françoises, Nikoli turned away from the window and joined his circle of cousins.

Ronan stormed toward Lucien, his black eyes growing darker by the second. "You had no business being over there in the first place. The two of you were supposed to be hunting Nosferatu at opposite ends of the river."

Lucien scowled. "Since when did you become my father? Did you not hear what I told you earlier? Nothing happened. The ball in this game is in your court."

Ronan stood and faced him, his jaw muscles working furiously.

Nikoli stepped between Ronan and Lucien and held a hand on their chests, nudging them farther away from each other.

"Chill," Nikoli said to Ronan. He turned to Lucien. "Now, what fucking ball are you talking about? 'Cause this sure ain't no game, cuz."

"I know it isn't a game," Lucien said. "Just something between Ronan and me."

"So he left it at the François home, what's the big deal?" Gavril asked. "We all know Lucien's been working as hard as the rest of us. Cut him some slack."

"You're taking his side?" Ronan asked Gavril.

Gavril snorted back a laugh. "Cuz, you sound like a five-year-old."

"Are you kidding me?" Ronan fumed. "You're actually pulling sides."

Nikoli dropped his hands. "Everybody shut the hell up and get a grip. This isn't about sides. We're a team. Benders. We're not here to piss in each other's boots. We've got enough problems to deal with." He turned to Lucien. "And you, no taking off your transmitter again. You had us worried."

"Sorry," Lucien said, and sat on the couch. "I don't

know why I took it off. Just muddled in the head at the time, I guess. We had a Cartesian attack out on the east bank. It nearly got Evee. I yelled to divert it, and it gave Evee time to run away. Problem was, she ran right into the river, and she can't swim. Had to pop the Cartesian, then rush into the water to get Evee before she drowned."

Nikoli looked at Ronan. "Where were you when all this was going on?"

"In the Quarter, searching for Originals."

"You mean to tell me that the three of you split up?"

Lucien looked down, feeling ashamed for a moment. "Yeah. It's all me, though, cuz. Sounded like a decent plan at the time. Split up and cover more ground."

"If the three of you were headed in different directions," Nikoli said, "how did you wind up where Evee was?"

Lucien shrugged. "Instinct told me to follow her. Good thing I did."

Gavril tilted his head, his brow knitted. "Isn't Evee the one who's supposed to have power over the element of water?"

"Yes," Ronan said.

"Then I'm lost," Gavril said. "If she has the power over water, how did she wind up nearly drowning?"

"I don't know," Lucien said. "She said she has power over water from a distance but is deathly afraid of going into it."

"Aside from controlling it, how does anyone not know how to swim?" Nikoli asked.

"A lot of people don't know how to swim," Lucien said. "And it really is none of our business as to why Evee can't. All I know is that she couldn't get her feet under her and someone had to get her out. Now, if we can put that issue behind us for a minute, you might want to hear about another problem that needs attention."

Nikoli scratched his chin and sighed. "More?"

"You talking about the scabior canopy?" Ronan asked Lucien.

"Yeah."

"What about it?" Nikoli asked.

"The one we set up in the catacombs started to wane," Ronan said. "We had to recharge it."

"Crap," Nikoli said, and leaned against the wall nearest him and swiped a hand through his hair. "Man, if those canopies go out, we've got nothing to keep the Originals that the Triad still have under their control... controlled."

The scabior canopies had been Nikoli and Viv's brainchild. The first one had been formed around the North Compound to keep the Loup Garous in check and the Cartesians out. It didn't take a genius to figure out that the Benders, with their four scabiors combined, couldn't watch over all the Originals at the same time and search for the ones who'd gone missing. To remedy some of the problem, Viv had used one of her Loup Garous to bend four steel poles that cornered the five-hundred-acre property at forty-five-degree angles. Each pole had a bloodstone placed at the top of it, just like the Benders' scabiors. The bent poles were aimed toward the center of the property, pointed at one another, then charged with Nikoli's scabior. That charge created an electrical dome over the entire North Compound, which kept the Cartesians from dropping down out of a rift into the compound. With the contained Loups protected, Nikoli and Viv were free to hunt for the ones that had gone missing.

The same protocol was used at the Louis I Cemetery,

where the Chenilles were kept, and the catacombs at St. John's Cathedral, where Evee kept her Nosferatu.

The fact that one of the domes had to be recharged worried Lucien, as it did his cousins. The others would have to be watched over closely to make sure they wouldn't need the same boost. That was all they needed. More to watch over.

As if reading his thoughts, Nikoli stood upright and stuck his hands in his back pockets. "Something else we're going to have to keep an eye on. I'll do a check on the compound before the feeding."

"Same here at the cemetery," Gavril said.

The room went silent for a moment, each cousin lost in his own thoughts.

Finally, Ronan cleared his throat. "There's more, guys."

Gavril's eyebrows arched. "More?"

Ronan nodded. "Earlier, when Lucien and me were in the Quarter, looking for Originals, we heard a woman screaming down one of the streets that branches off Bourbon. At first, she was making sounds like she wanted whoever was with her to fu…have his way with her. We checked to make sure she was all right, and saw one of the Nosferatu with her, transforming right there. Right in front of her. She started screaming so loudly I worried that people in the next parish might hear her."

"Man, oh, man," Gavril said, shaking his head in disbelief. "Don't blame her. What'd y'all do?"

"Jumped the Nosferatu. Gouged his eyes out with the back end of our scabiors. Unfortunately, we didn't make it there in time to save the woman."

"But Nosferatu heal themselves pretty quickly, don't they?" Nikoli asked.

"Oh, yeah," Lucien said. "And that one was regrouping double time. We were planning our next attack. I mean, the Nosferatu already knew we could get to its eyes, so I'm figuring it'd probably hit us from another direction, right?"

"Makes sense," Nikoli said.

"So what'd you do?" Gavril asked.

"Nothing," Lucien said. "Didn't have time. The next thing I knew, the Original jerked back, then fell over dead."

Gavril and Nikoli looked from Lucien to Ronan, waiting for a follow-up explanation. It wasn't like either to play a suspense card when relaying an incident.

Nikoli motioned with a hand for Ronan to continue.

"It was Pierre. Evee's head Nosferatu. He stabbed the rogue Original in the back with some kind of dagger. It went right through the Original. Came out the front of his chest, right through the heart."

Nikoli blew out a loud breath. "Bad for the Nosferatu, but good for us. Don't know how we'd have dealt with that one."

"You mean a Nosferatu has the ability to purposely kill its own?" Gavril asked.

"I'm no expert," Lucien said, "but I believe they do, if doing so serves a higher purpose. I know the Triad take the safety of humans seriously when it comes to the Originals. Guess that situation merited a higher purpose."

"There's more," Ronan said, and began to pace the room.

"Shit," Gavril said. "What?"

"There were witnesses, human witnesses. They saw the death and then the transformation of the Nosferatu to human after it died," Ronan said, frowning.

Lucien nodded. "And the police were summoned."

Gavril gawked at him. "You talked to the police? Were you interrogated? Did they consider you a suspect?"

Ronan and Lucien shrugged simultaneously.

"I have no idea what they thought or suspected," Lucien said. "As soon as we heard the sirens, Ronan and I took off for the hotel. How could we have possibly explained to the police what happened? They'd have thought we were totally drugged out or had some wires loose in our heads."

"Do the Triad know all this?" Lucien asked.

"Ten to one they do," Gavril said. "I was with Gilly looking for Chenilles when she suddenly said, 'Something's come up. I've got to go.'"

"She didn't tell you what the 'up' was?" Nikoli asked.

Gavril shook his head. "She just took off. Said we'd meet later at the docks when it's time to take the ferry to the compound for feeding."

Lucien got to his feet. "If the Triad know, surely they're together right now. Probably going to see their Elders for help, call in reinforcements."

Nikoli tapped the tips of his fingers together. "Maybe we should be doing the same thing."

Lucien, Gavril, and Ronan looked at him in unison.

Nikoli held out his hands, palm up. "You know, call for backup."

"Have you lost your—" Ronan began.

Gavril shook his head.

"I know, I know," Nikoli said. "But hear me out. There comes a time when we've got to suck it up, put pride on the shelf and call in our own cavalry. I mean, really. Look at where we are, for heaven's sake. I don't know about you three, but I feel like we've achieved little to nothing. We're being reactive instead of proactive."

"Our setting up the electrical canopies to create safe places for the Originals *was* proactive," Lucien said.

"True," Nikoli agreed. "But you said it yourself. The scabior canopy at the catacombs had to be recharged. What if something happens to the other two? What if they go out? Humans died, Lucien. Police are going to start crawling all over this."

Ronan rolled his left hand into a fist and punched it into the palm of his right. "No other Bender in our history has ever called for backup, and I, for one, am not about to start now. We've got to work the plans we've already set in motion." He turned to Lucien. "No more splitting apart more than we already have. It was stupid to allow Evee to go off on her own."

"Allow?" Lucien said with incredulity. "Evee is not a child. She's a strong and intelligent woman with a mind of her own. Just like her sisters. I don't believe any of them would allow anyone to force them in any given direction."

"Including yours?" Ronan snapped.

"My what?" Lucien asked, taken aback by Ronan's anger.

Without another word, Ronan stormed out of the hotel room.

Nikoli winced as the hotel door slammed behind his cousin.

"Who stuck a broom up his butt?" Gavril asked.

Lucien shook his head, indicating that he didn't have a clue. But he knew. Ronan cared for Evee. Wanted to protect her at all costs. Lucien understood that all too well.

Unfortunately, there was nothing Lucien could do about Ronan's feelings. He had given his cousin leeway to pursue his interest in her, and he planned to keep himself away until Evee either rebuffed Ronan or forced all of them out of New Orleans.

The only feelings Lucien had control over were his own. Whether he experienced guilt or fear, anger or frustration, the one thing he knew was that for now, he had to lay down what he felt for Evee and give Ronan space. Maybe even coach him a bit on how to approach Evee.

Even as he thought about it, Lucien looked down at the floor and shook his head slightly. Goddamn, he felt like an idiot. He wanted to be the one to pursue her, the one she'd run to whenever she was afraid or uncertain.

As stupid as it sounded, all he knew to do was play fair, help Ronan gain a bit of an edge and let nature take it course.

And for now, that had to be enough.

Chapter 7

It was nearing 10:00 p.m., and Arabella, Taka and Vanessa, the three Elders responsible for the Circle of Sisters and the Triad, were in their nightgowns huddled over cups of tea at the kitchen table. They lived in the Garden District of New Orleans, in an old Victorian about four or five blocks from the Triad.

"When did you hear about the humans being attacked, about the Nosferatu and the witnesses?" Taka asked. "Who told you?"

"Earlier," Arabella said. "About an hour ago and then a half hour later from Brunedee, a Circle sister from Plaquemine."

"Aw," Taka said, waving a dismissive hand. "I wouldn't lose sleep over that. Brunedee is a gossip magnet. Last I heard, she'd spread word that Brad Pitt met her at a gas station in Metairie, and he was so enamored with her, he up and left Angelina."

"And you believed that?" Vanessa asked.

Taka gave her a stern look. "What do you think I am, brainless? No way Brad would leave Angelina and all their kids for Brunedee. Nicholas Cage, maybe. But Brad, uh-uh."

"Everything, including the Nosferatu and witnesses, checks out," Arabella said quietly. "It's been confirmed twice."

"How on earth did Brunedee hear about it before us, especially with her living almost a hundred miles away?" Vanessa asked.

Arabella shrugged. "You know how the Circle of Sisters works. News travels fast. And news like this…" She shook her head. "Sisters in Argentina are probably hearing about it by now."

The Elders sat silent for a moment, each staring inside her teacup as if waiting for some apparition to appear.

"We lost three humans, too," Arabella said. "In case you hadn't heard."

Vanessa and Taka drew in deep breaths in unison.

"When? Where?" Taka asked.

"One in the Quarter, earlier this evening. The other two in Chalmette."

Taka gasped. "Chalmette? They're out of the city? Mother Earth, that means the Originals can go anywhere!"

"I know," Arabella said quietly.

"What happened to the human in the Quarter?" Vanessa asked.

"Word has it that a Nosferatu attacked her in some back alley. Two of the Benders were nearby, attempted to stop it."

"Well, that was stupid," Taka said.

"At least they tried," Vanessa snapped.

Arabella kept staring at her tea. "Got the Nosferatu

in the eyes. At least it served as a diversion. Too late for the poor woman, though."

"Yeah," Taka said, "but the Nosferatu heal themselves, like, super fast."

Arabella nodded. "That's what happened. Then it went after the Benders. Pierre had to take it down."

"Evee's lead guy at the catacombs?" Vanessa asked.

"Yes."

Taka shook her head. "Had to be bad for him to kill one of his own."

"Killing humans is serious business," Arabella said. "Pierre did the right thing. If he couldn't call the Nosferatu back into the fold, he had no other choice. That's just how it goes."

"Which Nosferatu got it?" Taka asked. "Sabrina? She's always been a hardheaded Original. Always liked to stir up trouble."

Arabella shook her head. "It was Chank."

"Aw, man, the redheaded one?" Taka said. "I always thought he was a sweetheart. Had great hair. Good-looking, too."

Vanessa gave Arabella an eye roll, which evidently wasn't missed by Taka.

"Well, he was," Taka said. With a look of frustration, she got up from the table and started to pace about the kitchen. Her open-back slippers slapped against her heels with each step.

"Arabella, you did contact everyone in the Circle about what's been going on here, right?" Taka asked. "I don't mean what just, just happened with the humans. I mean the deaths of Viv's Loups, the missing Originals?"

"Of course I did. I've summoned the Triad, too, to come this evening so we can discuss all this mess."

"And nothing's happened? The entire clan gets involved

and nothing? Why have we suddenly become so ineffective?" Taka demanded. "It's as if we've become nothing more than three old ladies living in a shoe."

"Stop talking like a nut job," Vanessa said with a huff.

"Nut job, huh?" Taka retorted. "The cops have already been here twice, and twice we ignored them. With witnesses to the Nosferatu death and transformation, who do you think will be knocking on our door next? Probably the FBI. The CIA. The IRS. Who the heck knows? News might travel fast among the Circle, but it flies like lightning through New Orleans. The city is going to be in an uproar. We could be looking at lynchings, like they did way back in the day. Witch hangings, burnings." The more Taka spoke the faster she walked, and the harder her slippers slapped against her heels.

"Stop being so melodramatic and working yourself up to a frenzy," Vanessa said. "We need to quit speculating and come up with a better plan. Isn't that right, Arabella?"

Arabella finally glanced up from her teacup, looked over at Taka, then Vanessa. "I'm concerned that Taka might not be exaggerating."

Vanessa did a double take at Arabella, and her brow furrowed. "What do you mean?"

Scratching the hives suddenly covering her arms, Arabella shook her head. "I'm concerned. Seriously concerned. If spells from the entire clan of the Circle of Sisters haven't helped, I don't know what else to do."

"No ideas at all?" Taka asked, fear creasing her face.

Arabella looked back down at her teacup. "Well… okay, maybe one, but the two of you won't like it."

"Spill it," Vanessa said. "We can't afford for things to get any worse."

Sighing, Arabella looked up. "You know how I said

I'd heard about the recent event earlier, then again from Brunedee?"

"Yeah," Taka said warily.

"Well, the first I heard of it was from Gunner Stern."

Vanessa gasped. "What were you doing talking to that stupid sorcerer? You know the rules. No collaborating with those idiots."

"Gunner isn't an idiot," Arabella said.

"He is if he hangs out with Trey Cottle and Shandor Black, the other two sorcerers in New Orleans," Vanessa said. "You may be sweet on Gunner, but he's still a sorcerer, and he may be a nice guy, but hanging out with those other two scumbags makes him a scumbag by association."

"Yeah," Taka said. "But he is a nice guy. I've got to admit, he's not like the other two."

"Oh, hush," Vanessa said. "You don't know any more about Gunner than you know where your reading glasses are right now."

Taka tsked. "Do, too. They're right here." She patted the top of her head and frowned when she didn't feel them perched there. She stuck her hands in her nightgown pockets. Empty. "Well, they're somewhere."

Vanessa rolled her eyes.

Arabella took a sip of tea, then said, "I happen to think that out of all three sorcerers in the city, Gunner is the most levelheaded. And for your information, I'm not sweet on him."

"But he is on you," Taka said.

"That's for sure," Vanessa agreed. "The way he looks at you…" She fanned her face with a hand. "Hot, hot, hot."

"Oh, please," Arabella said. "You're acting like a pubescent teen. I think Gunner has integrity, that's all. Now both of you stop with the attraction comments. We have to stay on track."

The three Elders fell silent for a moment, Taka still pacing, Vanessa sipping tea.

Arabella thought about Gunner, who lived in New Orleans proper. He'd called her in confidence to tell her about the incident with the Nosferatu and the human witnesses. During their conversation, he'd said that Trey and Shandor were out having dinner with a client.

Out of all the sorcerers, Gunner was the one Arabella trusted. Trey Cottle was a sorcerer whose entire world revolved around him, and him alone. He was a selfish twit. Overweight, sweaty, plump-faced with a band of gray, thinning hair that wrapped around the back of his head. And he wore thick black glasses that constantly slid down the bridge of his nose. Arabella guessed him to be in his late sixties, early seventies.

Shandor Black was Trey's partner at their law firm and his indomitable yes-man. He had a long, pinched face, a long beak of a nose, and if he ever had an opinion about any issue, he made sure it mirrored Trey's.

Gunner, although often seen in Trey and Shandor's company, carried himself quite differently. He appeared to be in his midsixties, had a strong, handsome face and blue eyes that twinkled whenever he spoke to Arabella.

When Gunner had called Arabella with the news, he'd offered to help in any way he could. And, oh, how she wanted to say yes. But keeping protocol in mind, especially being an Elder, she had to get a vote on the issue with the other two Elders and the Triad.

"It's late," Taka said, then yawned. "Are you sure the triplets are coming tonight? Can't they come in the morning, and we can discuss everything then? It's way past my bedtime. My brain works better in the morning." She ran her hands through her short white hair, making it poke up in untidy spikes.

"They'll be here," Arabella said. "I'm sure with all that's going on, they're trying to get their ducks in a row before coming here and then heading out again to take care of their feeding."

Taka suddenly stopped in midpace. "What if the cops come knocking at our door while the triplets are here?"

"Stop," Vanessa said. "Don't wind this up any tighter than it already is. We'll deal with that issue if it comes up. Until then, don't add it to our pile of worries."

Arabella nodded in agreement and took another sip of tea, noticed the cup shaking slightly in her hand. Of course she was nervous, anxious. Who wouldn't be under these conditions? Something was way off in their world of spells and ancient tried-and-true incantations. Most appeared to be useless. She had contacted each leader of the Circle of Sisters around the country and beyond, invoking their help. And for the first time ever, to Arabella's knowledge anyway, their powers combined seemed to have little to no effect on the situation here, regarding the Cartesians or the missing Originals.

Taka suddenly walked over to the kitchen table and slapped a hand onto it. "I think Arabella's right," she blurted. "We need some serious backup. I vote we bring the sorcerers in on this deal."

"Are you crazy?" Vanessa said. "The only thing they've ever provided us is trouble. They're into their own incantations and spells, and they're always having to do with benefiting themselves. When have you ever seen them use their powers for the good of others?"

"I think Gunner would," Arabella said, seeing in Taka's words an opportunity to create a slight opening in the door of impossibility. She had begun to give up hope that Gunner could ever be recruited in their mission. "He did offer to help."

Vanessa snorted. "Get real, old girl. You're only saying that because he's sweet on—"

"Stop it," Arabella said. "It's not about that."

"Bullshit it's not," Vanessa said.

Taka gasped. "You used the B word!"

"Oh, grow up," Vanessa said to Taka, then turned to Arabella. "You want us to be realistic and get back on track, then you have to admit that Gunner's got a thing for you. Whenever that man's around you he smiles so big that if he wore false teeth, they'd fall out."

"He's the only one I'd really trust," Arabella said. "Not only is he sensible, but I've seen him do good for others."

"When and for whom?" Vanessa asked.

Now Arabella rolled her eyes. "I don't remember the exact time, place or person, but he has helped."

"But what could only one sorcerer do to assist us when the entire clan of Circle of Sisters can't make a difference?" Taka asked. "I say we just roll the dice, bring all three in and make something serious happen. We can't deny that's something's out of alignment here. I don't know if it's the cosmos or something with the thinning ozone layer, whichever, whatever, we're in serious trouble."

Vanessa tsked. "Whether Gunner is sweet on you or not, Arabella, I seriously don't think one sorcerer can do the trick. And I sure as hell don't want those other two snot-ball sorcerers mixed up with us."

"How do you know one wouldn't make a difference?" Arabella said. "All you keep saying is, 'no, no, no, don't involve the sorcerers.' But seriously, look how deep things have gotten. The Triad and Benders haven't found any more missing Originals. Now humans are being attacked, they've witnessed the death of a Nosferatu, and more Cartesians are finding their way into our dimension. If we don't do something, and quickly, things are just going to get worse. Missing Originals means more humans are in danger, especially now. Feeding time is coming soon. The missing ones will be hungry and look for the first source of food they can find. And in this city, you know what that's going to be. Humans."

Taka raised her right hand. "I vote we start with Gunner, see what happens. He might at least offer some advice. Maybe there's a spell he can cast that is blocked from us."

"I think the whole idea is stupid," Vanessa said. "I understand the seriousness of this matter, but I think bringing in the sorcerers, even one, will only make things worse. That's what happens when you bring the devil into your ranks."

"Oh, for earth, water, air and fire's sake," Arabella said. "Gunner is not the devil."

"Maybe not, but he hangs out with Trey and Shandor. And you know what they say—if you mess with crap, you're going to get some on you."

"That's not true," Taka said. "I've smelled Gunner before. He smells real good. Not like poop at all."

"We'll discuss this in more detail when the Triad arrive," Arabella said. "I'm sure with all that's been going on, they'll have more to tell us. Once we get an update from them, we'll fill them in on what we've heard from this end, then take a vote regarding the sorcerers. One or all three, it doesn't matter. We just need everybody's input and vote. Otherwise, things remain just as they are."

"You mean in the shitter?" Vanessa said.

"Pretty much, from the sound of it," Taka said, and shook her head. "In all my years, I've never known things to be this bad. Maybe that's why we suck at this now. We've never been through it before."

"Experience has nothing to do with our spells not working," Arabella said. "The fact that they're not working is my greatest concern."

In that moment, a knock sounded from their front door. The three women froze, staring at one another.

"We're getting way too jumpy," Arabella said. "I'm sure it's the Triad."

"Check the peephole before you open the door," Taka whispered.

Another knock sounded on the door, and Arabella rose from the table and headed out of the kitchen, through the living room and into the foyer. She put her hand to the doorknob, felt a shiver run up her spin and decided to do as Taka suggested. She looked through the security peephole in the door.

Outside, standing near the door on their front porch, were two police officers. Both stood with hands on hips, heads slightly lowered, faces grim.

Hearing shuffling sounds behind her, Arabella turned about quickly and saw Taka and Vanessa standing at the end of the foyer.

"Who is it?" Vanessa mouthed.

Arabella held a finger to her lips.

"I knew it," Taka said, a little too loudly. "It's the cops, right?"

Arabella scowled at her and pressed her finger to her lips harder. Maybe if they didn't make any noise, the officers would go away. Hopefully they'd think no one was home.

Then a thought struck Arabella, sending another

shiver up her spine. She could only pray that the Triad didn't decide to show up at this moment with the police standing right outside their door.

Chapter 8

After meeting up with Evee, Gilly and Viv had chosen to go and check on their Originals to make certain the scabior canopies were still in working order. They'd agreed to reconvene at the house in a couple of hours, and then, just before feeding time, go and see the Elders who'd summoned them. It was Gilly's idea to extend the meeting time with the Elders by those few hours. The later it got, the more tired the Elders would be. The more tired they were, the better the chances were that the triplets wouldn't get their butts chewed out for one thing or another.

Although Evee wanted to check on her Nosferatu, she knew she had to get Lucien's watch, with all its buttons and gizmos, back to him as soon as possible. She had no idea if he remembered that he'd taken it off and left it on her washer. She had an inkling the fancy watch that also looked like a compass and some type of homing and navigational device, all rolled into one, had to be important to him. His cousins also wore the same device. If nothing else, bringing Lucien his watch was as good an excuse as any to see him now instead of later.

Evee left the house and took the trolley from the Garden District to the Canal Street intersection. She thought she remembered Lucien saying that they were staying at the Hotel Monteleone, and crossed her fingers that she was right.

When the trolley came to a stop on Canal, she hopped off and made her way down Royal Street. The Monteleone was barely a half block down Royal.

The hotel had been built back in the late 1800s, and time did nothing but add to the majesty of the structure, a favorite haunt of distinguished Southern authors. Its infamous Carousel Bar was a popular hangout in the city. Although Evee had been in the hotel more than once, she still took a moment to stare at its grandeur when she stepped inside. People milled about the lobby, and she heard laughter, music and the clinking of glasses in the Carousel Bar that sat just inside the lobby on the right.

After a moment, it suddenly dawned on her that Gavril, Nikoli and Ronan might be in the same hotel room as Lucien. If so, how was she going to explain why she had possession of Lucien's watch?

Feeling a few jitters settling in, she made her way to the registration desk and waited behind a pudgy, elderly gentleman as he spoke to the redheaded woman behind the desk.

When the woman finally handed the man his room key, Evee stepped up to the desk.

"Welcome to the Hotel Monteleone," the receptionist said. "How may I help you?"

"I'd like to speak to Lucien Hyland. I believe he's staying here," Evee said.

"Do you know his room number?"

Evee bit her bottom lip. "No, sorry. Maybe you could just ring his room and let him know I'm here? My name's Evee François."

The woman eyed Evee for a moment, then tapped some keys on her computer. "Hmm, are you sure he's staying at this hotel? I don't show a Lucien Hyland listed here."

"He's staying here with his cousins, so the room may be under one of their names. Either Nikoli, Gavril or Ronan Hyland."

The woman nodded, pressed more keys on her computer. Evee saw her right eyebrow arch ever so slightly before she picked up a phone and discreetly tapped in four numbers. She turned her back to Evee, and whispered into the phone. Her voice wasn't low enough for Evee not to hear her.

"Mr. Hyland? Yes…of course. There's a young lady here who'd like to speak to Mr. Lucien Hyland." A short pause; then the woman said, "Evee François." Another pause, this one shorter. "Yes, sir, I certainly will."

She turned back to Evee, hung up the phone and gave her a big smile. "Mr. Hyland asks that you please go right on up to his room. Number 1215."

Feeling awkward, Evee leaned closer to the registration table. "Would you happen to know which Hyland answered the phone?"

Not breaking her smile, the woman said, "No, I'm sorry." She glanced over Evee's shoulder. "May I help the next guest, please?"

Feeling dismissed, Evee turned to get a lay of the land and spot the elevators.

"Ms. François?" the receptionist called to her while tapping away on her computer. She stopped tapping long enough to point two, well-manicured fingers at a bank of elevators that stood beside the bar. "Those elevators will take you to the twelfth floor. Take a right out of the elevator and the room will be four doors down on the left."

"Thank you," Evee said, then hurried for the designated elevator bank. For some reason she felt skittish, wanting to bolt out of the hotel. What if Lucien's cousins were in that room? How was she to explain why she had Lucien's watch?

The elevator doors whisked open, and after taking a deep breath, Evee stepped inside and pressed the button for the twelfth floor. As the cubicle bumped its way higher and higher, Evee had to admit that her jitters had more to do with Lucien than his cousins. What if she went to the room and found him alone in there? That gave her more to worry about. His magnetism went through her like nothing Evee had ever felt before. In the short, intimate time they'd been together, it was as if Lucien knew how to read her mind, body and soul. Such a dangerous, erotic triathlon.

As the elevator came to a halt, dinging an announcement that it had reached the twelfth floor, Evee reprimanded herself. She wasn't a child. She was in control of her actions. All she had to do was return the watch, then confirm when and where she, Lucien and Ronan would meet for feeding time or hunt for Nosferatu. Simple.

She stepped out of the elevator and felt sweat beading on her forehead. If this was supposed to be as simple as she'd just tried to convince herself it was, why had she broken into a cold sweat?

It was then she realized she was standing in front of Ronan Hyland.

Evee hurried to hold the elevator door open for him.

"Thanks, but no need," Ronan said, swiping a hand

through his hair. He gave her a gentle smile. "I forgot something in the hotel room, so I have to go back there anyway. What brings you out this way?"

Evee hesitated for a beat, then decided the truth was never hard to cover. "Lucien forgot his watch at our house. I noticed the four of you always have them on, so I figured it must be important. Decided to bring it to him right away."

A dark shadow flitted across Ronan's face. It was quickly replaced by a warm expression, which suited the rest of him. His black hair, collar-length, was combed away from his angular face, save for a few strands that lay against his forehead. His seemingly constant five-o'clock shadow only highlighted the deep black of his eyes. He had a perfect nose that sat above full lips. No question Ronan was a handsome man. Any woman would be crazy not to want him, chase him relentlessly.

"No problem," Ronan said. "Come on. I'll take you to the room."

Chewing on her bottom lip, Evee followed Ronan, taking a right and heading down a maroon-and-gold swirled carpeted hallway until they reached room 1215.

She squared her shoulders and had lifted a hand to knock when Ronan produced a key card for the door. Without a word, he slipped the card into the door slot and pushed the door open.

Standing in the studio area of the suite was Lucien, all six feet three inches of him, wearing jeans and an olive green, button-down shirt. The color complemented his beautiful green eyes and his Mediterranean, caramel-colored skin. If his eyes had been a pool of water, Evee would gladly have dived into them, despite her fear of water, and not cared if she ever resurfaced.

For a moment, Evee wished she had taken a little more

time putting on a bit of makeup. She had just slipped into a pair of jeans, sneakers and a blue pullover. She suddenly felt self-conscious of her hair, which she'd pulled back into a half-hearted ponytail.

Evee heard the click of the suite door softly closing.

Lucien smiled when he saw her, and she stood transfixed, studying his full lips and straight white teeth. She would have given anything to have his mouth on her again.

"You okay?" Lucien asked, his smile fading. "Anything new come up?" He threw Ronan a questioning look.

"Uh...yes... I mean no." Evee held out his watch. "I thought you might need this before we hooked up again."

Lucien stared at her for a long moment before reaching for his watch and attaching it to his left wrist. "Thank you for bringing it. That was very thoughtful of you. My cousins gave me hell about not having it earlier."

At the mention of his cousins, Evee threw a slight glance around the sitting area of the suite, trying to see if anyone else was inside.

"Are Gavril and Nikoli here?" Evee asked.

A soft smile played around Lucien's lips. "No. Gavril went to meet Gilly to check on the scabior dome over the cemetery, where she's keeping the Chenilles, and Nikoli went for Viv. They're going to the North Compound to make sure things are set up for the feeding. I was about to go and check the catacombs."

"Is that where you were headed when we met by the elevator?" Evee asked Ronan.

He shook his head. "Had other business to tend to first."

Evee saw a look pass between Ronan and Lucien that she couldn't read.

Ronan cleared his throat. "Please excuse our rudeness. Make yourself comfortable."

Although Evee's mind said, *Time to leave, woman. NOW!* she ignored it. "Please don't let me stop you from whatever business you have to take care of," she said to Ronan.

"It can wait a bit longer," Ronan said, smiling softly.

Seemingly out of nowhere, Lucien grabbed a MagLite flashlight from the desk near the room's east windows, then quickly attached his sheath and scabior to the belt of his pants. His expression had turned hard, almost purposely so. Even worse, he avoided eye contact with Evee.

"I'll check the catacombs, cuz," Lucien said to Ronan. "Why don't you take some time to explain to Evee exactly how our watches work? I think it'll help her understand my deep appreciation for returning it to me so quickly. I'll meet the two of you at the docks later for the feeding."

With that said, and with no more preamble than a stiff nod at Evee, Lucien left the room so quickly you'd have thought a bomb had been set to go off in the hotel at any moment.

Once the door closed, and not so softly this time, Evee gave Ronan a questioning look. "What was that all about? Did I do or say anything to anger him?"

"Of course not," Ronan assured her. "Worry does that to him occasionally."

Evee felt Ronan's statement to be true, but it was the reason for his worry that concerned her.

Ronan motioned her to a couch in the living area of the suite. "Would you like a soda? Water? Something a bit harder perhaps?"

Evee gave him a shy smile. "No, thanks." She sat on the couch, not knowing what to do with her hands, feet or legs for that matter. She finally crossed her legs and held her hands in her lap. "I didn't mean to come here and interrupt whatever you're working on. Just wanted to return Lucien's watch, see if we were going to meet up later for the feeding."

"What would make you wonder that?" Ronan asked. "Of course we'll be there for the feeding."

Evee nodded and felt like a mentally challenged bobblehead. There was no way in hell she'd ever tell Ronan about the sexual experience she'd had with Lucien on the dryer. The question had actually been meant for Lucien, who'd already vanished. He'd left her house so quickly she wasn't sure if he even wanted to be around her anymore.

Ronan sat beside her and placed one of his large hands over both of hers. "I know there's a lot going on right now, Evee, but I swear we'll get to the bottom of it and bring your world back to order."

Evee blinked. Her thoughts and Ronan's words seemed to cross paths, which left her befuddled. She felt her cheeks go from warm to hot. "Thank you," she said quietly.

She glanced down and just then noticed that Ronan's hand covered both of hers. His touch was gentle, his large hands reassuring. He smelled of Coast soap with a hint of musk.

Holding her breath, Evee purposely turned away and surveyed the living room. "I'm sure you've heard about the attack on the human and the Nosferatu, right?" she asked, then immediately felt stupid. Of course he knew. He'd been there along with Lucien.

"Yes." Ronan sat back on the couch. "I was there. So was Lucien. We were able to slow the Nosferatu down, but not before he'd made his kill. He had to be taken down by your lead guy. What's his name? Pierre?"

Evee nodded.

"That's what sent my cousins here. They'd already heard about the incident and wanted to tell Lucien and me about it. They were able to reach me." He tapped the face of the watch on his left wrist. "This has a geo node in it that allows us to summon one another if an emergency comes up. Since Lucien wasn't wearing his, he never got the signal."

Evee chanced a glance his way. "I'm sorry about the watch. If I hadn't been so stupid and jumped into the river, Lucien wouldn't have gotten wet and—"

Unexpectedly, Ronan placed a hand to her cheek and gently turned it so she faced him. "Nothing was your fault, Evee. I don't know why Lucien took his watch off in the first place, and knowing now is pretty irrelevant. It was his responsibility. Not yours. Please hear me when I tell you, nothing was your fault. Do you hear me?"

She nodded ever so slowly.

"Why are you shaking?" he asked, his voice soft. "I can feel you trembling. Tell me. What's wrong? Besides the obvious, of course."

She looked up at him. "I—I guess I'm afraid that so much has gotten out of control that we won't be able to fix it. Nothing will ever be normal again, will it?"

In response, Ronan pulled her close to him. Evee stiffened slightly, then made a half-hearted effort to allow his lead.

Ronan kissed the top of her head, as a brother would a sister. "Evee, I know we're facing hell and damnation with all that's going on, and I don't want to add more to your plate."

Evee glanced up at him, steeling herself for more bad news. "What is it?"

"When…when this is over," Ronan said, "would you like to have dinner with me?"

Evee's eyes widened. "You mean like a dinner date?"

Ronan nodded, and he released her body as if bracing himself for the worst. A rejection.

His eyes were so expectant that Evee nearly felt sorry for him. Without question she would have given up half her powers to have Lucien sitting here, asking her the same question. She didn't know how the extreme attraction she felt toward Lucien started or why it was there, for all four Benders were drop-dead hunks.

Thinking about it now, Evee started to feel like a fool. Lucien hadn't asked her to dinner. There had been some odd sexual explosion that he seemed to know she physically needed and gave it to her. Ronan, on the other hand, was handling her like she was a lady. Maybe a bit too prim and proper for her taste, but at least she knew where she stood with him.

As for Lucien, she had no clue. Especially when she'd arrived at the hotel. He couldn't have left fast enough.

Evee smiled at Ronan. "I'd love to have dinner with you when this is over, and we can all breathe again."

A look of surprise flashed in Ronan's eyes, and then the smile he gave her lit up his entire face.

Ronan jumped to his feet. "I'll look forward to it."

Evee rose from the couch, as well. "As will I." She smiled at Ronan, but her heart didn't feel what her face expressed. Despite all the logic in the world, Lucien was the one man who filled her thoughts constantly. It was almost like they were two halves of one piece, only Lucien hadn't figured it out yet. And she couldn't have explained it if her life depended on it.

Regardless, without provocation or impetus, as far as

Evee knew, she rowed alone in her make-believe Lucien-and-Evee boat.

She *would* look forward to dinner with Ronan, and to prove it, she gave him a small kiss on his cheek.

Smiling, yet seemingly flustered, Ronan began grabbing things from the suite. His belt, his scabior... "I'll go and meet up with Lucien to make sure he doesn't need help at the catacombs. See you at the docks later?"

"Absolutely," Evee said, and grinned. All the while, all she could do was wonder why her smiles and grins and dinner date agreement felt fake. Like she was someone else making the promises. Giving out what was so desperately sought after by a wonderful, albeit quiet, thoughtful man.

No matter how many tongue-lashings she gave herself mentally, or how many logical explanations she forced into her brain about agreeing to date Ronan, Evee still couldn't help feeling like an asshole.

Chapter 9

Having been summoned by the Elders earlier, Evee, Gilly and Viv had little choice but to make an appearance. They'd put off the meeting as long as possible, but the inevitable had to happen.

They'd met up at an agreed-upon time about a block from the Elders' home. Surprisingly, each of their familiars had been there, waiting for them, when they arrived. When ordered to go home, they refused. Being too tired to argue, Evee and her sisters simply walked to their destination in silence, familiars in tow.

After a quick welcome, they'd been escorted into the dining room and motioned to sit at the table, which they did. The room had an old Victorian air about it, but felt comfortably lived in. The dining room contained a beautiful oblong oak table held upright by a large, claw-footed pedestal. Eight oak chairs surrounded the table, each covered with soft, albeit worn, pastel fabric. Against one wall stood a huge china hutch that held more bric-a-brac than china, and beside it sat a small oak table draped with crisp white linen. Atop the linen sat a blue, antique washbowl and pitcher.

Even at this hour, it was evident the Elders had taken the time to dress for the meeting. Vanessa, who appeared to be in her midsixties, the same age as Arabella, wore a black polyester pantsuit printed with red and yellow flowers, and pink slippers, the only type of shoe Vanessa ever wore. She was a constant worrier and often forgetful. Her hair had been dyed auburn, and she wore it in a chin-length sweep-over. Her aquiline nose sat perfectly between bright brown eyes, and wine-red lipstick covered her thin lips. Vanessa loved costume jewelry and a lot of it. Her ears weren't pierced, so she had black and white baubles, the same size and color of her necklace, clamped to her earlobes.

Taka, on the other hand, wore an electric blue overshirt on top of a black blouse and had accessorized it with a string of pearls and a turquoise necklace. Her earrings were turquoise, as well, but about the size of brooches. She was a week shy of sixty-nine, had snow-white hair, which she wore in a tousled pixie cut, blue eyes and a snub nose. Arabella had evidently chosen to dress a little more conservatively for the meeting. She wore a light lavender, silk blouse and white linen pants, and her makeup had been perfectly applied to her heart-shaped face. Her blond-white hair sat on her shoulders, curling under slightly. A classic look for a classy lady.

Arabella began the meeting by telling them about Gunner, Brunedee and more than Evee wanted to hear.

When Arabella finished her report, they sat around the table silent, the mood somber.

"So, let me get this straight," Evee said to Arabella, finally breaking the silence. "You originally found out about the human attack from Gunner Stern, one of the sorcerers?"

"Yes," Arabella said.

"How did he find out about it?" Gilly asked.

"Word travels," Arabella said. "And the sorcerers get around a lot more than we do."

"How can you trust anything any one of the sorcerers has to say?" Viv asked. "They've always been out for themselves. Since when have they ever shown the want or need to help the Triad or any member of the Circle of Sisters?"

Arabella held up a hand. "I know, but for some reason, I think we can trust Gunner."

"What makes you say that?" Evee asked. "He's always hanging around with Trey Cottle and Shandor Black. Both are snakes in the grass, in my opinion. Their power belongs to them and them alone. They use it to their advantage, and they very rarely, if ever, use their spells or incantations or whatever the hell else they do to better mankind."

"Gunner's not like that," Arabella insisted.

"Why are you so set on defending him?" Evee persisted.

"Well, first of all, he didn't have to share any information with me. He could have kept it to himself and gloated over it. In fact, we should have gotten the information from you before hearing it from any sorcerer or a sister who lives a hundred miles away."

"What sister?" Gilly asked.

"Brunedee."

Gilly sighed, and then everyone fell silent.

Evee sat with Hoot perched on her right shoulder, quiet for once, and felt anger start to bubble up in her chest. To her, having the sorcerers know about their problems just made things worse. She stole a glance at her sisters. Both sat, staring at the table, apparently deep in thought. Elvis, Gilly's ferret, had wrapped himself around his mistress's shoulders and Socrates, Viv's Bombay cat, lay across her lap.

"If it helps," Taka said, breaking the silence, "we only found out about the human and Original a relatively short time ago."

"Hours ago," Vanessa corrected. "Hours."

Taka glared at her and tsked.

"Okay," Evee said. "Gunner and Brunedee told you. What happened after that? I don't understand what's going on here." She looked from Arabella to Taka, then at Vanessa. These were their Elders, the women the Triad were supposed to go to when all else failed. Right now they simply looked like three tired old women.

"Weren't you supposed to contact all the leaders in the Circle of Sisters and ask for their assistance?" Evee asked Arabella. "Weren't they supposed to put out a collective protection spell around this city? A binding spell to protect us against the Cartesians and the disappearance of more Originals?"

"I did," Arabella said. "All of it. I can't explain why the spells have been ineffective. Occasionally, the three of us can get a spell to work. Then at other times they don't."

"Maybe it's the ozone layer," Taka said. "Or global warming. Probably both, since we have so much pollution, and glaciers are melting, you know."

"What the hell does that have to do with their spells?" Vanessa snapped.

"Well, if it can affect glaciers and the heating pattern of the earth, don't you think both or at least one can affect spells?" Taka said.

"I don't believe it's either," Arabella said. "Something

else is going on. We just haven't been able to put a finger on it. Tell us what's been going on with the three of you. What problems are you running into? How are the Originals?"

"I have the Nosferatu together in the catacombs," Evee said. "The Benders created this electrical dome with their scabiors to keep any Cartesians from getting to them. Seems to be working."

"Same with the Loup Garous," Viv said. "I've got them all together in the North Compound."

"The Chenilles are together in the Louis I Cemetery," Gilly said.

Arabella frowned. "How can you keep them cooped up like that without infighting?"

"Oh, we have infighting," Evee said. "At least I do. But so far, my calming spells seem to keep them under control."

"So your spells work?" Vanessa asked.

"Sometimes," Evee said. "Fortunately, the calming one did."

"Hmm," Arabella mused. "I guess those Benders know what they're doing. Electrical domes. Who'd have thought of that?"

"Yeah, it was a good idea," Evee said, "but we ran into a problem with the one in the catacombs earlier today. Its power began to wane. It had to be recharged. I'm concerned that whatever's affecting our spells will wind up dousing those domes until they're out and can't be recharged. We're taking advantage of them while they're still live. Keeping the Originals we have protected beneath the domes while we search for the missing ones."

"My word," Arabella said, the furrows in her brow deepening.

"Global warming," Taka said. "I'm telling you. Global warming."

"Oh, shut up with your global warming," Vanessa snapped.

"Stop, both of you," Arabella said to Vanessa and Taka. "We've got some serious issues to work through, and the problem is that I don't have a clue about what to do about them. I do know that we have to get this under control and fast. The police have already been here twice. They showed up not long after we heard about the human and the Nosferatu."

Evee felt her blood run cold. "What did you tell them?"

"Nothing," Arabella said. "I didn't even answer the door. We just stayed really still and quiet and waited until they left."

"They'll be back," Vanessa said. "I feel it."

"Why would they come here?" Gilly asked. "Why would they tie you to the Nosferatu or any of the Originals? We've spent years protecting the city from any knowledge of the Originals and of us. I mean who we were…are."

"I think our cover's blown," Taka said. "They're going to be hunting us like dogs. You wait and see. It'll be like back in the day. Lynchings, burning at the stake, the whole enchilada."

"Stop. You're overreacting," Arabella said.

"Oh, yeah?" Taka replied. "Then how come you refused to answer the door? I'm telling you, we're going to be riding the flashback train. People are going to come after us, wanting to burn the devil out of us."

Vanessa huffed. "You're going over the deep end, Taka. We have enough to deal with without your imagination jumping onto an express train to never-never land."

"I'm not on any train," Taka insisted. "It's the truth."

Gilly huffed. "Look, instead of spending so much time arguing, explain to me why an entire clan of the Circle of Sisters can't affect change in this situation. We're talking at least, what, fifteen to seventeen hundred witches around the country, all of them focused on our situation, and yet not only are we still fighting the same problems, but more are being added every day."

Gilly turned to Arabella, her expression hard with fury. "Why is that, Arabella? I mean, you're the head of this group of Elders. Why are spells from around this country turning out to be so ineffective? Why are ours useless, for the most part? What the hell are we supposed to do?"

Arabella returned her hard stare. "The first thing we have to figure out is why they're not working."

"And how are we supposed to do that?" Evee asked. "Anybody have a functioning crystal ball here?"

"Oh, crystal balls are so passé," Taka said.

Arabella suddenly sat upright in her chair. "Evee, have you tried channeling?"

"Huh?" Evee said, the question catching her unawares.

"Channeling. Maybe you can contact one of the dead Originals, some of the Loup Garous that were slaughtered or the Chenille that's passed on. Even Chank, your Nosferatu. Maybe they can see more from the other side than what we're seeing here. They might have some idea about what we can do with this."

Evee pursed her lips. She considered Arabella's suggestion. Thought it might have some merit.

Just as she was about to voice her agreement to try the channeling, Hoot began to flap a wing. He hopped off Evee's shoulder and landed on the dining room table and walked rapidly from one end of the table to the other, squawking the entire time. Among the Triad, Evee was the only one who understood what Hoot was shouting about. Unfortunately, she knew the Elders could understand him, as well.

"What?" Arabella asked, staring at Hoot.

The owl flapped his wings, and screeched until Evee thought he'd lose his voice. Hoot was ratting her out about her intimacy with Lucien. She wanted to duck under the table and hide from embarrassment.

Evidently deciding to join the rat wagon, Socrates scrambled off Viv's lap and jumped onto the table, along with Hoot. He began to meow, then caterwaul.

Although Evee couldn't understand what Socrates was saying, judging from the red blotches blooming on Viv's cheeks, it wasn't a good thing. She had a feeling Viv was being snitched on by her familiar, as well.

Knowing it would be useless to try and quiet Hoot, Evee had to wait until he ran out of steam. When both owl and cat finally stood quietly on the table, Arabella, Taka and Vanessa stared at the Triad with shocked expressions.

"Is—is it true?" Arabella asked. "They're saying the two of you have been intimate with the Benders. Those *human* Benders."

Elvis, Gilly's ferret, let out a small chitter and snuggled closer to his mistress.

Evee looked from Viv to Gilly, then back to Arabella. Words refused to come out of her mouth.

"I'm going to ask you one more time," Arabella said to Evee and Viv. "Have you two been intimate with the Benders?"

Evee wanted to take Hoot by the neck and pluck every feather from his body. After a long moment, she finally faced Arabella and said, "Yes, I have."

"Me, too," Viv said, her voice just above a whisper.

"In the name of all gods, are you kidding?" Taka said. "Oh, this is bad. Very not good."

Vanessa threw her hands up. "Figures. Hell, it might not be good, but at least we're getting closer to solving our spell problems."

"What do you mean we're getting closer to solving them?" Viv asked.

Arabella aimed her chin at Evee. "Your familiar claims you've been intimate with Lucien, and you," she aimed her chin at Viv, "with Nikoli." She looked at Gilly. "Your familiar has given us no indication of any transgression on your part, so I'm assuming you have not, as of yet, been intimate with the human Bender you're paired with?"

"Don't be ridiculous," Gilly said. "I have not."

Arabella leaned into the dining table. "I think we've found the problem as to why some of our spells aren't working. Why we're being inundated with such chaos and mayhem." Her voice rose an octave, and her eyes sparked with anger. "You know the rules about humans, do you not, Vivienne and Evette?"

"Yes, I do," Evee said. "But the Triad curse says that we're not to marry a human or live intimately with one. Neither Viv nor I have married a Bender, nor are we living intimately with them."

"That may not make a difference," Taka said. "It's all in the interpretation. It's possible that sleeping…no, having sex with a human counts, as well. For all we know, it could be the reason why the ozone layer is thinning."

"Drop the damn ozone layer," Vanessa snapped.

"Yet it could be enough to cause our spells to not work," Arabella said solemnly.

"But not all of our spells are ineffective. Remember,

I told you my calming spell worked on the Nosferatu," Evee pointed out.

"Were you intimate with the Bender before or after you cast that spell?" Arabella asked.

Evee glanced away and chewed her bottom lip. She remembered how Lucien had touched her as she sat on the dryer, still soaking wet after having jumped into the river. How his thumbs found their way between her legs, crisscrossing, circling, rubbing across her jeans until she'd exploded beneath his hand.

"Before or after?" Arabella asked again.

"I didn't have sex with him before or after the spell," Evee said, feeling a tinge of guilt. It wasn't like she lied. They really hadn't had sex. Not yet, anyway.

Arabella narrowed her eyes. "But were you intimate with him in any way?"

Evee threw up her hands, hating the interrogation. "Yes, yes, we were intimate. No sex, but intimate, yes. And I wanted more, damn it!" She wanted to grab the blue pitcher perched inside its matching washbowl and throw it across the room.

The Elders turned to Viv.

"Yes, we had sex," Viv said, anger in her voice. "Lots of sex. Good sex. The I-want-more-of-it kind of sex. The three of you happy now?"

With her back ramrod straight, Arabella placed both of her hands, palm down, on the table. "It's not enough that we're having to fight these Cartesians, who are becoming more numerous by the day. Yes, we have the Benders to ward them off, but this electrified canopy they supposedly set over your Originals has begun to weaken. Your own words. I have a feeling that the growth in the number of Cartesians and the weakness of our spells are directly related to your intimacy with the Benders. We must regroup, re-empower ourselves so we're up for the struggle. This means no more intimacy with the Benders, do you understand?"

"Yes," Gilly said.

Arabella ignored her. "Vivienne, Evette, do the two of you understand?"

Evee gave her a half-hearted nod.

"Vivienne?" Arabella said.

"Yeah, I'm not deaf. I understand."

"If the two of you don't take this seriously, we will lose this battle and probably all of the Originals. And trust me, it's not hard to figure out that if the Cartesians plan to take out the Originals, they plan on taking you, as well. This is bigger than the six of us. Bigger than the entire clan of the Circle of Sisters. The Cartesians mean to control the entire netherworld. I can see that as clearly as I see my own hands. How any of you can think of sex at a time when so much turmoil surrounds us is beyond me. You should be ashamed of yourselves."

Tired of the harangue, Evee finally spoke up. "I'm not ashamed. I have nothing to be ashamed of. I broke no mandate of the curse. I haven't married Lucien, and I'm not living with him intimately."

"But you almost had sex with him," Taka said. "I'm sure that counts for something. Maybe it's just a part of the curse the first Elders didn't clarify. Maybe that's part of it and why things have gone so haywire."

Evee rolled her eyes, then looked down at the table.

Seemingly satisfied that he'd done his job appropriately, Hoot hopped across the table and jumped back on Evee's shoulder. She shooed him off, and he landed on the floor beside the table, squawking.

Socrates attempted to settle back into Viv's lap, and she swatted him off and onto the floor alongside Hoot.

Evee and Viv looked at each other simultaneously and nodded. Their familiars were supposed to protect them and be loyal. There obviously was a clause in the familiar journal, because Hoot and Socrates had just betrayed them.

Evee had never felt so lonely as she did in that moment. Except for her two sisters, she was utterly alone and lost. She didn't know what to do next, which wasn't like her. She had thought herself to be levelheaded, and been sure that she could always see the next step that needed to be taken. Now all that seemed visible to her was a vat of mud that gave no direction as to what they should do next.

Arabella looked around solemnly. "Now that everything's out on the table, so to speak, we're going to fix this. So much has gotten out of hand that I'm considering having one of the sorcerers help us."

Evee felt her mouth drop open. "The sorcerers? Are you kidding?"

"You can't!" Gilly said, alarm making her voice shrill. "Those men aren't interested in anyone but themselves."

"Gunner's different," Arabella said.

"That's because he's sweet on you," Taka said.

Gilly's head snapped to attention. "Is that why you want to bring that sorcerer into our circle? You hammer Viv and Evee about the Benders, yet you want to bring in a sorcerer who has the hots for you?"

"Watch your mouth, young lady," Arabella warned. "Gunner is not like Trey or Shandor. They may be together often, but I think it's simply because like hangs about like. Gunner was the one who warned me about the humans and the death of the Nosferatu. He told me on the QT, not when Trey and Shandor were around. He might be able to offer some form of advice, have some spell that isn't used by the Circle of Sisters. His viewpoint will be once removed, clearer, which in and of itself may be of help."

Evee lightly tapped a fist on the table. "I refuse to let the sorcerers get involved with my Originals. They'll make it worse. I don't trust any of them. I don't know how you can even suggest it, Arabella. Ever since I can remember, you've drilled into us that we take care of our own problems."

Arabella clicked her tongue against her palate and turned her head to one side.

"I think Arabella's idea has some merit," Taka said. "We've lost our footing, even if it's because you two were doing the dirty with the Benders, and we have to find a way to stand up again."

Evee sighed and looked at Vanessa. "And you? Do you feel the same way?"

"I'm on the fence about it."

Evee looked at Arabella, who turned back to face her. "Look, we are the ones out there fighting these Cartesians with the Benders, despite any sexual events. They have saved many Originals since they've been here. We're out there constantly, with little sleep, forgetting to eat, hunting for the missing Originals. Fighting to keep the other Originals safe. All I ask is that you don't add to our chaos by bringing any sorcerers into our situation. We don't need any more problems."

Arabella studied Evee's face, and from the look in Arabella's eyes, Evee knew the Elder was considering all she'd just said.

"You know the rules in matters like this," Arabella said. "Majority vote determines the decision. However, since you and Vivienne were intimate with your Benders,

I'm releasing the majority vote. I'll take full responsibility for what should be done."

"Good thing because you already have my vote," Gilly said, not breaking eye contact. "Hell no on the sorcerers."

Arabella gave her an infinitesimal nod. "I will think on this. I know it's getting close to feeding time, and that the three of you have to go."

"Promise me," Evee said. "Promise me you won't bring a sorcerer into our circle."

"All I can promise you, Evette, is that I will think on it and let you know my decision, which will be soon."

"Why not now?" Gilly asked.

"Enough," Arabella said. "I said I'd think on it, and I will. End of discussion."

"What will you do if the police show up here again?" Viv asked, diverting everyone's attention. "Keep hiding?"

"Of course not," Arabella said. "We're going to have to eventually face them."

"Does facing them mean you tell them we're witches?" Gilly asked. "That we're responsible for the Originals that are running about the city?"

Evee squirmed in her seat, grateful she hadn't told the Elders about the Cartesian that tried grabbing her by the river.

"No way would Arabella tell the police that," Taka said. "All we have to tell them is that we're three old ladies living here in the Garden District and have no idea about what they're saying."

"So you plan to bold-face lie to them," Gilly said.

"Absolutely," Taka said. "That way they'll move on, look in a different direction."

"I don't understand what would cause the police to come here in the first place," Viv said. "Do you think they suspect we're witches?"

"No way, Jose," Taka said. "We've kept that secret under wraps forever."

"What if the sorcerers said something to them, directed them here?" Evee said. "Why else would they be way out here in the Garden District? It happened in the Quarter and Chalmette. Why aren't they searching out there?"

"We can what-if until dawn," Arabella said. "Don't worry about the police. I'll take care of that situation. Now go about your feeding."

As Evee, Viv and Gilly left the Elders' home, Evee couldn't help wondering if they were the ones being fed—to the police, to the Cartesians, to annihilation.

Chapter 10

Lucien stood outside St. John's Cathedral, pacing in front of the massive structure, waiting for Evee. Every time he spotted a person with bold black hair, he felt his heart stop and then kick-start again. He had to admit he was absolutely smitten by the woman, and he feared his feelings for her might cloud his judgment. He'd all but handed her over to Ronan, for heaven's sake. What business did he have wishing, wanting anything regarding Evette François? Still, Lucien couldn't help wondering what had happened between Ronan and Evette. What did he say? What did she say?

As if the cosmos had been listening and chose to answer, Lucien spotted Ronan a block away.

Lucien felt his jaw tighten reflexively.

"All clear?" Ronan asked when he reached Lucien on the steps of the cathedral.

"So far. Scabior dome is still holding up."

Ronan checked his watch. "Evee's running a little late," he said more to himself than to Lucien.

"Mmm," Lucien said, trying to sound offhand. "We've still got plenty of time." What he really wanted to know was what had happened between Ronan and Evee once they'd been left alone. Knowing Ronan, however, that information would never pass his lips unless someone directly asked. So he did.

After checking both sides of the vast concrete walkway that fronted the cathedral, and still not spotting Evee, Lucien asked, "So, how'd it go?"

At first Ronan looked at him questioningly, as if he had no idea what his cousin meant. When realization dawned on him, a slow smile brightened his face. "You were right."

"About?"

"You know, being more assertive. Telling Evee how I felt and sort of letting the chips fall where they may."

Lucien felt nausea wash over him. "And where did they fall?"

Ronan gave him a small shrug. "I didn't bring up how I really felt about her. You know, it seemed too brash, too soon. Hell, I've barely spoken to Evee. But I did ask her to go on a dinner date once this was all done."

Lucien watched him expectantly.

"She said, yes, cuz. She really did. Even gave me a small kiss on my cheek." Ronan looked down at the ground and tapped the toe of his boot against one of the concrete steps of St. John's.

Every bone in Lucien's body felt like it went limp at one time. "Sh-she kissed you?"

"Yeah. Nothing big, you know. A kiss on the cheek isn't like a whole French job, but it was sweet. Perfect, in fact.

Thing is… I don't know… I could be overthinking things, but she didn't seem really thrilled about the prospect."

"What do you mean?"

"You know, it came across kind of…plastic. Almost like she was doing me a favor."

"You are overthinking it. Evee's not like that. If she said she'd have dinner with you, then you've got a dinner date."

Forcing a smile, Lucien fist-bumped Ronan's fist. "You go, big man."

Something inside Lucien felt like it wanted to explode. He was anxious to see Evee again, especially after the last time they'd been together. There was no question as to what he felt for her, and it was more than sexual. All of who she was consumed him, body, mind and soul. All he could think about was her. And he had no idea when those feelings started or how they grew so intense so quickly.

Lucien paced nervously up and down the cathedral steps, needing to work off excess energy. He feared that the moment Evee appeared, he'd take her into his arms, as he thirsted so much for her full, luscious lips. He needed to kiss her, to feel her skin against his. He hated being away from her, even for a moment. And that frightened him. He had no business feeling this way. Now he had no choice but to wait until time passed and the dinner date between Ronan and Evee occurred. Only then would she be able to fairly compare.

Lucien chewed the inside of his right cheek. He'd never felt this way about any other woman before. The ones he'd had before Evee had been easy to let go. Too easy. Most of the time he'd found them too clingy, which made him all the more anxious to be on his way. Lucien didn't consider himself a cad. He was a realist. Why lead a

woman on, allowing her to believe there was more between them than what he felt? He couldn't, wouldn't toy
with a woman that way.

With Evee, Lucien felt like he wore a new pair of
shoes, ones that felt a little snug around the toes, but became more comfortable with each time he put them on.

"Where should I take her?" Ronan asked. "There're
so many great places to eat—"

"Three o'clock," Lucien said suddenly, and motioned
with his eyes for Ronan to look to his right.

Evee was on her way to them.

Ronan's face broke out into a huge smile when he saw
her. Lucien's heart skipped two beats.

As usual, during feeding time, Evee was dressed in
black jeans, a pullover T and sneakers, with her hair
pulled back into a ponytail.

When she met Ronan and Lucien at the upper step
of the cathedral, Lucien frowned. There was something
in her eyes that bothered him. A hard, dismissive look.

She nodded at him, then at Ronan. The action couldn't
have been more aloof.

"What's wrong?" Lucien asked.

"Nothing." Evee's voice had an angry snap to it. "Let's
get to work."

Lucien took Evee's arm, turned her toward him. She
pulled away.

"What's wrong with you?" Lucien asked. "Have I done
something to upset you?"

Evee sighed, her eyes softening a little. "You haven't
done anything. I have."

"What are you talking about?" Ronan asked.

She eyed Lucien, her expression serious. "All the
chaos we're going through—more Cartesians coming
out of seemingly everywhere, human attacks, human

witnesses, the deaths of some of the Originals, the missing of many more… The only thing we can figure out is that all of it has to do with our being…" She glanced at Ronan, then seemed to check herself. "With the two of you being human. It has to stop. We can't handle everything that's going on now. What the hell are we going to do as things get progressively worse?"

"I'm a bit confused," Ronan said. "What has to stop? Our helping you?"

Evee threw a dismissive hand in the air as if to encompass the entire vocabulary of the English language. "Anything other than business," she finally said. "Nothing intimate, like talks about dinner or dates. It's business at hand or nothing. Everything else clouds our judgment."

Lucien felt his heart thud painfully in his chest. He knew she'd meant to say that their being intimate in her home had caused most of this, and he knew in his heart of hearts that it couldn't be further from the truth. He couldn't lose this woman. But as soon as he had thought, he wanted to flog himself for even thinking it. Not only was Ronan looking forward to spending time with her, but Lucien had never "pined" for any woman. And especially not over some stupid curse, whether real or exaggerated. He needed Evee in his life. The admission of that, even in his own mind, caused his breathing to grow labored.

"You and your sisters met with the Elders, haven't you?" Lucien said.

"Yes, but what does that matter?"

"Were the Elders the one who came to this conclusion? That you're to stay away from us? I mean, in any capacity other than business? No small talk, nothing off topic?"

Evee turned and gave him a hard look. "Not in those exact words, but yes. They were adamant about focusing on one thing. The problems facing us now. They already knew about the human attack and death in the Quarter and the killing of the Nosferatu by its leader. The police even came to their house. Twice."

Ronan's head jerked up. "What did the Elders tell them?"

"Nothing," Evee said. "They ignored them. Didn't even answer the door." She shook her head. "I just don't get what the police were doing all the way out there. How they knew where the Elders lived."

Setting the police issue on a back burner, Lucien took Evee's arm again, and though she tried to pull away once more, her effort felt half-hearted. He pulled her closer to him, touched her chin with a finger and turned her head so she faced him. Peripherally he saw Ronan bristle.

"Evee, you didn't do anything wrong," Lucien assured her. "As I've known and you've reiterated, the curse of the Triad is that they were not to marry a human or live intimately with one. I haven't done either with you, nor has Ronan."

"Yeah, well, according to the Elders, there surely had to be a clarification error with the original Triad and first Elders. I spouted the curse as I'd been taught it, verbatim, to the Elders, but they're convinced an error of omission occurred back then. They're convinced that our—any intimacy, however small, creates more chaos, despite what the curse specifically states."

Frustrated, Lucien looked from Evee to Ronan. "It'll soon be time to leave for the feeding. Cuz, would you mind doing one final check in the catacombs?"

Ronan stared at him. It didn't take much for Lucien to read the expression on his cousin's face.

Dude, if I'm supposed to try and get closer to Evee

why don't you check the catacombs so I can be alone with her?

Ignoring the blatant glare, Lucien said, "We'll head over to the docks. Make sure everything's good to go. Once you check the catacombs, you can meet us there."

With a scowl, Ronan turned on his heel and headed into the cathedral.

As soon as they were alone, Lucien asked Evee, "How did the Elders find out about you and me, anyway?"

"My familiar ratted me out. So did Viv's."

Lucien did a double take. "Viv's been with... Nikoli?"

"Evidently, because Socrates, Viv's familiar, sang like a canary, telling the Elders all he knew about the two of them. Same thing with Hoot regarding you and me. I swear I wanted to pluck that owl bald."

"Evee, you have to hear me out here," Lucien said. "I realize there's a Triad curse, and that it's real and significant. But I think something as serious as that curse set by the first Elders wouldn't have been left to interpretation. It was stated in the way they meant for it to be understood. They wouldn't have carelessly thrown out any curse that could be misread. It would have been direct. I honestly believe that our small sexual encounter doesn't have a doggone thing to do with the turmoil that seems to be growing daily."

"How can you know that for sure?"

"Because I know the Cartesians, and they're the ones responsible for all this. Viv may have brought the Originals and the Triad to the Cartesians' attention when she offhandedly and in anger said she'd quit caring for her Loups. But I know the rest of it, everything we're experiencing now, has to do with the Cartesians. You have to remember that they have a leader, and that the leader has an agenda. It wants to be the sole power in the netherworld, then of the entire universe. It wants to control the stars, the weather, inhabit the earth and populate any other planet with Cartesians. In order to do that, it has to control and take all the Originals to absorb their power. It wants the Triad for the same reason. Then it'll take possession of all the power of every creature in the netherworld, those that are the offspring of the Originals. And the way that leader plans on accomplishing this is to create chaos and turmoil. To confuse us and have us running in circles so it can accomplish that goal. Don't you get it? This is much bigger than anything you or I could have created by what happened on the dryer."

Evee stared at him, eyes wide, blinking back tears. "Who's this leader? Why aren't we looking for it? If we take the leader out, wouldn't the rest of them scatter?"

"I've always believed the same thing," Lucien said. "The problem is we don't have a clue as to who or where this leader is. It never makes an appearance. Always sends its minions to do its dirty work."

"Then how do you know what to look for?" Evee asked. "Shouldn't that be our focus, finding the leader?"

Lucien nodded. "Of course. But, Evee, we've been looking for the leader for ten generations. Right now our priorities have to be caring for the Originals you have and finding the ones that are missing. Killing Cartesians along the way will be a given. Hopefully, we'll luck out and find the bastard that leads them."

A tear slid down Evee's cheek. "This so-called leader has to be the first Cartesian created by the original Triads. The ones who took certain matters into their own hands and turned their betrothed into the Originals, and did it out of spite and anger." She sighed heavily. "Regardless, I can't take any more chances. We have to get this straightened out. I don't know if the curse regarding

Triads and humans was misinterpreted or not. Whether something was misquoted as it was handed down from generation to generation or not, I just can't take any more chances. It can't simply be coincidence that after we became intimate, things seemed to jump further out of control. So, please, let's drop this for now and get to work. Like you said, it's getting close to feeding time, and I need to get the Nosferatu ready. Make sure they're not trying to massacre each other again."

Lucien took a deep breath, nodded, and let go of her arm. He had so much more he wanted to say to her. He longed to tell her how much he needed her. But he said nothing. Only led the way to the docks.

They hadn't walked a hundred feet when Lucien suddenly grabbed her arm.

"Wait," he said, catching a whiff of clove in the air.

"What?"

"A rift," he said, looking up at the sky. The first hint that a Cartesian was nearby was the scent of clove, followed by the smell of sulfur as it worked its way through a rift.

He suddenly felt Evee at his side, holding on to his arm. She looked up, seemingly searching the sky, as well.

"Where?" Evee whispered. "I don't see anything."

"Clove. I smelled it as we were leaving the cathedral. That scent is the first sign a Cartesian has found a rift and is working its way through it." He felt Evee's grip tighten on his arm.

"Do you see anything?" she asked, still looking skyward.

"No. But it's close. Just hasn't broken through the rift yet. Once it does, I'll smell sulfur along with the clove." Lucien wished he had a giant spotlight to aim at the sky. Stars were out, but every black distance between the Big

Dipper and the next cluster of stars seemed darker than the one above it. All of them looked like rifts.

Just then, Lucien heard the sound of pounding, running feet behind them. He swirled about and saw Ronan headed their way.

As Ronan pulled up alongside Lucien, he said, "I smelled it from the catacombs. Clove."

"Yeah," Lucien said. "I just caught a whiff of it a moment ago."

Lucien was about to tell Evee to go into the cathedral for safekeeping when a loud boom sounded from overhead. It was immediately followed by the overwhelming stink of sulfur.

In that moment, three rifts opened up overhead. A Cartesian hung from each rift, leaning over by its waist. Each had a massive, matted fur head, huge black eyes with no pupils. Mouths open, every tooth a lethally sharp incisor. Their claws, long, sharp talons, all of them reaching, searching, clawing.

Lucien shouted for Evee to go into the cathedral and into the catacombs. He and Ronan simultaneously pulled their scabiors from their sheaths, snapped their wrists once, then twirled the scabiors between their fingers faster than even Evee's eyes could track.

Lucien aimed it at one of the Cartesians, and for the first time since he could remember, he missed. Ronan aimed the electrical beam from his scabior at the same Cartesian and caught it right between the eyes. He kept his scabior aimed at it until the rift from which it came closed up as neatly as a zipper.

In that moment, another rift suddenly tore through the sky, then another and another, with Cartesians worming their long arms through each opening. Within seconds, their massive heads poked through the rift, and like their counterparts, they began to stretch and swing their long arms and claws toward them.

"Go into the catacombs," Lucien shouted again at Evee. "Hide out there with the Nosferatu!"

"Bullshit!" Evee shouted back. "I'm not about to leave you and Ronan out here by yourselves."

"Go!" Ronan insisted. "There're too many out right now. Stop being stubborn, damn it. Go! You don't have anything out here to use for protection."

Lucien palmed the handle of his scabior once more, snapped his wrist once, then twirled the scabior at breakneck speed between his fingers. He took aim at the Cartesian closest to them. Lightning exploded from the bloodstone atop the scabior and, this time, struck the Cartesian in the forehead. With an ear-piercing howl, the Cartesian flew back, and Lucien heard a loud pop, an indicator that he'd pushed the Cartesian back one dimension.

Keeping his aim steady, Lucien shot again, then again. After a third sound of explosion, the rift that had held that Cartesian zipped closed.

Just when he thought he was down to three Cartesians, another boom sounded and another rift appeared overhead, farther to the left. The Cartesian coming from this rift obviously didn't plan on wasting any time. It immediately thrust itself from the rift to waist level and swung an arm at Evee.

One thing with Cartesians, they were so massive that they had no need to fully leave the rift. Half of them hung out, vulnerable, while the other half stayed safely out of sight. They didn't need to make a full body appearance, however. Their arms were so long and their talons so sharp that they simply had to swipe at their victims and could easily gore, grab, kill anything they desired.

"Now!" Lucien yelled at Evee. "For heaven's sake, go!"

"I'm not leaving the two of you," she insisted.

Lucien couldn't take his eyes off the sky to argue with her, reason with her. Cartesians seemed to be dangling from every corner of the night. Long yellow incisors bared, talons spread and reaching, reaching.

A feeling ran up the back of Lucien's back, and it took a second for his brain to register it as concern, a sense of being overwhelmed, overpowered.

It surprised Lucien when he'd missed the first shot at one of the Cartesians because it'd never happened to him before. But what surprised him even more at the moment were the feelings oppressing him. They all balled up into one emotion. Fear. Too many Cartesians, not enough scabiors. Evee.

Before Lucien knew it, Evee suddenly appeared between him and Ronan. He opened his mouth, planning to scold her for being so hardheaded, but snapped it shut when he saw her hold out her hands, palms up, aimed at the sky.

"Double, thrice, by tens ye shall see.
No longer one to be seen by thee.
Thine eyes shall fully confuse thy mind.
Making all evil intentions blind.
Blunder thee, blunder now.
I call upon Poseidon, Tiamat and Apsu, bring strength to my command.
So it is said.
So shall it be."

When Evee was done, Lucien stood dumbstruck, watching as the Cartesians who had been aiming directly for them were now swinging wildly in every direction but theirs.

A look of confusion filled the Cartesians' grossly huge

black eyes. Each looked from right to left, up and down, and swung its arms in random directions.

From what Lucien saw, it was as if either the Cartesians had lost their eyesight or Evee's incantation had performed Cartesian lobotomies.

"Shoot," Evee shouted at Lucien and Ronan, snapping both out of a stupor.

Lucien aimed at another Cartesian, shot it back four dimensions. Ronan targeted one, and managed to push it back five. Finally, Lucien took aim at another and sent it back three, which he gladly settled for because it was the last Cartesian and all the rifts had vanished.

Drawing in an exhausted breath, Lucien replaced his scabior in its sheath, then turned to Evee, who appeared to be mildly shaken by all she'd just witnessed.

"What did you do?" Ronan asked. "They looked confused, like they'd gone blind or something. Is that what your spell did? Cause them to go blind?"

Evee grinned. "Something a little better. I did an illusion spell. Instead of the Cartesians seeing just one of you, me and Lucien, I made them see twenty of all three of us, running in different directions. They couldn't tell what was real from illusion. That's what caused the confusion. That's why they were swinging in every direction. Because they saw us everywhere."

Lucien shook his head in disbelief and took Evee's arm. She didn't resist this time. He walked her slowly toward the docks. Ronan took hold of her other arm as though it took two to steady her walk. She didn't protest.

When they reached the dock, Ronan said, "I'll pull anchor and slip-tie the mooring rope."

"I'll have a look at the motor," Lucien said. "Don't want to run out of fuel."

Lucien kept one eye on Evee as she stood a few yards

away from the dock. There was amusement on her face. He figured she knew that at the end of a crisis, men had to do something, anything, to calm their nerves. Which was exactly what he and Ronan were doing.

Suddenly, catching a strong scent of cloves and sulfur that seemingly came out of nowhere and without preamble, Lucien and Ronan froze in the middle of their nerve-calming work and looked up and about.

Evee was looking, as well, into a rift that had formed right over her head. She seemed frozen in place.

"Evee, run!" Lucien yelled.

"To the cathedral," Ronan added. "Get inside the cathedral!"

As Lucien and Ronan scrambled off the ferry, reached for their scabiors, the Cartesian that had managed to sneak up on them was hanging from his waist, his large arm and claws swinging back, ready to strike Evee.

Running and trying to aim a scabior so it hit the right spot were two things that didn't work well together.

Lucien saw Evee's hair brush across her face as the Cartesian reached but missed her. It quickly swung back, wiggled over the rift until it was nearly below waist level, and aimed at Evee once more.

Lucien's brain kicked into overdrive. It might take a scabior to rid a Cartesian from this dimension, but they wouldn't stand a chance with this one. It was too close to Evee. He had to get her out of the way.

Evidently realizing the same thing, both Lucien and Ronan sprinted and ran as fast as their legs could carry them toward Evee. Lucien saw Evee's mouth move, but no words came out and she remained glued to her spot. Only now she looked over at Lucien and Ronan running at full speed toward her. Lucien saw the resignation on her face.

Just as the Cartesian drew his arm and claws up from his back swing, Lucien and Ronan reached Evee at the same time. Lucien tackled her to the ground even as the creature's claws raked through her ponytail, yanking out a bit of hair. Lucien kept his body covering hers as he worked his scabior out of its sheath.

It was then Lucien heard an ear-piercing scream.

"No!"

Lucien rolled over in time to see the Cartesian lifting Ronan into the rift. After the Cartesian had missed Evee, it had found Ronan in midrun toward Evee, right in its target area. It had skewered Ronan in the head. In one temple and out of the other. There was no mistaking, Lucien's cousin was dead.

Lucien stumbled to his feet, and this time he was the one screaming, "No! No!" He aimed his scabior at the Cartesian. Blasts of lightning shot the creature in the forehead, in the chest, which caused it to howl in pain and fold back into another dimension. No matter how many times Lucien struck the beast with the scabior, Ronan remained stuck to its claws.

Roaring with fury and shooting the Cartesian again and again, Lucien knew he must have looked like a wild man ready to take on the world.

But the world soon came to an end.

For the rift closed, taking the Cartesian and Ronan with it.

Chapter 11

It had taken Evee some time to convince Lucien to leave the docks and the cathedral. He kept looking up at the sky, as if hoping by some miracle Ronan would drop out of it, and he'd be there to catch him. She couldn't blame Lucien for not wanting to leave. Had the Cartesian taken one of her sisters, Evee would probably have spent the rest of her life in the spot she'd disappeared from, waiting for her return.

Aside from Ronan's death, the worst part now was the lack of closure. There was no body to return to his cousins or his family back home. All Lucien had was a story to tell and memories to live with. Evee couldn't imagine how difficult that must be for him. Her heart ached, not only for Lucien but for Ronan. The man had died so she might live. She'd never have the chance to thank him, to offer gratitude or restitution.

Just before they left the docks, Lucien signaled for his cousins from the geo node on his watch. He gave them the coordinates to Evee's café, which sat only a few blocks away in the Quarter. Evee also summoned her sisters, using special signals they'd refined since they were children. Whenever any of them found trouble, they'd summon the other two by using the distress calls innate to their familiars. For Evee, it was a high-pitched screech, the same sound Hoot made when he was afraid or sensed mortal danger. They'd refined the calls, making each sound so natural that another human would never associate the sound with them. Evee had no coordinates to give Viv and Gilly, but having gone through this drill on more than one occasion, they knew the first place to look for her was the café.

Evee held Lucien's hand as they walked the few blocks to their destination. The café would be closed at this hour. A good, private place to break the news to the other Benders and her sisters.

When they reached Bon Appétit, Evee unlocked the door, switched on the lights and motioned Lucien to sit anywhere he pleased. He chose a table, sat and remained mute, only shaking his head to turn down the drink Evee offered him. She wanted to sit by his side, to hold him and ease some of the pain he carried. But she felt that at this moment, the one thing he needed was to be alone with his thoughts. He'd be forced to talk soon enough. Forced to relive that horrible moment when the Cartesian had taken his cousin. For now, the most helpful thing Evee could do for him would be to leave him with the solitude he seemed to desire.

As she went behind the counter to prepare drinks for Gavril, Nikoli and her sisters, a thought suddenly struck Evee. What if Lucien blamed her for Ronan's death? Had it not been for her, there would have been no reason for him to run in that direction or block anyone from danger. The Cartesian would never have reached him.

Just thinking about that made Evee feel weak in the knees. She pulled up a stool near the register, kept one eye on Lucien, who sat with his head bowed so low it nearly touched the table. Tears welled up in Evee's eyes. The truth had been staring her in the face all along and either shock or shame had kept her from seeing it. And that truth was Ronan would still be alive this very minute had it not been for her. If she'd only listened when Lucien told her to run. But fear had kept her frozen in place. What kind of Triad did that make her? To freeze up in the face of danger?

A stupid and useless Triad, that was what it made her.

Evee felt shame and remorse consume her and felt tears flow down her cheeks. The only sounds within the café were the coffeepot brewing, the ice machine dropping a fresh load of ice into its bin, Lucien drawing in a deep, ragged breath from time to time and the occasional creak of a floorboard. Evee kept her tears silent.

Over the next twenty minutes, the only thing that changed in the café was the smell. It was now filled with the scent of freshly brewed, dark-roast, chicory coffee. Evee had remained seated on the stool and Lucien at the table he'd chosen when he first walked in. He'd yet to raise his head or speak since they arrived.

Evee was debating on whether or not to offer him coffee when the front door of the café opened and the rest of their troupe stormed in. Gavril, Gilly, Viv and Nikoli. Out of habit, Evee found herself waiting for Ronan to bring up the rear, then felt fresh tears fill her eyes.

"What's wrong?" Gilly and Viv asked simultaneously, both staring at Evee.

Instead of answering, Evee motioned to Lucien with her eyes.

Obviously catching the signal, Gavril and Nikoli walked over to Lucien, each standing on either side of him.

Nikoli placed a hand on Lucien's shoulder, which caused him to finally lift his head.

The look on Lucien's face was one of a man whose soul had just been ripped in two. His eyes were red-rimmed, yet no tear tracks ran down his cheeks. It broke Evee's heart to see him this way.

"What's going on, cousin?" Gavril asked, squatting next to Lucien.

Lucien looked at him, opened his mouth to speak, then shook his head.

"Hey," Nikoli said. "Where's Ronan?" He looked at Evee. "Is he in the restroom?"

She shook her head.

Gavril got to his feet, pulled out the chair beside Lucien and sat. Nikoli walked over and sat opposite them at the same table.

"Would somebody tell us what the hell is going on?" Gilly said. "We're here because you sent out an emergency call. The same goes for Gavril and Nikoli. The four of us nearly broke our asses getting here as quickly as we could. Now we're here. So somebody say something."

Lucien opened his mouth, looked from Gavril to Nikoli, then snapped his mouth shut and shook his head.

Nikoli reached over and put a hand on Lucien's arm. "Cousin?"

Gavril suddenly drew in a sharp breath and sat bolt upright in his chair. "It's Ronan, isn't it? Something's happened to him?"

Viv and Gilly looked over at Evee, the same question in their eyes. She didn't signal a confirmation or a denial. She felt it was up to Lucien to break the news to his cousins first.

Lucien lifted his head, placed both hands on the table, looked from Gavril to Nikoli. "Yes," he said, his voice hoarse and hollow.

Gilly and Viv, both frowning, went over to a second table, grabbed two chairs, then brought them over to the table to sit near the Benders.

"What happened? Where is he?" Gilly asked.

"Dead," Lucien said.

Evee worked hard at keeping her tears in check. Lucien had to be the one to break the news. If she started crying, her sisters would pounce on her with a hundred questions.

Everyone around the table stared at Lucien, their expressions ranging from disbelief to confusion, as if they hadn't heard correctly.

"Ronan is dead?" Nikoli asked, his voice holding a note of incredulity. "Where is he? What happened?"

"How'd it happen?" Gavril asked.

"When did this happen?" Viv asked.

Seemingly at a loss for words, Lucien looked over at Evee, his eyes begging for help.

"A Cartesian attack," Evee said. "About an hour ago. The three of us were waiting until it was time to send the Nosferatu to the North Compound on the ferry when all hell broke loose. Lucien and Ronan were fighting a shitload of Cartesians. Then just when we thought it was over, a rift appeared over my head, literally."

"Holy Mother Earth," Viv said. "What did you do?"

"I couldn't do anything," Evee said. "The moment I spotted it I froze. Like some half-brained ass, I froze. It was as if every muscle in my body tensed up and held me in place. The Cartesian took a swing at me, so close

I felt the wind from its movement ruffle my hair. Lucien yelled for me to run, but I couldn't. It was as if the Cartesian had me mesmerized."

Viv frowned. "That so doesn't sound like you," she said. "Freezing up, I mean. If anything, you'd usually be the first to react. Go for the jugular."

"I can't explain why I couldn't move. Maybe it was shock. I truly don't know. The Cartesian kept swinging for me, and I felt it getting closer to me each time. I actually watched it pull back for another strike and knew I'd be a goner with that one."

"You knew that and still didn't move, run, anything?" Gilly asked.

"Yeah," Evee said. "I was actually contemplating what it might feel like to die as the Cartesian started a downward swipe with its horrible claws. Then, out of nowhere, I felt myself being shoved down to the ground by a flying tackle. It was Lucien. He knocked me down and away just in time. For me, but not for Ronan. He must have been only inches behind Lucien, because he caught the downswing from the Cartesian just as Lucien tackled me."

Everyone around the table gawked at her, except for Lucien. He was looking in her direction, but Evee knew it wasn't she he saw. The faraway look in his eye told her he was reliving Ronan's death.

"Is that what happened?" Gavril asked Lucien. "Ronan isn't…wasn't that stupid to get caught in a Cartesian's backlash."

Evee looked over at Lucien, whose focus seemed to be back, front and center.

"Yeah, that's how it happened. Just like Evee said. I knocked Evee down so she was out of harm's way. I think Ronan was following too close to have it come down any other way. In a matter of seconds, the Cartesian swung out again. It—it skewered Ronan in the head. Its claws went into one temple and out of the other."

"Jesus," Gavril said, and then both he and Nikoli got up from the table and began to pace the dining area.

Except for the sound of Gavril's and Nikoli's footsteps, the only other thing Evee heard was sniffling. Her sisters were crying openly.

"Wh-where's his body?" Nikoli asked, breaking the silence.

"The Cartesian never released him," Lucien said. "I blasted it with my scabior, hoping to shake Ronan loose from its grip, but it wouldn't or couldn't let go. I struck it again and again, mostly missing. I was too shaken up that it had Ronan. Before I had a chance to figure out any other way to get it to release him, the Cartesian disappeared into the rift, taking Ronan with it."

Evee felt tears well up in her eyes. "Ronan was doing the same thing Lucien was doing. Trying to save my life. If it hadn't been for me, none of this would have happened."

"Suck up the self-pity, Evee," Gilly said matter-of-factly. "There's enough going around this café to last a lifetime. It went down the way it was supposed to go down. There are no coincidences."

"Where were you when all this was going on?" Nikoli asked Lucien.

"Lying on top of Evee on the ground, trying to keep my body over hers to protect her. When I heard Ronan scream—"

"Jesus, he screamed..." Nikoli said as if trying to envision the incident in his mind's eye.

"I rolled over and fought the Cartesian, trying to get it to release Ronan, but it wouldn't or couldn't let go. Man, had all those Cartesians showed up while Evee was crossing the Nosferatu, there'd have been a serious bloodbath. They'd have been wide-open targets in the water. Easy pickings for the Cartesians." Lucien's eyes suddenly brimmed with tears. "Before I knew it, Ronan... it all happened so fast, I didn't have time to close the rift in time to help him."

With tears still streaming down her face, Evee said, "It's my fault Ronan got killed."

"Why the hell do you keep saying that?" Viv asked.

"Because Lucien had yelled for me to run for safety, and all I did was freeze in place. If I had done as he asked, Ronan would probably still be alive right now. I'm so, so sorry. I should have listened."

"Stop beating yourself up," Lucien said. "As Benders, we put our lives on the line every time we confront and attempt to destroy a Cartesian."

"Yeah," Evee said, "but if it hadn't been for me freezing in place like an idiot, Ronan would still be alive."

"Stop. It's not your fault," Lucien insisted. "Ronan chose to be there to help you, to run after you and knock you out of the way. I was only seconds earlier. There truly is no blame here. Those ugly Cartesian bastards are determined to kill whatever and whomever they please. That Cartesian was already in midswing, aiming for you. Ronan acted quickly, but unfortunately couldn't get out of the way fast enough. That Cartesian was aiming for you, not Ronan. Pushing you down to safety was both Ronan's and my choice. I simply reached you first."

It broke Evee's heart to see so much pain in Lucien's eyes. Nikoli and Gavril seemed to be at a loss for words.

Despite Lucien claiming it wasn't Evee's fault, she couldn't help feeling a ton of guilt resting on her shoulders. She was trying to find the right words to offer her condolences when Gilly suddenly sat bolt upright in her chair.

"The feeding," Gilly exclaimed. "What time is it?"

"We have a couple hours yet," Evee said.

Viv nodded after glancing at her watch.

Gilly pushed himself away from the table. "With all this Cartesian talk, I'm going to look in on my Chenilles. Hang out there until it's time to get them to the docks."

Gavril got to his feet. "I'm going with you."

A look of surprise crossed Gilly's face. "There's no need for you to come, Gavril. What with Ronan and all. I'm sure you have family to tend to and notify. I'll be fine on my own."

"I said I'm going with you," Gavril said, and walked over to her.

Viv rose from the table. "I hate that business has to take precedence at such a horrible time, but the Loup Garous need to be set up in the back of the property and kept there until the Nosferatu are done feeding. We're going to have to do this quickly. If there are as many Cartesians as Evee and Lucien are saying, all the Originals taken out from under those electric domes will be sitting ducks."

Lucien nodded. "I understand."

"We—we're so sorry for your loss," Viv said. "And I'm sorry that we were the cause of it. I know you think otherwise, but had it not been for me saying I quit to my Loups in the first place, none of this would be happening."

"No need for anyone here to assume any responsibility for Ronan's death," Lucien said. "He was a Bender through and through. Sometimes braver than all of us put together. But in reality, as with all things, there's a time to live and a time to die. I suppose Ronan's time here was done. If it hadn't been here, fighting to protect the Triad and the Originals, it probably would have been somewhere else."

Nikoli shook his head slowly. "It's not going to be the same without Ronan. But he would have wanted us to keep fighting. To bring back order and safety to the Originals and Triad." Nikoli turned to Lucien. "I hate to leave right now, cuz, but duty calls. I need to make sure Viv doesn't run into any Cartesian problems while she moves her Loups out from under the dome in the North Compound."

Although Gavril, Gilly, Viv and Nikoli spoke their piece about having to leave, not one of them moved toward the café's front door.

Lucien looked from one to the other. "You need to go and tend to your broods, and, cousins, you need to make sure they don't run into problems with the Cartesians. Make sure they stay safe. I'll go back to the hotel and contact Uncle Charles, Ronan's dad, and let him know what's happened."

"Maybe we should simply pack things up and head to Buffalo Grove and be with the family," Gavril said, his voice doing an occasional hitch. "They may need our support. This is a big loss. Not just because Ronan was a Bender. We grew up together. We were like brothers."

"I know," Lucien said. "This will not only hurt Uncle Charles, but it'll affect all of our families. But neither Ronan, Uncles Charles, nor our own fathers would want us to head back. We're Benders, and we have to stay and complete what we've set out to accomplish. That's been a given oath since we arrived here."

Gavril nodded hesitantly. "You're right, cuz. Neither Ronan nor Benders before us would want us to bail right now."

Lucien nodded.

With nothing left to say, Viv, Gilly, Nikoli and Gavril were about to leave the café to tend to the business at hand when Lucien suddenly said, "Wait!"

Everyone turned in his direction.

"I just thought of a way to get the Nosferatu and Chenilles to the compound without having them exposed to the Cartesians."

"What?" Gavril asked.

"How?" Evee asked.

Lucien stood from his place at the table and tapped a finger to his lips. "Viv, can you and Nikoli chance exposing one of your largest Loups for a project?"

"What project?" Nikoli asked.

"Yes," Evee said, not waiting for Lucien to answer Nikoli's question. "If it'll help the rest of the Originals get safely to the feeding grounds, we can make it happen." She looked at Nikoli. "You'll be there with your scabior, right?"

Nikoli nodded, then turned and frowned at Lucien. "What project are you talking about?"

"If we can build electrical domes over the safe zones for the Originals, nothing says we can't build one over the ferry, right?"

"Oh, great call, cuz," Gavril said. "That narrows the kill zones to a much shorter distance. Their safe place to the ferry, then off the ferry into the compound. Same on the return."

"That should work," Nikoli said.

"But can it be done in such a short time?" Gilly asked.

"My Loups can make anything happen," Viv said proudly. She turned to Lucien. "We'll get started now. I still have steel pipe from the other domes we created, and we still have plenty bloodstones to anchor to the top ends of the pipes."

Gavril nodded. "Mission on," he said, and he, Nikoli, Viv and Gilly high-stepped out of the café like a troupe on a mission.

When the café had emptied, save for Lucien and Evee, Evee walked over to Lucien and took his hand. "Great call on the dome for the ferry."

Lucien abruptly let go of her hand. "I have to go to the hotel now and make that call to my uncle."

His abruptness confused Evee. She stood and went to his side. "I—I'm so sorry for your loss. If I hadn't defied the curse on the Triad, this probably wouldn't have happened. I've been trying since you arrived to brainwash myself into thinking it was all right to sidestep the curse, because I allowed myself to use semantics, taking the curse verbatim. Since then, so much has escalated, worsened, I can't afford myself the luxury of thinking I'd found a way to circumvent the curse. I haven't." Evee felt tears fill her eyes again. "I can only be responsible for my actions, which means we can't be together anymore. Ronan's death is proof of that. If it hadn't been for me, in more ways than one, Ronan would still be alive."

"You don't know that," Lucien said.

Evee glanced down at the floor for a minute, then looked into Lucien's pure green eyes. She stood on tiptoe and kissed him on the cheek. "I care for you more than you'll ever know. That's the biggest reason why I can't allow 'us' to happen."

Lucien studied her face, and she saw that his eyes had grown flat, expressionless. "Ronan cared for you, too."

Without saying another word, Lucien left the café.

Evee stared at the closing door, and her heart felt like

it had split wide open within her chest, leaving sharp edges that stabbed her with each thought.

He'd left without saying goodbye. Nothing.

Evee sat down heavily on one of the chairs at the table. There was no holding back tears this time. She sobbed openly for Ronan, for the pain his death had caused so many. And no matter how many times the Benders had said otherwise, she still felt responsible for Ronan's death.

Now she was experiencing a death of her own. A life without Lucien. The thought consumed her with so much pain she didn't think she'd have the wherewithal to leave her chair and stand on her own two feet.

Much less stand for anything again.

Chapter 12

Score!

Well, almost.

The target had been the Triad, which his Cartesian missed completely. He still couldn't believe it. How close his Cartesian had come to grabbing such a choice morsel and wound up missing again and again.

The only thing that saved the creature from receiving severe punishment at his hand was the kill it did manage. The Bender.

A Bender wasn't exactly what he'd hoped for, but taking one out of commission had a significant benefit. One less to worry about. One less running around with his little baton-twirling act that somehow managed to shove his Cartesians to other dimensions.

He wished he knew where the power of the Benders' batons came from. Oddly enough, for as long as they'd pestered him, it was a wonder he'd never considered that before. Someone or something had to give those little batons power. Did they have a leader with powers who made those batons deadly? If so, that was someone he needed to add to his list. He must find the answer to that. The answer might come from the next Bender.

If he instructed his Cartesians properly, they'd capture a Bender without killing him. He didn't know if a human could survive a dimensional change without harm, but it was worth a shot. If a Bender did survive the change, he'd make certain to interrogate him at length. Torture him if necessary to find out who had infused their batons with power.

Now that all was said and done, he reviewed his initial plan to see where'd he'd gone wrong and how he might get better results next time.

He'd meant to take out the Triad near the church while she waited to cross her Originals over the river by boat. With her out of the way, the Nosferatu would reach the shore of the compound with no one there to remove them—except him. Permanently. With that in mind, he'd aligned part of his army along rifts that he'd already had them working on for some time. It was to be a rush, surprise attack. The Benders had taught the Triad about the rifts, how they slowly opened. How the Cartesians wormed their way through the rifts. The last thing they'd expect was an immediate opening and Cartesian drop.

The surprise attack had worked as expected, but, alas, he didn't wind up with the prize he'd craved.

Regardless, there had been a kill.

And it meant at least one lesson had been learned, although it needed refinement, for the underling Cartesian had brought the essence of the Bender to him. Had dropped his lifeless body at his feet, as all Cartesians were expected to do after any kill, and then he'd opened his mouth and sucked the essence from him just as he did with every kill.

The taste of the Bender initially was too sweet, like sugar melting into rotten tooth. The aftertaste was bitter like lemons, so much so it made his lips pucker.

He wasn't sure what the sweet and bitter meant. He'd never eaten anything with such contradicting tastes.

After pondering it awhile, he'd waited to see if it might make him sick. Or maybe the Benders had been created so that if they were captured and killed by a Cartesian, their very essence might kill him. Had he been the leader of the Benders, that would have been his plan.

But after a while, when nothing happened and he had only the bad aftertaste left in his mouth, he'd shrugged it off. Maybe all humans tasted that way. Sweet and sour. Maybe it depended on who they'd been in life. What they'd accomplished. What purpose they'd served. Despite the taste, he hadn't felt any measure of additional power transferred to him. If he felt anything at all, it had been remnants of the man's brave heart, which did him no good. His heart was already the bravest heart he knew in existence. For whom or what else in existence would have the wherewithal to not only create and grow the most vicious beings in the universe, but lead them?

He supposed he could get used to the taste if he had to...and he would. For after all, once the Triad and Originals were taken care of, humans were next on his list.

After he'd emptied the Bender and tossed the shell of his body away, he made a point of gathering his Cartesians, all of them, to instruct them once more on their method of attack.

Earlier he'd noticed that one Cartesian had literally pushed one of his legs through the rift, which made it all the more vulnerable to the Benders. Of course, the action that followed only confirmed his orders, for the overzealous Cartesian had been one of the first to get zapped by the Benders.

Not wanting to take anything for granted, he planned on going over how his Cartesians should attack so there wouldn't be any further errors.

So far, none of his Cartesians had dared to lean over the edge of a rift far enough to cause them to fall out. For one thing the Benders did not know, and if it was up to him, would never know, was that if a Cartesian fell from a rift to earth, it became nothing more than an animal. Its protective scales would shed like that of a snake, only its scales would never return. Covered only in fur, it would be vulnerable to any form of death. A bullet, an arrow, a hammer blow to the head. Once on the ground, a Cartesian couldn't make its way back to any dimension. It was doomed to fight out its remaining days on earth, hiding from any and all who hunted its kind.

His army needed to be reminded that the rifts were their haven, their protection. From a rift, a Cartesian had all the power it needed to conquer anything.

Reviewing the mistakes made in the recent kill, he couldn't help thinking of the Bender who'd been skewered instead of the Triad. A look of shock had been the man's death mask. The kill had been so instantaneous, had happened so quickly and unexpectedly that the Bender never uttered a sound, save for one scream before he was impaled. Nothing followed. No more screams. No yells for help. Black and white, immediate death.

That had left him with some regret. He would have liked to hear the gurgle of death, screams of pain, to have seen the Bender attempt to fight his way free of the Cartesian, and then, when that was unsuccessful, watch him writhe in the throes of death. But he'd been denied it all.

The only screams and cries he'd heard had come from the Bender left behind.

He knew to expect one of two things to happen. When an enemy lost one of their own, the rest of its team either dispersed from the weakness of having lost one member, or they grew stronger and became more vengeful. Determination on steroids to annihilate whoever or whatever had killed one of their own.

Unsure yet as to which to expect from the Benders, he could only wait and see. Of course, he hoped the former would happen and not the latter. If weakened by the death of their team member, the Triad and Originals would be left to their own devices.

He'd think positively. Sadness, extreme sadness had a way of eating away at humans until they were little more than shells of their former selves. If that happened to the remaining Benders, he'd have much to rejoice over. They might remain in the city, but their grief might cause them to become lax, which was perfect, as far as he was concerned. There'd be no more hunting, searching for missing Originals. He'd simply collect them all and take their powers unto himself. Once the missing ones were consumed, it wouldn't take much effort to collect the rest. The weakened Benders would weaken the Triad who'd become dependent on them.

Now that he thought about it, the Cartesian who'd missed the Triad and killed the Bender instead had done him a favor. The process would speed up now.

He already had big notions and big plans. Much bigger than anything the small Bender lying like a ragdoll at his feet drained of life, of the essence of anything and everything he once was, might have come up with.

Oh, yes, this death, although regrettably not a Triad's,

would more than likely give him what he craved with his whole being faster than he could ever have hoped for.

He'd bet on it.

He was getting closer, so close to his goal. It took all of his mental powers to keep his excitement in check. He knew the Triad faced serious roadblocks, were at a total loss regarding any plan of action, especially now that humans had been brought into the picture. He couldn't have been more excited.

It had been his plan all along. Well, not the summation of the plan, but the journey toward it.

He was pleased with his work and the work of his ever-growing army. Create chaos, mayhem and destruction. And all was happening gloriously, independently and collectively. It created more rifts, more opportunities to get to the Originals and the Triad.

He had to admit that he carried a tinge of disappointment with one of his soldiers. The one who'd come inches from grabbing a Triad. That soldier had been stupid, allowing itself to get distracted and let the Triad slip away. Oddly enough, the stupid wench had all but killed herself after that. Running into a muddy river without a clue of how she'd retreat from its depths.

He'd watched in amusement as she thrashed, flailed, yelled, her head dunking into the water again and again. Each time she managed to surface, less of her head appeared.

Then, of course, the Bender who took out the distracted Cartesian, the one that had come so close to capturing his prize, jumped into the water to save her, protect her, take her away. He couldn't think of a son of a bitch he hated more, except the other Benders keeping him from realizing success faster than it was occurring.

Except for the river incident, the Benders had kept the

Triad so far up their asses his army hadn't been able to squeeze in for a shot, a taste of any of them.

The Originals, though, were a different story—sort of. His soldiers, his pets, his creations had managed to get some of the Originals. And the taste of the first Original capture had created such a feeding frenzy among his creatures, it had taken him some time to get them back on track—in line.

As always, his Cartesians were allowed a taste, a small morsel of their captures as a reward before the capture was brought to him to devour. He alone absorbed every ounce of energy that the victim possessed. It not only caused him to grow in his own power but also allowed him to create new Cartesians. That was how he'd grown his army, one new Cartesian at a time. And now they stood at the ready, eagerly awaiting his command. Hundreds of them developed, molded by his own hand. His beloved creations.

After centuries of trial and error, he'd perfected their looks and abilities. Their appearance, in many ways, mimicked his own. He wanted his creatures to create such fear and a sense of foreboding that the sight of them alone would stop a prey's heartbeat, leave it motionless and easy to capture.

For the most part, that strategy had worked, but mostly with the subspecies of the Originals. Vampires, werewolves and the like. But the fear factor had proved useless when it came to Benders. Those meddling infidels had been meticulously trained to purposely seek out his Cartesians, not avoid them. Not once, in ten generations of Benders, had he seen any Bender freeze or hesitate at the sight of his hideous beauties.

In fact, the opposite seemed to occur. The Benders seemed to glory in the sight of the Cartesians, anxious, heart racing with excitement as they aimed what looked like toy batons at his creations and pushed them out of this world's dimension.

To make matters worse, the Benders appeared competitive, all eager to be the first to send a Cartesian to the farthest dimension possible.

So far, this generation of Benders had managed, on one occasion, to send two of his Cartesians back seven dimensions. This meant it would take decades for them to make their way back to him. They'd have to claw, tear, rip through the tiniest hole in each dimension to return. Since other dimensions were not as active and restless as the one now containing the Originals and Triad, rifts were more difficult to locate. This problem alone caused a severe time lapse for the Cartesians that had been pushed back that far.

Fortunately, no Bender, thus far, had accomplished the ultimate goal—shoving the Cartesians back to the eleventh dimension from which there would be no return. The eleventh dimension contained nothing but a void, a place that had no rift potential whatsoever.

And the Benders' second goal, capturing him, the leader of the Cartesians, had always been an act of futility. His army made sure of that. He was their leader—the master and god of his glorious monstrosities.

Capturing him and pushing a Cartesian to the eleventh dimension hadn't happened in the past Bender generations, and he sure as hell wouldn't allow it to happen with this one.

The current Benders assigned to protect the Triad and Originals were proving to be quite ingenious, however. Much more so than the ones who'd fought before them. Enemies though they were, he had to give credit where credit was due. The electrical domes the Benders had created to protect the Originals in their safe places had been a well-thought-out plan and, for a while anyway, an effective barrier.

Ingenious as it was, however, he'd discovered, albeit by happenstance, that the electrical currents of the domes could be affected, minimized. And the key to doing so was simply to allow nature to take its course.

The sexual distraction of the Triad owing to the Benders seemed to be one catalyst, and the second was allowing the Originals that had gone missing to do what they did best when left to themselves—attack humans.

The Nosferatu that had thirsted for the drunken harlot in that dark alley could have been easy pickings for his Cartesians. For a while, the Nosferatu had been left to its own meanderings. He'd watched as it found its prey and had lured her into the alley.

In that moment, he'd been torn between having his soldiers snatch the Original then and there and watching the kill of the human. Then, once the Nosferatu was engorged with the woman's blood, he'd have his Cartesian snatch it from the same dark alley.

His curiosity had won the coin toss. He wanted to watch the kill, thinking that once it was glutted with blood, capturing that particular Nosferatu might prove to boost its overall power, thus allowing him a bigger bang for the capture.

Sadly, neither had occurred.

Once again, the opportunity had been lost at the hands of a Bender. As disappointing as that had been, it did wind up being quite the fascinating show. Nosferatu against Bender—then watching an Original leader kill one of its own. He'd watched with glee as humans gathered, witnessing the event—creating more chaos. More problems.

It was then he realized that the increase of chaos some-how affected the electrical domes, causing their power to wane. That had been an unexpected bonus.

And now that humans were involved, he anticipated all hell to break loose. He couldn't have asked for any-thing more perfect.

Now the Triad, who had already been running from pillar to post, protecting their sequestered Originals, hunting for the ones who'd gone missing, which had been his master plan, would come unglued. This was one way he would get all he wanted, demanded, which was su-preme power over all. To do so, he had to set the stage to make it happen. Create turmoil, weaken and distract the Triad, confuse the Benders.

With humans thrown into the mix, one having seen a Nosferatu in all its glory, many witnessing the death of that Nosferatu by its leader, soon the entire city would be in a state of commotion.

Man would wind up killing man. Original would kill Original.

Once that mayhem heightened, all would be his for the taking. All the Originals, the Triad, every bastard offspring hiding beneath the Originals' skirt—vampires, werewolves, the rest of the netherworld. He'd even cleanse his palate between consumptions with a sorcerer or two. No, he'd definitely take all three. And, of course, the Triad Elders were on his checklist.

Finally, he'd have it all. After all the years of working, waiting, his plan was coming to fruition.

Oddly enough, the closer he came to accomplishing his goal, the more bittersweet if felt to him. He so en-joyed watching the Triad and Benders running in circles, chasing their own tails, accomplishing little more than adding to their own frustration.

As he often did, he wondered what pleasure he'd experience when consuming a Triad. He imagined the taste to be as exquisite as the finest chocolate, something to be savored on the tongue. He'd allow it to melt slowly so every morsel would be experienced to its fullest extent. He'd take his time, let the sensation wash over him. Allow the scent of it to fill his nostrils, his lungs.

Even now he could almost feel it on the flat of his tongue, washing through him, rolling over all his senses. And once that time came, which he knew would be oh-so-soon, he imagined the height of the sensation to be greater than any human orgasm ever experienced.

The completion of it, the longing and desire he'd carried for it, finally meeting. How could anything compare to such glory?

No human emotion, need or desire could possibly match something of that magnitude.

And the culmination of it was so close, just within reach now.

In the meantime, he still had work to do. More heartache, worry and desperation to create for the Triad and the foolish Benders who followed them like puppies.

He anxiously awaited the perfume of their terror, their uncertainty to waft over him like the fragrance of an entire field of summer flowers.

Little did the Triad or Benders know that their own fears and indecisiveness, their own questioning of themselves as the Triad's powers continued to diminish—all of it was their own worst enemy.

Soon there would no longer be the waving of hands, lighting of candles, useless charms and incantations. All would belong to him.

Once again, feeling as giddy as a child awaiting a

much-desired treasure, he forced himself to stay in check. To remain stoic, strong.

He'd only allow his Cartesians to see him as a pillar of strength, a force never to be questioned. Whose orders were to be followed without a second's hesitation.

He must always be seen as their master, not a foolish twit who succumbed to emotion.

And soon, very, very soon, the world would view him the same way. Master of all that existed.

And every knee would bend at his feet.

Chapter 13

Taka Burnside knew she was going to be in big trouble
with the other two Elders, Arabella and Vanessa, but she
couldn't just sit around doing nothing anymore. The police had returned to their house not long after the Triad
left. And once again, they'd stood in silence, hiding, not
answering when the police beat on the door over and
over, seemingly forever, trying to get someone to answer.

That had scared Taka. She didn't want to go to jail. She
didn't want to be hanged by the neck in a tree or burned
at the stake. And it would happen, she was sure of it. The
past would revisit the world of witches.

Despite what Vanessa and Arabella told her about
being overly dramatic, Taka knew better, and she knew
what needed to be done. Arabella and Vanessa just didn't
have the courage she did.

Taka had to wait quite some time after the triplets
left before Arabella and Vanessa had gone to bed. It was
about two in the morning before Taka felt it safe enough

to move around without stirring the two awake. She'd quickly dressed in a pink polyester pantsuit and white orthopedic shoes. She'd slicked her hair down with a comb, then grabbed her white faux leather purse and sneaked out of the house. She'd gone through the back door, since it didn't squeak as loudly as the front door did when opened.

Her mission was clear, her steps sure. She intended to find Gunner Stern, the sorcerer that Arabella claimed they could trust. If Arabella trusted him, then they had a real possibility for help. At least there was some merit in finding out. Arabella's word counted for something. She wasn't an airhead.

Taka knew that if Vanessa and Arabella thought anyone in their group to be an airhead, they'd point to her. But nothing was further from the truth, as far as she was concerned.

It was true that occasionally words kind of slipped out of Taka's mouth before she'd thought them through. And sometimes she had an issue with expressing what she meant in the right order. But she had a brain. A good one. And she planned to use it to do what must be done.

As she made her way through the Garden District, counting on streetlamps and moonlight for direction, she hoped her knees wouldn't give out from the long walk ahead. The trolleys didn't run at this hour of the day.

Keeping her head up and her attitude positive, Taka kept a single mantra running through her head. *Feet, don't fail me now!*

She planned to find Gunner, explain that their issues were much bigger than the problem he'd reported to Arabella, then ask for his help.

She knew that in doing so, she was spitting right in the eye of the Elders' protocol, the one that insisted on a majority vote when faced with a decision of this magnitude. And she knew that asking a sorcerer for help was no small matter. Taka had little doubt that Vanessa and Arabella would be furious with her. They might even consider dismissing her from the order of Elders.

Right now Taka didn't care what they did to her. Arabella was taking far too much time to make a decision. Something needed to be done now before all they knew and loved was destroyed. The Triad, the Originals, the humans in this city.

How long could they stand in silence in their home, hiding like mice from a cat, every time a police officer pounded on the door?

As far as Taka was concerned, everything they'd attempted so far to help the Triad and the Originals had failed miserably. They couldn't simply sit around wishing, hoping something would change.

The one thing that had really set Taka on this quest was the fact that all the leaders in the Circle of Sisters around the country had collectively set a spell in motion to help them, and nothing had happened.

Arabella had made a point about Gunner. Having someone outside the Circle of Sisters might be able to bring a new perspective to their problems. Being a master of his own incantations and spells, Gunner just might have an idea on how to help them.

Taka kept reminding herself about Arabella's point as she walked, seemingly forever. When she finally reached Canal Street, there were very few people milling about. A few homeless men sleeping near door stoops, a couple of drunks singing nonsensical songs.

When she reached Evee's café, Bon Appétit, which, of course, was closed at this hour, she stood near its front door and studied the lay of the land. From here, she at least had a sense of direction. Trey Cottle's law office was across the street, and she knew he lived in an apartment right above the office. Shandor Black lived in an apartment about a block away. Although she didn't know Shandor's exact apartment name or number, it wouldn't have taken much to find him. A few knocks on a few doors, some irritated people having been roused from sleep. No big deal.

It was then that Taka realized she didn't have a clue as to where Gunner lived. She'd just assumed he lived next to Trey and Shandor since they were together so often.

Yet, in that moment, Taka remembered that she'd never heard Gunner mention where he lived.

She sat on the stoop of the café, clutched her purse to her breasts, and slapped herself on the forehead. She was a damn airhead. She should have thought this out more thoroughly before taking off. For all she knew, Gunner could live in Baton Rouge, a city over an hour away. Many people commuted to work in New Orleans from surrounding cities.

What was she supposed to do now? Taka sighed heavily, her feet throbbing from having walked so far. The Elders made a habit of walking the Garden District area from time to time for exercise and fresh air. But at her age, Taka's brain had lied to her, convincing her that her body could easily make the walk to the Quarter.

She sat, staring at Trey Cottle's office, at the apartment windows above it. They were dark, which meant Trey was either asleep or out for the night. As she stared, an idea struck her. The only way she'd be able to find out where Gunner lived was to ask one of the two sorcerers that the other two Elders didn't trust.

As far as Trey was concerned, Taka held no opinion one way or the other, except that she considered him ugly with his round belly, triple chins and the snooty nose with glasses always resting at its tip. Then there was his balding, sweaty head. But looks weren't what she was after. She needed information, and if anyone knew where to find Gunner, Trey would certainly know.

If Trey was up there in his apartment, sleeping, she could wake him and at least ask for Gunner's address. Certainly he wouldn't get upset for that small bother. All he'd have to do was give her the address and go right back to sleep.

Taka got to her feet and crossed the street to Trey's office. Alongside the building was a wrought-iron gate, which was locked. Beyond it, down a short alley, she spotted a stairwell and landing that obviously led to Trey's apartment. The fence stood at least eight feet tall. No way she'd be able to climb it and jump over.

Standing back a few feet, Taka studied the darkened apartment windows again. With the gate in her way, how could she get Trey's attention? Knocking on his office door wouldn't do any good, as it also had a wrought-iron security door over the mahogany one that led into the office.

Frustrated, Taka looked down both sides of Canal. Only a straggler or two walking on the opposite side of the street. She paced for a moment, head lowered, rubbing her chin between a thumb and finger.

That was when she happened upon a pebble…then a second, slightly larger one. She picked them up, rolled them over in her palm. In the movies, when a boy wanted to get a girl's attention in an upstairs bedroom without her parents knowing, he'd toss pebbles at her window until he got her attention.

Excited that she might have found a way to reach Trey, Taka took the smallest pebble and threw it at one of the upstairs windows. She missed by a foot, hitting the brick siding of the building instead.

Sticking her tongue between her teeth, she took the larger pebble, closed her left eye to get a better sight on her target, then threw it as hard as she could.

The rock not only hit the window but shattered it.

Gasping, Taka jumped left, then right, not knowing whether to run away or just wait out the tongue-lashing she was sure she'd get from Trey.

Within seconds Trey Cottle's face appeared at the window. From the streetlamps that lined Canal, Taka could easily see the fury on the man's face. When he looked down and saw her, however, his expression changed.

It went from anger to surprise to oddly soft and curious.

"Why, Ms. Burnside, were you the one who broke my window?" Trey called down to her.

Taka began to wring her hands, her purse swinging in the crook of her right arm. "Y-yes. I—I'm so sorry. I didn't mean to throw it that hard. I wanted to get your attention because I need some help with something."

Trey lifted an eyebrow and said, "Wait. Wait right there. I'll come down and let you in."

"No, no, that's not necessary," Taka said, anxiety riding her body like a bull just let out of a chute.

Before she could say more, Trey had already disappeared from the window, and she saw lights flooding the rooms upstairs.

Taka stood on the sidewalk, shifting nervously from foot to foot, needing to pee. She shouldn't have come here. Something in her gut told her that coming to Trey Cottle's place had been a big mistake. Then again, it could just be her paranoia running amok. The only other option she'd had was to find Shandor, which would have meant knocking on more doors, waking more people. She took long, deep breaths, trying to remember the bigger purpose as to why she was here. That all she planned to get from Trey was an address. Gunner's address.

The longer Taka waited, the more she needed to pee. She crossed her legs to keep from letting go right there on the sidewalk in her pink pantsuit.

Trey suddenly appeared to her left, at the wrought-iron gate that closed off the short alley. He wore a maroon silk robe over maroon pajamas. Their pant legs clung to his chunky thighs.

He quickly unlocked the gate and motioned Taka inside.

She hesitated. "I—I really don't need to go inside. I hate to bother you. I know it's late or rather very early morning, but I'm a little desperate. I need Gunner Stern's address. Do you know where he lives? I really need to contact him."

Trey cocked his head to one side and shoved his glasses up the bridge of his nose. "Why would you be looking for Gunner at this hour?" he asked.

"I need... I just need to talk to him," Taka said, being careful about what she relayed to Trey.

Trey sighed. "He lives out by the Causeway, Ms. Burnside, which is quite the distance from here." He looked down both sides of the street. "I don't see any vehicle nearby. May I call you a cab? And while I do so, I'll write down Gunner's address for you."

Taka was about to say yes, please, then remembered she hadn't taken any money with her. All she carried in her purse was tissue, a compact, a hairbrush and a can of pepper spray. She hadn't thought about bringing money.

"I appreciate you offering to call a cab for me, but it seems like I left home without any money. I know the

Causeway's a long way from here, but I'll figure out a way to get there. If you would be so kind as to just give me his address."

Trey tsked and said, "I know you said it's important, but if you can't physically make it to him, you're certainly welcome to use my telephone and call him. I have his number, and I'll most certainly give you as much privacy as you need while you speak to him."

Taka thought about it for a moment, feeling out Trey, trying to get a sense of whether he was sincere or not.

Remembering her initial mission, Taka squared her shoulders and walked past the gate, which Trey closed behind them. She then followed him down the short alley and up the stairs into his apartment.

As he ushered her inside and led her through the apartment, Taka saw a neatly kept kitchen and a living room decorated with mahogany and leather furniture.

Trey motioned to a room on the right, just past the living room. "My phone is right in there. It's my home office." He opened a pair of French doors and led her into a large room that held a circular desk, two wingback chairs in front of the desk and a tall leather-back chair behind it. The desk itself held a computer, a telephone and mountains of paperwork. Bookshelves lined every wall of the room, each overflowing with books.

Trey pointed to the telephone. "There you go. You're welcome to it." He leaned across the desk, picked up a pen and wrote a set of numbers on a yellow Post-it note. He handed the note to Taka. "This is Gunner's number. He's probably asleep right now, so just let it ring. I'm sure he'll eventually answer. I'll be out in the kitchen if you need me for anything."

"Thank you," Taka said, feeling a bit uneasy as soon as Trey left the room and closed the door behind him.

She listened to his footsteps as he made his way down the hallway. When his footsteps finally faded to nothing, Taka picked up the receiver of the phone and punched in the number Trey had written down for her.

On the fifth ring, a man answered the phone. "H-hello?" His voice sounded thick with sleep.

"Is this Gunner Stern?" Taka asked quietly.

"Who is this?" he asked.

"Taka Burnside. I'm one of the Elders, you know, along with Arabella. I've met you a few times at the Bon Appétit Café."

The man cleared his throat. "Oh, yes, Ms. Burnside, I know who you are. I apologize that it took me a while to recognize your voice. It's a bit early in the morning."

"I—I know," Taka said. "I'm so sorry for waking you, but we desperately need your help."

Taka heard shuffling on the other end of the phone, and when Gunner finally responded, his voice sounded strong and alert.

"How may I be of help?" he asked.

"I'm not sure," Taka confessed. "I was hoping you might have some ideas."

"Regarding...?"

Taka glanced around the room, making sure she was alone. She cupped the mouthpiece of the receiver and lowered her voice even more. "Mr. Stern, the Elders need you. Things have gotten out of control for us. We're losing some of the Originals, and humans are being attacked. We've had the entire clan of Sisters casting spells to help us, but their incantations don't seem to be working. You're the only one of the sorcerers I trust to ask for help. Arabella trusts you, too. At first no one wanted any sorcerer involved, but we're running out of options, and if we don't do something soon, I'm afraid we'll lose everything. The Originals, the Triad, the people in this city." Taka stopped her blabbering and listened for a response from Gunner.

A few seconds passed before he said, "You are in quite the fix, aren't you? Is there somewhere we can meet to discuss this in person?"

"I—I don't know." Taka fretted that if she waited to meet him face to face, went over the entire story again, the other Elders would wake and find her missing.

"Where are you now?" Gunner asked.

Taka whispered into the mouthpiece while eyeing the room. "At Trey Cottle's apartment."

"What are you doing there?" Gunner asked quite loudly.

"I didn't know where you lived. I wasn't sure where Shandor lived, either. I just knew Trey's apartment was on top of his office, so it was easy to find. I figured he'd know your address, so I got his attention. Sort of in a bad way, though. I threw a rock at his window and it shattered. Trey was nice about it. He didn't get angry at me or anything. He told me you lived out by the Causeway, and I wasn't able to make it there by cab because I forgot to bring cash with me. I didn't know you lived that far away. So Trey offered to let me use his phone. Gave me your phone number."

"Listen carefully," Gunner said. "Don't say anything more. Just hang up the phone, leave Trey's apartment and head straight to your house. I'll meet you there."

"No, I can't meet there," Taka said frantically. "The other two Elders don't know I'm out here. Can we meet at Evee's café? The Bon Appétit? It's not open now. No one will be there."

"Can you get inside the café?"

"No, I don't have a key."

There was a moment of silence before Gunner said, "I don't like the idea of you standing out in front of the café at this time of night…morning."

"I'll be fine," Taka said. "I've got Mace with me."

Another moment of silence, then Gunner said, "All right. Just leave that apartment this minute and go to the café. I'll be there as quickly as I can."

Taka nodded, then realized he couldn't see the gesture. "Yes, I will. Thank you. Thank you so much for speaking with me."

"Leave now," Gunner insisted. "I'll be looking for you, and I promise I won't keep you waiting long."

"Thank you."

A second of silence made Taka wonder if she should hang up now. Before she did, Gunner's voice came to her ear. "Taka?"

"Yes?"

"Before we meet, I want to give you an important piece of advice."

"Certainly. What is it?"

"Don't ever return to Trey's apartment again. Understand?"

Now it was Taka's turn to bleed silence into the line. Only when she finally said, "Yes. I understand," did Gunner hang up his phone.

She hung up, sitting behind Trey's desk in the large leather chair. Taka had a sinking feeling in the pit of her stomach that she'd just crossed a line she'd never be able to return from. Not only had she contacted a sorcerer, but she done it from Trey Cottle's apartment.

Something inside her didn't feel right. She did as instructed, leaving the apartment as quickly as possible.

Taka ran into Trey as she followed the route he'd used

to bring her to his home office. He stood near the stove with a kettle of water he placed on a burner.

"Ah, Ms. Burnside, just in time. Would you care for a cup of tea?" Trey asked. His brow furrowed slightly. "You seem a bit rattled. I hope all is well. Maybe some chamomile tea will help settle your nerves."

"No, thank you," Taka said quickly. She noticed Trey's eyes grow darker. "I appreciate the use of your phone. And I do apologize again about your window."

"Then please do me the courtesy of allowing me to help calm your nerves. You don't have to talk about whatever's bothering you if you don't want to."

Taka felt the hair on the back of her neck stand on end, and her body tensed, ready for fight or flight.

"I'd love to, really, but I can't. Arabella and Vanessa will be worried about me. I need to head back home. So, thank you. Thank you again for your kindness," Taka said while making her way to the kitchen door. When she opened it, ready to fly down the stairs, Trey called out to her.

"Wait a moment," he said, and followed her to the door. Taka felt her insides tremble and prayed it wasn't obvious to Trey. "I'll need to unlock the alleyway gate so you can leave."

"Ah." Taka forced a smile. "Of course. I'm sorry to inconvenience you again."

"No problem, Ms. Burnside."

They made it to the gate, and Trey unlocked it, then opened it wide so Taka could leave.

As she squeezed past him and felt she could breathe again now that a fence separated them, Taka said, "Thank you again. And I'll be happy to pay for your window, Mr. Cottle."

Trey tsked. "No need, Ms. Burnside. I understand

emergencies. The window's on me. Have a good evening." He smiled at her, and the look came across more like a smirk.

Taka hurried away, wanting to throw up and wishing more than ever that she'd never gone to Cottle's apartment.

Chapter 14

After Lucien left the café without saying goodbye, Evee had sat there for a while. And then, finally managing to pull herself out of her despondency, she went home to dress for the feeding. She put on a fresh pair of black slacks and a black pullover sweater and brushed her hair back into a ponytail.

She left the house weary but also somewhat cautiously. Her illusion spell with the Cartesians had worked. But to what end? Ronan had died anyway. Why did that spell work and not others? She didn't have a clue. She was only grateful that it had worked.

She'd never seen so many Cartesians hanging from the sky, roaring, clawing, all of them like vultures starving for fresh meat. Although Lucien and Ronan had faced them bravely, Evee didn't have to be a Bender to realize they were seriously outnumbered. Evee had been certain that through their years of experience as Benders, Lucien and Ronan would have figured their way out of the calamity. But despite her confidence, Evee had refused to leave them out in the open, alone, with so many enemies eager to kill.

The illusion spell had come to mind unbidden, and although she had had issues with previous spells going south or simply fizzling out altogether, she hadn't hesitated to stand by Lucien's side and speak her incantation.

Oddly enough, she wasn't surprised that it had worked. She didn't know if the ferocity she'd felt to help Lucien and Ronan had given the spell the extra kick it needed to work. For all intents and purposes, the reason the spell worked really didn't matter now. What mattered was that it had worked. Only too little too late. If only it had saved Ronan's life, as well.

After leaving her house, Evee decided to look in on the Nosferatu in the catacombs once more before she checked on the ferry and the electrical dome they'd discussed building over it to protect the Originals en route to the compound.

The walk to St. John's was a long one, but it gave her time to think.

The Elders had given her and Viv hell when the Triad's familiars had ratted them out about Evee's intimacy with Lucien and Viv's with Nikoli. They'd reprimanded the sisters, and warned them to forgo all intimacy with the Benders.

She and Viv had given the Elders a half-hearted agreement that they'd stay hands off, but that didn't do a damn thing to keep her from thinking about Lucien. The man could wear an Eskimo coat and hood over an armored bodysuit, and Evee would still be able to feel the strength of all that made up the man. The bulk of his muscular arms, the ripples of muscles that ran down his chest and stomach. The width of his hands. The length of his fingers. How he towered over her, a gentle, protective giant that turned her insides into mush.

After meeting with the Elders and all but being blamed along with Viv for the turmoil and suffering unleashed in the city, Evee had tried to stay resolute.

She'd met Lucien at the cathedral as they'd agreed upon, and attempted to keep her distance from him. Remain aloof. Her resolve had vanished, however, the moment she saw his strong, finely chiseled face and the fierce emerald of his eyes. Every time Lucien had spoken to her, Evee had trouble concentrating on his words. She'd watched his lips, which made her thirst for him in the worst way. She wanted to kiss his full, beautiful lips again.

The fight with the Cartesians had been fierce, and it had terrified her. But for the first time since they'd been paired together, along with Ronan, she felt they'd operated as a team. It made Evee feel good to contribute the way she did.

Still feeling a sense of remorse over Ronan's death and with Lucien on her mind, Evee soon found herself on Canal Street before she knew it. She took a right on Chartres, then made her way to the cathedral and into the catacombs.

The electric canopy that Lucien and Ronan had recharged with their scabiors was still intact. The Nosferatu beneath it paced restlessly. They all looked over at her questioningly, and Evee could almost hear their collective mental questions.

Now? Is feeding time now? Will you release us from here—now?

The only one Evee made eye contact with was Pierre, her lead Nosferatu. Evee mouthed to him, "Very soon."

Pierre gave her an almost imperceptible nod, then went about his business.

With that, Evee quickly left the catacombs and cathedral and headed for the docks to check on the ferry.

Evee had barely walked fifty feet when she heard someone call her name. A man.

"Miss François."

She froze, then turned slowly in the direction of the man's voice.

Standing about a half block away was Shandor Black, one of the three sorcerers who lived in New Orleans. He walked in her direction, his tall, lanky body stiff in motion, a body that appeared more comfortable settled in a chair than chasing a Triad in the wee hours of morning.

Shandor was one of the sorcerers that the Elders had mentioned often. One they didn't trust any more than they trusted Trey Cottle, Shandor's usual sidekick.

As he drew closer, Shandor pushed his eyeglasses up on his long, hooked nose, closer to his beady eyes. The glasses did little to enhance the man's thin, drawn face that carried a perpetual scowl.

"How lovely to meet you out here, Miss François," Shandor said when he finally reached Evee.

Evee nodded politely. "Mr. Black. What brings you out at such an early hour?"

"Well, actually," he said, pressing his glasses against his eyes again, "I was looking for you."

Evee felt her head jerk up in surprise. "What on earth would you want with me?"

"I hear that you and your sisters were facing quite a dilemma," Shandor said. His voice held a nasal stuffiness to it. "I wanted to offer my assistance."

"Where did you hear about this so-called dilemma?" Evee asked, eyes narrowing.

"Oh, you know," Shandor said, absently rubbing his chin. "Word gets around rather quickly in this city. Well, the Quarter, anyway." He attempted a smile, but the gesture appeared to make his face hurt.

"So," Evee said, and put a fist on her hip. "If I understand you correctly, you've heard a rumor about me and my sisters and decided to seek me out at what…two thirty in the morning?"

Shandor shrugged. "I don't sleep well these days. Insomnia. I often walk the city at night when I can't sleep."

"And what made you think I'd be out here this early?"

"Oh, I've seen you out in this area this early from time to time on nights when I can't sleep. Figured it'd be worth a shot, looking for you here, I mean."

Evee felt gooseflesh rush along her arms just thinking that Shandor had been watching her without her knowledge. And now confronting her here.

Stiffening her spine, Evee said, "Tell me what it is you think you know."

"I'd be happy to," Shandor said. He pointed to a stoop near a darkened building. "Why don't we sit over there for a chat? I'll tell you what I've heard, and you can decide whether or not my services might come in handy."

They walked the few steps to the stoop, which was little more than three cracked brick steps, and Evee said, "Feel free to sit. I'm fine standing right here."

Shandor shrugged again and sat on the stoop with a grunt, then drummed his fingers on his knees. "Aging is no fun, I've got to tell you. These old knees have seen better days."

Anxious to get to the ferry and wanting to rid herself of Shandor, Evee put her hands on her hips. "Please get to the point. I have business to take care of."

Shandor squinted up at her. "Oh, of course, of course."

He looked down, continued to drum his fingers against his knees. "Well, let's see. I've heard that the Originals, not all of them, but some, have gone missing. I've also heard about the human and the Nosferatu killed. Plenty of human witnesses from what I was told. Plenty."

Evee felt fury roil through her body. "When did you hear such things?"

"Today."

"From whom?"

"As I said, word travels, and my source for the information is very reliable."

"Bullshit!"

Shandor stopped drumming his fingers and peered up at Evee. "Why, Miss François, such language from a nice young lady like yourself. I must say, it's not very becoming."

Evee's hands rolled into fists on her hips. "Tough tits, Shandor. Your 'word travels fast' excuse is bullshit. We both know it. You had to get that information from someone specific, and I want to know who."

Shandor held up an indignant chin. "Who gave me the information is truly irrelevant, especially with the problems all of you are experiencing now. And really, Evette, I truly believe I can be of service to all of you."

Evee remembered the discussion she and her sisters had had with the Elders. How they'd argued back and forth about getting any of the sorcerers involved. Evee had felt strongly about not allowing them into their lives.

She glared at Shandor, who still sat on the stoop, his back resting against the building behind it. He crossed his arms and placed them in his lap. As relaxed as a man waiting for the city bus.

"Hypothetically," Evee finally said, "suppose what you heard was true—and I'm not saying it is. What do you possibly have to offer anyone who might be in such a state?"

Shandor let out a snort of laughter. "We have many spells and incantations that are different from yours. And since we're sorcerers and not witches—and I'm not meaning that in any sexist way or implying any inferiority of one to the other," Shandor assured her, "we might add some extra punch."

Evee opened her mouth, ready to ream out Shandor, but he blabbered on before she was able to get a word in edgewise.

"Just hear me out," Shandor said. "Don't think that me, Trey or Gunner don't know how the Triad feels about sorcerers. No matter those feelings, wouldn't calmer heads prevail? I know that collectively we can put a stop to all this. No more deaths. No human deaths. You, once again, in full control of all that's yours. I'm quite confident we can help make that happen."

"We *are* in control of our Originals and each other," Evee said through clenched teeth. "Thank you very much for your concern, but I assure you it's unwarranted. Your information and whatever reliable source you think you have are wrong."

"You're only saying that because I won't reveal my source," Shandor said, then struggled to his feet. "Let me assure you, Miss François, despite what you think, my information source is as reliable as your familiar."

Evee frowned. "What about my familiar?"

Shandor held out a hand. "Nothing, really. Only a point of reference. Think about what you're asking. It would be quite crass of me to divulge the name of my source who specifically asked to remain anonymous. I'm only here to offer my help, and I don't know how my revealing that information, thus breaking my promise, would

cause you to trust me more. In fact, the opposite would
be true, would it not? It would cause you to mistrust me
all the more."

"You're right," Evee said. "I don't trust you. Any of
you. Why should I? All I've ever seen from you and
Trey are spells and incantations that served no one but
yourselves. Not once have I seen either of you open up
to help other people in the community. Your motives
have always been self-serving. Why come to me now if
you think there are issues? What would you gain out of
this, Shandor?"

"Truthfully," Shandor said, looking wistfully down
the street, "to save this city, the one we both love. Look,
Evette, we both play baseball, so to speak, only we play
in separate fields. It only makes sense that if one team
winds up in trouble, trouble big enough to affect both
playing fields, both teams should merge to conquer the
problem."

Evee sighed, noting time getting further and further
away from her. "I appreciate your metaphor and offer
to help, Mr. Black, but I assure you that we have things
firmly in hand."

Shandor pursed his lips and studied Evee for a few
seconds. "Do you plan on assuring the police officers
who've made numerous trips to the Elders' home in the
same way?"

Evee felt her brows lift in surprise. She didn't allow
herself to give Shandor the satisfaction of asking how he
knew about the police.

Shandor clicked his tongue against his crooked front
teeth. "What do you think the Elders will tell them when
they finally do decide to open the door? Or worse, if the
officers obtain a warrant and force their way inside?"

Evee only stared at him, working hard to remain expressionless.

"If we join forces, Miss François, we can certainly have the police officers turn the other cheek, so to speak. Point them in a completely different direction. The Triad and Elders remain safe that way."

Unable to stop herself, Evee huffed. "Trust me. Whatever you think you can do with your powers, we can do three times as much. The Triad is not a simple cluster of witches. We have our own ways and powers."

"So I've heard," Shandor said. "But from what I've heard recently, those powers seem to be slipping, for whatever reason. If that's true, then imagine you having the help of the sorcerers in this war you're fighting. You would be able to conquer these problems in a day, two at the most. Think of it. No more sleepless nights. No more having to watch the catacombs, where you're keeping the Nosferatu cloistered."

"How do you know where my Nosferatu are?" Evee demanded.

"Oh, there are many things I know. I'm aware that the Chenilles are collected in the Louis I Cemetery, and the Loup Garous have been gathered in the North Compound out in Algiers."

Without a second thought, Evee spat, hitting the ground and missing Shandor's shoes by a couple inches. "I'm going to ask you once more, Black. Where are you getting your information?"

"And once more, I have to reiterate that I cannot divulge that information. But all of it's true, isn't it?"

Evee heard a low growl come from the bowels of her throat. "In a million years, how can you possibly expect me to ever trust the likes of you?"

Shandor eyed her. A glint in his milky brown eyes.

"Because you have no one else to turn to. Because you're at a loss and afraid. Because we're your only hope. There's no one else who could possibly understand where you're coming from or how the challenges you face affect you."

"Except the opposite sex of witches?" Evee nearly shouted. She leaned into Shandor to make certain he heard every word she said, and that he wouldn't miss the determination in her eyes. "This is the last time I'm going to repeat this. I don't know what you've heard or who you've heard it from, but it's all bullshit. We take care of our own. It's not like sorcerers don't ever run into challenges of their own. When was the last time you called on any of us for help? Never! Whatever situation we may face, we'll conquer it as a Triad with our Elders."

"And your new friends?" Shandor smirked.

"What the hell are you talking about?"

"Oh, we see more in this city than you give us credit for. I've seen those four handsome young men following the Triad's every footstep."

"Who told you about the Benders? Your fastidious, reliable source?" Evee taunted.

"What was there to tell? Who could possibly miss those handsome men in this city? They truly stand out, and I've personally seen two of them following you through the Quarter. Their appearance here is certainly no secret. They're—"

Evee finally held up both hands, stopping his rant. "As I stated before, Black, I have business to tend to. I would ask that you mind your own business, and we'll take care of our own."

With that, Evee turned on her heel and stormed away from Shandor Black. She had to let her sisters, the Elders and the Benders know that word was on the street, and worse, in the hands of the sorcerers. That was a problem they certainly didn't need. For this one held the potential to turn things a lot uglier than they were now or make them far worse than anyone expected.

Chapter 15

After making his call to Ronan's father and the rest of his family regarding his cousin's death, Lucien paced about the hotel room, unable to think. All his brain focused on was the sight of Ronan, the long black claw that had been shoved into his left temple and came out of his right. His face bloody, eyes open and void of expression, mouth slightly open from the shock.

The only comfort Lucien had to offer Ronan's family and his own was that Ronan's death had been quick. There'd been no struggle, no death throes. Lucien's cousin had simply hung from that goddamn claw like a ragdoll.

Aside from his cousin's death, the worst part would be the lack of closure for Ronan's family. They'd have no body to bury. Only memories, which they planned to share in a memorial mass to be held as soon as the Benders' mission was over.

Gavril and Nikoli had been right. Although he was

grieving, Ronan's father had insisted that the other Benders carry on with their tasks despite this horrid event. He specifically said Ronan would have wanted it that way, as well. When Lucien had spoken to his father about the news, he also reminded his son to complete their mission. It was the Benders' way. Always had been. Always would be. They'd make time for emotions later.

Still, Lucien couldn't help remembering the huge smile Ronan had had on his face when he'd announced that Evee would have dinner with him once the mission was over. Lucien wished Ronan had spoken up sooner, at least to show Evee he was interested in her. The problem was, and aways had been, that doing so wasn't Ronan's style. He wasn't like the rest of his cousins. He looked at life much more seriously and quietly than they did.

Shaking off the thoughts of Ronan and women, Evee specifically, Lucien began to feel like a caged animal in the hotel suite. He left the room and the hotel.

Since the front of the hotel emptied out onto Royal Street, he had but a block to walk before he reached Bourbon. Not that he felt like looking for Originals. He simply needed to hear people right now. Normal people. Laughing, singing, talking, all of them seemingly without a care in the world.

Lucien couldn't remember ever feeling that way. Not only did he go about life with many cares, but sometimes it felt like the entire world rested on his shoulders. Feeling the stirrings of self-pity, he frowned and forced himself to study the streets. He walked down alleys, peered behind buildings, looking for any of the missing Originals.

It was eerily quiet in the Quarter at this time of morning. Aside from a handful of drunks, some singing while staggering along the sidewalk, a couple of others puking in the middle of the street, the streets were all but empty.

The air smelled of garbage, booze, vomit and urine. Not a place anyone would care to hang around in for very long.

As hard as he tried to keep Evee off his mind, she popped back in without his permission, and this time, Lucien couldn't shake her off.

He wished he could turn back time and do things differently. Instead of playing the martyr and suggesting that Ronan ask her out, Lucien should have shot his own gun straight and on target. He really liked Evee, thought she was one of the most beautiful women he'd ever known.

Lucien knew that Ronan's slow approach to women was due to fear. Fear of rejection. He had easily faced Cartesians, one of the most dangerous creatures in the netherworld. Yet when it came to speaking his mind to a woman, he froze. Out of all the other cousins, Lucien was probably the only one who knew that Ronan had been more afraid of being rebuffed by a woman than of getting attacked by the monstrous creatures the Benders had hunted for years.

Some years ago, Ronan had told Lucien in confidence that he felt something had to be wrong with him. Some trauma he couldn't remember that made him so slow and uneasy about even asking a woman on a date. He'd been raised on the same street as his cousins, all four of them damn near connected at the hip since they could walk and talk. You would have thought that some of their bravado, their fearlessness with women had rubbed off on him. But it hadn't. He'd always seemed to be the odd man out.

Fortunately, regardless of all the odd theories Ronan had ruminated on regarding women, he'd known he served a purpose. Ronan had been good at his job, a job that was serious. It saved people's lives. Kept the universe in sync, and preserved the harmony between the humans and netherworld. The importance of that mission had to mean more to him than losing out on any woman. Including Evette François.

As logical and stoic as that sounded in his own head, it didn't stop Lucien's heart from aching. And he knew it would do so for some time.

Suddenly, a scream broke through Lucien's musings.

It sounded like a woman, and her screams seemed to be coming from a couple blocks away. Possibly down St. Ann Street.

Lucien broke into a run, taking a right on Ursuline, a quick right on Dauphine, then two blocks onto St. Ann.

Just as he turned onto the street, he saw a dark-haired, petite woman running out into the street, her face bloody, her clothes shredded. And right behind her was a Nosferatu in full natural form.

Although the streetlamps on St. Ann's were few, there was no mistaking the Nosferatu's lanky form, his large white bald head with the large vein across its forehead.

Lucien took off for the woman, meaning to shove her to safety and distract the Nosferatu. But the Original was gaining ground quickly, which meant it was actually toying with the woman. A Nosferatu had the ability to easily move from place to place in the blink of an eye. The fact that he allowed the woman to run and he simply trotted after her proved the creature planned to toy with its prey before taking her.

"Hey!" Lucien yelled, attempting to get the Nosferatu's attention. He suddenly had a sense of déjà vu, remembering how he'd had to do the same with two Loup Garous. Although he'd distracted the Loups by yelling at them, he'd failed to rescue their prey. However, he had managed to blind the Loups, keeping them from easily hunting other prey.

The Nosferatu was different, though. Even if Lucien

blinded the bastard, a Nosferatu healed itself quickly, and it would only take a matter of minutes before it would regain its sight.

When he failed to get the Nosferatu's attention, Lucien yelled again. "Hey, you ugly fuck. Over here!"

This time the Nosferatu stopped and looked over at him. He stood, hunched over, looking from the woman to Lucien. Probably trying to figure out which would be an easier target.

Unfortunately, the woman won the Nosferatu's coin toss. He spun about and knocked her down to the ground before Lucien had time to blink.

Lucien took out his scabior. It was all he knew to do. Without question, the Nosferatu had ten times more strength than he had, but if he caught it by surprise, he might be able to do enough damage, cause enough of a distraction for the woman to escape.

At that moment, Lucien heard voices behind him. A shriek, gasps, curses.

He glanced back and saw that three people now stood at the corner of St. Ann and Bourbon, watching the action.

The Nosferatu looked back at them and let out a guttural growl. Its long fangs bared, its face twisted with fury.

Lucien turned to the three onlookers. A chubby man wearing a Who Dat T-shirt and stained jeans, an average-size man with glasses and no teeth, and an elderly woman in a very short skirt and halter top.

"Get back!" Lucien yelled at them. "Get out of here!"

Instead of listening to him and dispersing, the crowd seemed to grow thicker with onlookers. Five or six more people had joined the original three to watch the show.

Even with the crowd watching, Lucien feared that if he

didn't get the Nosferatu away from the woman, she'd have no hope of survival. Worse, if the Nosferatu did manage the kill, it would go after the next human in line. That could be him or anyone standing in the growing crowd.

"Get out of here, damn it!" Lucien shouted at the on-lookers.

No one moved. They stood, mouths agape, watching the events unfold. Lucien heard bits and pieces of their conversation, their words jumbling over each other.

"What's going—"

"What is that ugly—"

"—at that ugly son of a bitch!"

"—some kind of monster."

"Somebody call—"

"He's going to murder her! Stop—I—"

"—the police! Somebody call the—"

"Shit, look at—"

"Somebody help her!"

"Fuck me—"

"—not going over there! Look at that thing!"

"—like a horror story."

As people continued talking over one another, Lucien decided to take the Nosferatu by surprise as it had the woman on the ground and its fangs bared, ready to latch on to her neck.

Just as Lucien was about to make the leap for the Original, he suddenly caught a strong scent of clove and sulfur.

Instinctively, he looked up at the sky, and right over where the Nosferatu and woman struggled, Lucien saw a rift open up wide, which surprised him. Usually a rift appeared as a slit in the sky, and it took a bit of time for a Cartesian to work its way through the opening. This one, however, seemed to burst open like a pustulant wound, and within seconds, a Cartesian's fur-matted head appeared. It didn't take long for it to hang from the rift by the waist, lower its massive arms and swipe down with its claws toward the Nosferatu, who was already draining the woman of her blood.

With scabior already in hand, Lucien found himself in a conundrum. He had been willing to put his life on the line to save the woman from the Nosferatu, but now with a Cartesian aiming for a Nosferatu he had to choose. Get the human to safety or blast the Cartesian back into other dimensions.

Choices, always choices. And never easy ones.

Although it hurt his heart, Lucien had little choice but to choose the bigger cause. He had to get rid of the bigger danger. The Cartesian.

Despite the crowd of onlookers still whispering, squealing, gasping, now shouting at the sight of the Cartesian overhead, Lucien held on to his scabior, gave a quick flick of his wrist, then twirled the scabior lightning fast between his fingers. He heard comments from the crowd growing louder.

"What's that guy doing?"

"What's that thing in his hand?"

"What—"

Lucien forced himself to tune out their blabbering and focus on the task at hand. With the scabior charged, he aimed it at the Cartesian and hit it square in the face. It shrieked and jerked backward. A loud noise followed its retreat.

With the rift still open, Lucien kept his scabior aimed at it, concentrated only on the Cartesian, then heard a second and third pop, which meant he'd been able to push the Cartesian back two more dimensions. Only then did the rift in the sky disappear. It closed so quickly, it was as if someone had zippered it shut in one fell swoop.

With that done, the sounds from the crowd reached Lucien's ear once more. Some women were crying, men were cursing, yet not one of them stepped a foot closer to the Nosferatu, who was now draining the woman on the ground dry. Lucien had only to look at the locked expression of terror in her open eyes to know she was already dead.

Evidently oblivious of the Cartesian who'd come so close to attacking it, the Nosferatu had chosen to finish its meal with gusto.

With the Cartesian taken care of, Lucien knew he still had to deal with the Nosferatu. The gawking crowd had refused to disperse, and he feared that once the Original finished with the woman, it would spring lightning-fast for yet another victim.

The problem was he wasn't sure how to effectively stop the Nosferatu. Not with its ability to heal so quickly.

Instead of taking the chance of riling the Original while it fed and have it focus on the others in the crowd, Lucien took one more shot at getting the gawkers to move on.

"Get the hell out of here," Lucien shouted at them. "I can't stop this creature. And when it's done, there's a good chance it'll come after one of you. Go! For the love of God, get the hell out!"

This time, at the sound of Lucien's voice, the Nosferatu looked up from its prey and screeched a warning to Lucien. Its mouth was covered with blood, which dripped down its chin. The sight of that alone sent the men and women crowded near the end of the alley screaming and running off in different directions.

Lucien stood his ground, scabior in hand, waiting for the Nosferatu to turn on him.

Oddly enough, the Original didn't. It turned back to the woman, attached its fangs to her neck, obviously determined to drain every drop of blood from her body.

Although Lucien had managed to get rid of the Cartesian, he still felt like a failure. A woman had died because he hadn't been able to handle both the Nosferatu and Cartesian at the same time.

Knowing there was nothing he could do to permanently stop the Nosferatu without Evee's help, Lucien started to head for the docks, where he knew a dome was being built to transfer the Originals across the river to feed. He'd make sure to let Evee know of the sighting. With any luck, she'd be able to reach the Nosferatu and bring him back into her fold.

Turning away from the sickening sight and the sucking, licking sounds coming from the Nosferatu as it fed, Lucien started for the docks.

That was when he heard the wail of sirens and horns. Evidently, someone had called the police. And once again, just as he'd had to do when tackling the Loup Garous and the Nosferatu with Ronan, Lucien quickly left the site. For there was no way in hell any explanation of what truly happened would satisfy the police. They'd take him in for questioning, wasting time he didn't have to spare.

Hurrying down St. Ann to Chartres, Lucien started to feel like a pathetic loser. A wuss.

Always running. Away from love, away from himself, away from the police.

Chapter 16

Instead of going to the docks as she had initially intended to do once she left Shandor, Evee chose to detour. She turned off Dumaine, then onto Bourbon. Fury still roared through her from her confrontation with Shandor. She had to let her sisters and the Benders know about the sorcerers.

She was sure Viv was already at the North Compound, getting the cattle set up for the feeding. But Evee knew Gilly would be at Snaps, the bar-and-grill she owned off Bourbon. She counted on Gavril being with Gilly. If that proved true, then Gavril would be able to summon the other Benders, hopefully. That way everyone except Viv and Nikoli, who had to remain at the compound, would be able to huddle up at Snaps and discuss the new challenge facing them.

When Evee arrived at Snaps, she found it packed with people, even at this hour of the morning. Drunken laughter echoed off the walls of the building, and loud music pounded from the jukebox.

Evee spotted Gilly at the far end of the bar, taking an order from an already too drunk customer, as the other two barmaids hustled from one end of the bar to the other.

When Gilly saw Evee she sent her a wave, pointed to the customer in front of her, then held up a finger, signaling for her to wait.

As soon as Gilly served a Crown and Coke to the man, she rounded the corner of the counter and went over to her sister.

Gilly leaned in close to Evee's ear, obviously wanting to be heard above all the ruckus of yelling, laughing, music and talking. "I was just getting ready to leave for the docks. We're slammed tonight, and I wanted to make sure my people had a handle on this crowd."

Evee turned so her mouth was next to Gilly's ear. "I have something to tell you before we go to the docks. Where's Gavril?"

Gilly aimed a thumb over her right shoulder. "Back in my office. Guess the noise in here was getting to him."

"We need to include him in this conversation," Evee said.

"What's up?" Gilly asked, frowning.

"Can we go somewhere quieter?"

Gilly nodded, took Evee's hand and led her through the crowd, down a short hallway, past the men's and women's restrooms, to her office, which was at the end of the hall. Gilly opened the door, motioned Evee inside.

The office was basically a ten-by-twelve-foot room that held a desk and two chairs. Paperwork overflowed on a small credenza.

Gavril sat behind the desk and smiled when he spotted Evee. His smile quickly faded, however, and Evee suspected it had something to do with her expression, which probably read "urgent and ugly."

Sitting upright, Gavril asked, "What's wrong?"

"I need for you to use the watch thingy that you and your cousins wear and contact Lucien. Have him meet us here ASAP," Evee said.

"What about Nikoli?" Gavril asked.

"Nix him. I'm sure he's with Viv at the compound, and we need them there to get the cattle ready. I'll fill Viv in on the news when we get to the compound."

Instead of questioning her further, Gavril immediately punched two buttons on his watch, then looked at Evee. "Done. He should be here any minute."

From what Evee had gathered after Lucien had left his watch on the dryer at her house and she'd returned it to him, the Benders' watches contained geo nodes that emitted a signal. Whenever one of the Benders was in dire straits and needed help from the cousins, he activated the geo node. Once the signal was emitted, the Benders who received the signal were to drop whatever they were doing and go to the signaling Bender's aid.

Gilly sat in one of the chairs, swiped a hand over her face. She seemed utterly exhausted, which made Evee feel a bit guilty about bringing her more bad news.

"What's going on?" Gilly asked, then held up a hand. "Yeah, yeah, I know you want to wait until everybody gets here, so never mind. But really, Evee, with all that's going on right now, I can't take much more." She narrowed her eyes. "You didn't...you know..." Gilly threw Gavril a quick glance before turning back to Evee. "Do anything that the Elders told us to stay away from?"

"I don't have anything to do with this one," Evee said. "It just popped up, and I think it's important that we all know about it. It could be a game changer."

"Good changer?" Gavril asked.

Evee shook her head. "I wish."

"Man, oh, man, oh, crap, fuck, shit," Gilly said in one long breath. Then put her head in her hands.

"You mean like more missing Originals?" Gavril asked. "Dead ones?"

"I don't know," Evee said. "Something's come up that might very well twist us way off track."

"How's that possible when we're off track now?" Gilly asked.

Evee studied her sister's face. "We may not have solved the problem yet, but we're working hard to get a handle on it. The problem is that somebody else has suddenly got their hand on the wheel and is trying to steer."

"Who?" Gilly asked.

Before she had a chance to say more, the office door opened and Lucien hurried inside.

"What's the emergency?" Lucien asked, anxiously looking about the room.

Evee closed the door behind them.

"Why did you summon me?" Lucien asked Gavril. His eyes suddenly grew wide. "Where's Nikoli? Is he hurt? Is he okay?"

Gavril held up a hand and patted the air, signaling for Lucien to bring his anxiety down a few notches. "Nikoli is fine. I purposely didn't signal him because he and Viv, along with one of her Loup Garous, are building a dome over the ferry. It's getting closer to feeding time. I didn't want to take him away from the task. We'll fill him in on whatever news Evee has as soon as we see him."

"Evee?" Lucien looked at her questioningly.

"Evee has some news she feels we all need to hear," Gavril said. "According to her, there's company intending to join us in the troubles we're trying to work through."

"What are you talking about?" Lucien asked, still looking at Evee.

"I'd ask all of you to sit," Evee said, then held out a hand, indicating the shortage of chairs.

"We're fine standing," Lucien said. "Please, continue."

Evee nodded. "Earlier, I was headed to the docks to check on the progress of the dome when I heard someone call my name. It was Shandor Black."

"No frigging way," Gilly said.

"Yes, way. He claimed he had been looking for me. Had seen me walk the route to the ferry on many occasions."

"What?" Gilly said, her brow furrowing deeply. "You mean that son of a bitch has been stalking you?"

"Claims he suffers from insomnia and often walks the streets in and around the Quarter when he can't sleep."

Gilly bared her teeth as if she meant to attack and gnaw through the first thing in sight.

"Was that the emergency?" Lucien asked. "That you'd been followed?"

"No," Evee said. "It's what Shandor said."

Everyone remained quiet, waiting for Evee to continue.

"He claims that he heard from someone that we were having issues with the Originals," Evee said. "He knew about the human attack, the Nosferatu death, about the missing Chenilles, Nosferatu and Loup Garous. He even knew about the police going to the Elders."

"The police have been to see your Elders?" Lucien asked. "This puts a whole new twist on things. We'll have to do double time on discretion. I mean, I couldn't help what happened in the Quarter, when Pierre had to put down one of the Nosferatu, but with the police snooping around, that means we'll have to limit our exposure during the day. If we don't, I'm sure we'll be spotted by one of the witnesses, who'll wind up going to the police. They'll ask difficult questions. To the Triad and the Benders. What did the Elders tell them?"

"Nothing," Evee said, a bit put off with Lucien's pessimism, although it had reason. "When the police knock on their door, they don't answer. So nothing's been said… yet."

Lucien nodded, his lips a thin line of worry.

"Anyway," Evee said, "the bottom line of all this is that Shandor knew too much." She looked from face to face. "Did any of you tell him anything?"

"Of course not," Lucien said. "I don't even know the man."

"As if!" Gilly exclaimed, pounding a fist on the chair arm.

"I don't even know who Shandor Black is," Gavril said. "So I know it wasn't me and would bet my life that none of the Benders have said a word to anyone. We're here to help you, not spread gossip to people we don't even know."

"Who exactly is this Shandor Black?" Lucien asked.

"One of the three sorcerers who live in New Orleans," Evee said. "He's partners in a law firm with Trey Cottle, one of the other sorcerers."

"And neither of them can be trusted for shit," Gilly said. "Both of them have only done spells and incantations to serve their own needs. I've never known either of them to reach out and help anyone else."

"Who's the third sorcerer?" Lucien asked.

"Gunner Stern," Evee said. "He's not a business partner with Trey or Shandor, but he seems to hang around them pretty often, so there's a question about him there. He seems like a genuinely nice guy, and our Elders, well, at least one of them appears to trust him. But Shandor is Trey's yes-man and his right hand. And for the exact reasons Gilly just mentioned, there was no reason for Shandor to approach me. Too out of character. Claimed he wanted to help us. Join forces for the sake of the city."

"Bullshit," Gilly said.

"My words to him exactly," Evee said. "But despite Shandor, it seems we now have someone on the streets spreading rumors about us."

"Do you think it might have been the Elders?" Gilly asked.

"With the fight we had with them earlier about the sorcerers, I seriously doubt it," Evee said. "And you know Arabella. When she says she's going to think on something and then get back to us, that's exactly what she's going to do. There's no pushing a go-button with her until she's ready."

"So, I assume you haven't heard from her yet?" Gilly said.

"Right. No update."

"Me, either. Maybe it was one of the other Elders," Gilly said, then stuck her thumbnail into her mouth and chewed on it.

"You know they don't do anything without Arabella's approval. Even without that, Vanessa hates all of the sorcerers. She'd rather cut off her head than run to one for help. As for Taka, well, she's a few crayons short of a box. I just don't see her having the wherewithal to simply take to the streets and start spreading rumors. Besides, you know how fearful she is about being found out. She's probably having nightmares about being hanged, then burned at the stake."

"Then someone else has to be watching us...closely," Gilly said.

Evee shuddered at the thought.

"Just how big is the threat if the sorcerers do get involved?" Nikoli asked.

"It's a trust issue," Evee said. "There's no telling what kind of spell or incantation they'd cast. Remember, Trey and Shandor are infamous for only using their powers for their benefit. Anything that gives them more power, more control over the world of magic. It's always seemed like they were in competition with the Triad or anyone from the Circle of Sisters. They jump in, screw things up so it turns bad for us and looks good for them. I swore I saw a smirk cross Shandor's face. I wanted to spit on him. He tried to sound nonchalant, of course, even look worried, concerned about us. I didn't bite."

"We need to keep a close eye out for those guys," Gavril said. "What do they look like?"

Gilly snorted. "One looks like a pig, the other a rotting twig with glasses."

Evee couldn't help grinning at Gilly's short, but relatively accurate, description. She filled in the blanks for the Benders. "Trey's kind of short and dumpy. Balding head, gray hair wrapped around the back of his head. He wears glasses that always sit near the tip of his nose. Always wears a suit. Except for wearing a suit and glasses, Shandor is Trey's mirror opposite. Tall, lanky, thinning gray hair that he combs back, away from his forehead. And he has a thin face that holds a perpetual scowl. Both in their late sixties, early seventies. As for Gunner, he's a white-haired gentleman, late sixties, I'd guess. Pretty average in appearance, except for his eyes. They're bright blue. Average height and build. Nice face. Very different from Trey and Shandor."

"Different doesn't always mean different in a good way," Lucien said. "For all we know, this fellow, Gunner, because he's so different from the other two, might be the one finding out information and spreading rumors. If he's as different from the other two as you say, it would be easier for him to collect data. You know, nice guy, no one suspects a thing."

"Maybe we do have to look at what seems least obvious," Evee said. "Honestly, though, right now we don't have time to hammer through this. We've got a feeding to do. I just wanted to warn all of you. Give you a heads-up. It's not like it's not tough enough that some of our spells don't work, but now we've got to watch out for spies."

"But your spell did work," Lucien said. "Remember the illusion spell earlier?"

"You did an illusion spell?" Gilly asked, gawking at Evee. "Wow, I haven't seen you do one of those in years. How'd it go?"

"She saved my life," Lucien said with no hesitation. "We'd just come out of the catacombs when it seemed like the entire sky opened up with Cartesians. I tried to get Evee to go back into the catacombs, but, being who she is, she was determined to stay and help. That's when she did the illusion spell. Confusing those Cartesians was brilliance in the making. They didn't know where to aim. It gave us time to push all the ones who'd crawled through rifts back."

"You go, girl!" Gilly said, giving a little clap of congratulations.

"Just something that had to be done," Evee said. "I'm thankful it worked. Now let's get ready for the feeding. I'm sure the dome's done, since the ferry isn't that big, and Viv's probably getting the cattle ready."

Gavril put a hand on Gilly's shoulder. "Guess we'd better get our lineup ready for the Chenilles."

She nodded.

Lucien grabbed the doorknob to leave, then turned to Evee. "I know this sorcerer thing has everyone concerned. We just have to take this slow. I don't mean in speed, but slow as in being mindful of every decision we make, so it's the right one. And, of course, keep an eye peeled and look over our shoulders from time to time. Don't worry. I've got your back, and I know Nikoli has Viv's."

"And I've got Gilly's," Gavril said.

"Glad we're all up to speed," Evee said. "Hopefully things will start heading in the right direction and quick."

With that, everyone left the office single file.

Evee felt Lucien's body close behind hers as they made it into the main room and squeezed through the crowd of people. A six-foot transvestite, wearing black fishnet stockings and a shorter than short red glitter dress with accompanying four-inch red glitter heels, and one of Gilly's waitresses were walking at a furious pace. The waitress carried a tray filled with nachos smothered in cheese and jalapenos, three margaritas and two glasses of beer. Evee came to an abrupt halt to let her hurry by. Lucien pulled up short right behind her, and in that moment, a drunk sideswiped the waitress, and her tray flipped out of her hand, its contents landing all over Evee.

With a gasp, Evee stood stock-still, feeling melted cheese slide from her hair down to her cheeks, the front of her clothes. She felt like a garbage dump and smelled like a margarita gone bad.

"Oh, God, I'm so sorry!" the waitress said. "Somebody bumped into me and…please let me help. Get something to clean you up."

"I've got it, Darnelle," Gilly said, and turned to Evee.

"Is it as bad as it feels?" Evee asked.

"Worse," Gilly said. "You look like a walking disaster. I've got a clean pair of jeans and shirt in my office that I keep there for emergencies. You can use those. We wear the same size, so no problem there. No way you're going to get all that goop out of your hair in the bathroom sink, though."

"You know the Monteleone's just a block away," Lucien said. "You're welcome to shower in our room."

"Plan," Gilly said. "I'll go get the clothes. Then Gavril and me will head out to do our thing." With that, Gilly hurried off to her office.

Evee felt like an idiot, standing there with cheese and booze dripping all over her body. She refused to look at Lucien. Too many people were staring at her and laughing as it was.

Within minutes, Gilly was back with jeans and a green-striped sweater. She handed them to Evee. "Here. Go, shower."

Thinking about taking a shower in Lucien's hotel room gave Evee pause. But only for a moment as another glob of cheese dripped down from her hair and slid down the middle of her face.

Holding the clean clothes at arm's length, Evee gave Gilly a look, which she hoped her sister could read. *You know this shower thing is sending me into dangerous territory, right?*

Gilly lifted an eyebrow, and the hint of a smile played around the corners of her mouth. "Shower, then off to the docks, right?"

"Right."

"A little cheese and booze isn't so bad, considering," Gilly said. "What else could possibly go wrong between here and the hotel?"

It wasn't the distance between Snaps and the Monteleone that Evee worried about. It was the distance between her and Lucien in the hotel. She made a mental note to remind her bright-eyed sister to lose the words "What else could possibly go wrong?" from her vocabulary.

Evee knew all too well that many things could go wrong…and probably would.

Chapter 17

Lucien led Evee down Bourbon Street, then Royal toward the hotel. Unfortunately, she'd suffered a few cat-calls along the way. A drunken jerk yelled, "Hey, lady, watch out for the big-ass birds out here! Oops, too late. One already gotcha!"

Lucien had to hold back his temper because he'd wanted so badly to punch the guy out. And anyone else who made a negative comment. He knew how embarrassed the remarks made Evee because she stayed close behind him, nearly pasted to his back, trying to stay out of sight as much as possible.

When they finally reached the hotel, Lucien went straight to the bank of elevators, placing Evee in front of him so she was sandwiched between him and the elevator door. As they waited for the elevator to ding open, Evee wrung her hands every time someone walked in or out of the lobby.

As hard as he tried to give Evee some sort of safe refuge, inevitably somebody would walk by, do a double take at her, then move on with a laugh. He couldn't blame them for staring, really. She was quite the sight. Cheese covered most of her head, and her face was smeared with it despite the many napkins she'd used to try and clean her face. Her clothes were a lost cause. Her black pants and shirt had been doused with alcohol and dribbled cheese.

Lucien kept his fingers crossed that there'd be no one else in the elevator when it opened.

Two seconds later, he found that his luck held out. The doors whispered open with not a soul inside.

He hustled Evee into the elevator, hit the button for the twelfth floor and jabbed the close button numerous times, wanting the doors to close before anyone else stepped inside.

Lucien let out a sigh of relief as the doors closed, with him and Evee the only riders. Only then did Evee take a step away from him.

"This has got to be one of the most humiliating things I've ever been through. I smell like a bar and garbage dump all mixed together," she said, and for a moment, Lucien thought she'd start crying. Instead, she lifted her chin and stared at the floor numbers illuminated one by one over the elevator door.

As the tiny cubicle began moving upward, Evee kept her eyes on the floor number lights.

"It's not so bad," Lucien said, and swiped a string of nacho cheese off her left cheek, then licked the cheese from his finger. "Doesn't taste bad, either."

Evee gave him a light punch in the arm, and the smallest of grins.

He smiled softly, and held the clothes Gilly had given Evee to change into closer to his chest. The conversation about the sorcerers in Gilly's office played over in his mind, but, for some reason, it didn't concern him as much as it seemed to bother the Triad. Of course, he didn't know the sorcerers as well as they did, so his radar on the matter could be way off. Right now his thoughts were on Evee. How close she was to him, no matter the cheese and booze. The thought of Ronan tumbled across his mind, causing Lucien to remember how enamored Ronan had been with her. It saddened him that Ronan would never experience the dinner date he'd made with Evee.

Fate had taken Ronan out of Evee's life. And although guilt over Ronan pressed against his heart, he had a choice to make. Either mourn what might have or could have been between Ronan and Evee or wait for fate to deal a double hand. His last choice was to make certain this woman would always be by his side, safe, protected... loved. A word that felt strange to Lucien even when he thought about it. He'd never uttered the L word to any woman before, and although he'd yet to say it to Evee, there was no denying that somehow, in the midst of all they'd gone and were still going through, he'd managed to fall in love with her.

As the elevator took its time making its way to the twelfth floor, he noticed that Evee had her fingers of both hands crossed at her sides. He guessed that she was hoping that the elevator wouldn't stop on another floor before it made it to the twelfth.

To break the silence, Lucien asked, "You really think those sorcerers are a threat to us?"

"I do. Just don't know how big. I don't know what their agenda is, but I know that two of them for sure are trouble."

"The Trey and Shandor duo?"

"Yeah."

The elevator finally bounced to a stop, and the doors

swished open. Lucien stuck his head out to check for people and gave Evee a thumbs-up, indicating the coast was clear.

Evee grabbed on to the back of Lucien's shirt and clung tight as they left the elevator, hung a right in the hallway, then all but ran fifty feet before Lucien came to a stop. He dug into his back pants pocket, pulled out a key card, then stuck it into the appropriate door slot and pushed the door open. He hoped the maids had already taken care of business for the day. Not that he and his cousins were slobs, but Gavril had been the last to use the shower, which usually meant towels strewn all over the floor and toothpaste spit in the sink.

Lucien breathed a sigh of relief when he walked in and saw the beds neatly made, and everything smelled lemony fresh and dust-free.

He pointed to a room on the left. "Bathroom's right in there. Help yourself."

"Thanks," Evee said, then grabbed the clothes out of his hands and hurried off to the bathroom, closing the door behind her.

Half expecting it, Lucien thought it a bit odd when he didn't hear the lock click on the bathroom door.

Not knowing what else to do with himself, he walked over to one of the beds and sat on the edge of it. He ran his fingers through his hair, hearing the sound of water now coming from the bathroom. The sound made him fidget. He wasn't sure what all the sorcerer information really meant, but if Evee considered them worrisome, then he'd trust her judgment. Enough to see them as another part of an equation, which only meant more trouble. The last thing they needed.

Growing more restless by the second, Lucien got off the bed and went into the sitting area of the suite. He picked up a magazine that highlighted the have-to-see lo-cations in New Orleans, then sat on the couch and flipped through the magazine, not paying attention to any of the pictures or articles. He couldn't stop thinking about Evee in the next room.

He imagined her in the shower, wanted more than any-thing to be in there with her. Touch her, hold her, reassure her. he just needed to be near her; cheese or no cheese, booze or no booze, it made no difference to him. Beneath it all was the essence of Evee, and that always filled him with need and desire. It made his heart grow so huge it felt like it wanted to burst from his chest.

Lucien continued to flip through the magazine. First forward, then backward, still not seeing a damn thing on its pages.

Suddenly, unexpectedly, Lucien heard Evee call out to him.

"Lucien, do you have any shampoo? I don't see any in here."

He jumped to his feet, went to his travel bag and grabbed the shampoo he normally carried with him when traveling. Hotels rarely handed out enough shampoo and cream rinse to handle four grown men sharing a suite.

Lucien stepped up to the bathroom door and said loudly, "I have some here. Do you want me to leave it outside the bathroom door?"

A moment of silence followed before Evee said. "The bathroom's pretty big and cold. Is there a way you could, like, bring it in here?"

Surprised with her answer and confused by the hesi-tation in her voice, he asked, "Do you have the shower curtain closed?"

"Of course I do," she said.

He waited a beat, then said, "Do you want me to bring it to you?"

A hesitant moment passed before Evee said tentatively, "If you don't mind, you can just sort of stick your hand around the curtain and hand it to me."

"Sure," Lucien said, then wondered who in the hell had taken over his body and mind. Like it would be no big deal for him to be but a curtain's distance away from her, hand out shampoo, then leave. Sure, no problem.

Biting the inside of his cheek, Lucien opened the bathroom door. The room was filled with steam.

Obviously hearing the door open, Evee said, "I tried using soap, but it didn't work. Now my hair's caked with clumpy soap and cheese goo."

"I'm sure the shampoo will help," Lucien said. He pushed the bottle around the edge of the shower curtain. "Here you go."

Lucien saw her silhouette move in the shower, behind the white, translucent shower curtain. Seeing the outline of her naked body took his breath away.

She took the shampoo bottle from him, and in the translucent glory he'd found as his window, Lucien saw her bring the bottle up to her nose.

"Smells good. Thank you."

Not wanting to leave, Lucien tried to think of something, anything to say so she wouldn't send him immediately away.

"Glad you like the shampoo," he said, and wanted to slap himself for how ridiculous he sounded. Now all he could do was follow up the asinine statement with more stupidity. "I usually carry that brand with me whenever we travel. Can't ever have too much shampoo when you're traveling with three other guys."

"I'm sure," she said absently, and Lucien saw the silhouette of her tilting the shampoo bottle into her hand, then leaning over and placing the bottle on the side of the tub. The sight of her heart-shaped ass became clearer as it moved closer to the shower curtain, and Lucien thought he'd have a heart attack. He stifled a groan.

He watched arm shadows move to her head, hands folding up shoulder-length hair, scrubbing, scrubbing.

"Are you still in here?" Evee suddenly asked.

"Oh…uh, yes, sorry. I'll leave you to your shower."

"Wait. Before you go, could I bother you for a comb? I don't think I'm getting all the cheese out. Combing it out might help. I promise to clean the comb when I'm done."

"No problem," Lucien said, then reached for his comb, which happened to be sitting on the counter near the bathroom sink.

With comb in hand, Lucien slipped it around the edge of the shower curtain. "Here you go. Hope it helps."

He saw the shadow of her hand reaching blindly for the comb.

"Sorry. I've got shampoo in my eyes. Can't quite make out where your hand is."

Lucien stretched his arm in farther. She finally latched on to his hand.

"Got it," she said, probably more to herself than to him.

Figuring he'd either go into the living area of the suite and die a slow death or take a chance while he had it and remain by the shower.

"Do you need any help in there?" Lucien asked. "Do you want me to check your hair? Make sure all the cheese is out?"

"Do you have any cream rinse?" Evee asked, evidently avoiding his indirect lead.

"I think so," Lucien said. Reluctantly, he turned to the

vanity and checked the small hotel bottles neatly lined up on a narrow silver tray. He found one labeled conditioner and grabbed it.

He stuck his hand with the conditioner back behind the shower curtain. "Here you go. It's the hotel's brand. Sorry I don't have anything better."

"Thanks," Evee said. "Trying to get this comb through my mop of hair without conditioner is hell." Once again her hand reached blindly for his. As her hand wandered along the shower curtain, it pushed the curtain aside a bit more. Lucien stood transfixed, seeing her naked body standing before him, her eyes closed, her hand searching. He aimed the bottle of conditioner at her hand, and she grabbed it.

Out of respect, Lucien backed away, allowing himself only a shadow's view once more. He watched her bathe her hair with conditioner, work it through with her fingers, then lean over again for the comb she'd placed on the edge of the tub. As soon as she touched it, the comb fell into the tub.

"Shit," she said softly.

Reflexively, Lucien reached into the shower. "I'll get it." He didn't think about what he'd just done until he looked up and saw her looking down at him.

They stared at each other for a long moment, neither uttering a word. Water still pelting her body.

Lucien silently handed her the comb.

Evee took it from him, her eyes never leaving his face. He saw her lips move, heard her whisper his name. Fire seemed to melt the copper color of her beautiful eyes. Need was written in the expression on her face. He allowed his eyes to move slowly, blatantly down her body. Watching water splash over her breasts, her stomach, her thighs…between her thighs.

Determined not to give it a second thought, Lucien took a step back from the shower and removed his clothes in record time.

Before either of them had a chance to say a word, Lucien stepped into the shower, picked up the bar of soap that sat at the bottom of the tub, and rubbed it between his hands. When his hands were completely lathered, he dropped the soap, put his hands on Evee's naked shoulders and turned her so she faced the shower wall.

She moved without hesitation, and Lucien began to caress her shoulders and back with his soapy hands. He worked down to her buttocks, taking his time, moving his fingers over and in every private part of her. He heard her groan with desire, which only flared his need to white-hot.

Lucien lathered his hands again and began to work his fingers down her legs, reached her right ankle, then moved to the left and worked his way back up, his fingers kneading, fluttering over her. When he reached the top of her thigh, Lucien pressed against both of her thighs ever so gently, and Evee immediately placed her hands on the back shower wall, threw her head back, and spread her legs slightly. Enough for Lucien's fingers to work their way between them.

He brushed his fingers lightly between her legs, barely touching the mound that emitted so much heat even in the shower that it sent a shiver of pleasure through Lucien's own body. As his fingers slid across the slit of her heat, Lucien knelt in the midst of the shower spray and placed his lips on her beautiful, heart-shaped ass. He kissed and licked one cheek, then the other, nipping occasionally, which caused her to moan.

When he press a finger inside her, only a knuckle's depth, she called his name.

"Lucien…yes, more!"

Her body began to shake, and once again, Lucien was amazed at how responsive she was to his touch.

He slowly moved one hand around her waist so it rested between her legs only from the front. Then in one fell swoop, Lucien ran the finger he'd been teasing her with from behind deep inside her, captured her clitoris between the thumb and forefinger of the hand now in front of her, then nipped one cheek of her ass.

Evee cried out, and shuddered, and as she shook with the force of her orgasm, he bit down harder. The bite seemed to hit a reset button in her body, because Evee screamed his name and rode his fingers like her life depended on it.

As the waves of her pleasure began to wane, Lucien gently ran his hands over her ass, especially over the bite mark he'd placed there.

He heard her breathing, still labored, her head now down, hair hanging like black curtains along the sides of her face. Lucien grabbed the soap once more, lathered his hands, then stood.

He stood and turned Evee so she faced him. The look in her eyes lay softly on his face, and he brushed the hair away from her cheeks with a finger.

Looking her in the eye, Lucien moved his lathered hands over her breasts, taking her nipples between his thumbs and forefingers, squeezing gently, pulling gently. Evee's eyes closed and she moaned loudly, always a signal for Lucien.

With no further preamble, Lucien grabbed her around the waist and lifted her. Evee's legs automatically wrapped around his waist. Moving his hands to her ass, holding her in place, Lucien pressed the hard length of him into the swollen, open, ready and eager mouth between her legs.

Throwing her head back, Evee, groaned. "More, God, Lucien, more!"

Lucien gave her what she craved. He thrust the full length of his manhood into her body, holding her up and thrusting her forward, matching his every thrust. He lowered his head to her right breast, put her nipple in his mouth, ran his tongue around its stiffness, then bit down ever so gently.

Once more the bite seemed to trigger an inner animal that hid within Evee, for she grabbed handfuls of his hair, urging him to move harder, faster within her.

Lucien didn't hesitate to oblige. He lowered his head, bit his bottom lip to control the explosion teetering within his body.

"Yes! Yes!" Evee cried, and hot lava soon bathed him. Lucien felt it overflow from her, sending warm rivulets down his own legs.

"All of it," Lucien demanded. "Give me all of it... now."

With a wail of pleasure, Evee's body bucked again, and more flowed from her body. Only then did Lucien allow himself to let go, and the force of his orgasm was so powerful Lucien felt his legs weaken. He fought to stay upright, still holding Evee up and against him.

When they were both spent, Lucien lowered Evee slowly, carefully to her feet, still holding her close to him. She rested her head against his chest, and he cupped the back of her head, pressing her in closer.

They stood there, holding tight to each other, so many emotions flooding Lucien that he couldn't name them all. He kissed the top of her head. Kissed it again.

Evee lifted her head, brought her hands to the sides of

his face and drew his lips to hers. It took seconds before the kiss became as ravishing as the sex they'd just had.

Knowing they had responsibilities to tend to, Lucien reluctantly took her face in his hands and moved it a micro inch away. He kissed her cheek, her chin, nuzzled her neck. Then he simply held her, feeling the heat of the shower beating into his back for a moment longer. He'd never felt such satisfaction or any of the other rumble of emotions inside him with any other woman. He'd always—always been able to walk away without regret.

But this time—this time, Lucien feared this was one woman he'd never be able to walk away from...ever.

Chapter 18

Arabella paced the length of her foyer, waiting, waiting. Vanessa stood nearby, at the bottom landing of the stairs, holding on to a newel post, tapping a slippered foot against the floor.

"Where could she have gone?" Arabella asked Vanessa.

"Maybe somebody kidnapped her," Vanessa said.

"Stop talking like that," Arabella said.

Vanessa tsked. "You're right. We wouldn't be that lucky anyway. The kidnapper would bring her back."

Arabella shot her an angry look, then glanced over at the old grandfather clock ticking at the end of the foyer.

"She's never gone out this late before," Arabella said.

"Well, we are talking about Taka. Something doesn't have to make sense for her to do it. We both know she's a little loose in the goose," Vanessa said. "For all we know, she might have simply gotten bored and gone for a walk through the District. You know how she loves to make new friends."

"At three in the morning?" Arabella said. "I don't think so."

Arabella shook her head and paced the foyer again.

Suddenly a noise that sounded like a creaky hinge echoed from the back of the house, near the kitchen.

Arabella froze, listening intently, and heard the unmistakable sound of a door gently closing. She took off for the kitchen.

"What is it?" Vanessa asked.

"Can't you hear the back door?" Arabella said. "I just heard it close."

"Well, that little sneak," Vanessa said.

"We don't know that it's her," Arabella said. "Somebody could be breaking into the house."

"Oh, for the love of earth, get a hold of yourself. It has to be Taka. She's the only one besides us with a key. We'd have heard glass shattering. A window breaking, and remember, the door doesn't have a window. The only windows are over the kitchen sink. So, see? It has to be Taka."

Arabella and Vanessa took off, nearly colliding into each other as they turned the corner into the kitchen. Both came to a sliding stop as the kitchen lights flickered on.

There stood Taka, right inside the back door, her eyes deer-in-the-headlights wide. "Oh…hey. What are you two doing up?"

Arabella put a hand on her hip, felt a huge flood of relief flow through her. "Where have you been?"

"No," Vanessa said. "Where the hell have you been? Do you have any idea what time it is?"

"I couldn't sleep," Taka said. "So I went for a walk."

"At this hour, in this city?" Arabella said. "Are you crazy? You could have been murdered or kidnapped."

"Oh, I wasn't worried about that one bit," Taka said, patting the patent leather purse she had clutched to her chest. "I took Mace. Got it right here, in my purse."

Vanessa snorted. "By the time you'd have dug through all the junk you keep in there, anybody could have hauled you over a shoulder and shoved you into a van before you managed one squirt. Think about it. You could be on your way to Missouri right now and not even know it."

Taka rolled her eyes. "Really, so melodramatic. I went for a walk. That's it."

Arabella pointed to the kitchen table. "Sit."

Sighing, Taka did as she was told.

When they were all seated around the table, Arabella jabbed the tabletop with a finger. "We deserve an explanation," she said to Taka. "You had us worried sick. You didn't put on a pantsuit to stroll the District. And you never do that alone. We always go together."

Vanessa nodded. "Safety in numbers."

"I've already told you," Taka insisted. "I couldn't sleep and needed some air."

"And I can tell you're lying," Arabella said, leaning back in her chair.

Taka blinked at her. "What do you mean you can tell?"

"When you lie, your left eye twitches," Vanessa said. "And right now it's twitching to beat the band."

Taka glanced over at Arabella. "What band is she talking about? I didn't see any band out there."

"Oh, quit acting like you're innocent," Vanessa said. "You know that your left eye twitches when you lie. Stop acting like you're senile or trying to make us think you're stupid, because you're not."

Taka huffed and hugged her purse closer to her chest.

"Neither of you are my parents or guardians. I'm quite old enough to choose when I want to go out and take a walk outside or not."

"Not in this city, especially with all that's been going on lately," Arabella said. "That was a stupid move, Taka. You could've been seriously hurt out there. So I want the truth now. What did you do?"

"Walked," Taka said.

Arabella sighed. "Where?"

"Through the District."

"And?" Vanessa asked.

Taka looked down at the table. "And then I sorta found myself down on Canal."

"Oh, mother of marbles. Canal Street!" Vanessa slapped a hand against her forehead. "All right, it's official. You *are* senile! Nobody but the homeless roam that street at this hour."

"Not true," Taka said. "Had a great time people-watching."

"How long were you out there?" Arabella asked.

"What's it matter? I'm back."

"Because we've been so damn worried about you all night, all right?" Vanessa said.

"Baloney," Taka said. "I wasn't out there all night."

"You two stop bickering," Arabella demanded, then studied Taka. "I woke up about half an hour ago from a bad dream. I got up and checked on Vanessa, then looked in on you, saw you were gone. So I woke up Vanessa, and we've been pacing the floor ever since, sick with worry. Now you're telling us you were out on Canal Street."

Arabella gave Taka a stern look. "Walking out there this late is bad enough, but why do I get the feeling that there's more to this than you're letting on?"

Taka pursed her lips and looked nonchalantly around the kitchen.

"Taka Burnside, you either spill everything or else," Arabella said.

"Or else what?" Taka asked, a defiant tone to her voice. "What're you going to do? Put me over your knee and spank me like I was a kid?"

"Don't be ridiculous," Vanessa said. "I'd be the one to do that."

Arabella shot Vanessa a warning look to shut up.

"Taka," Arabella said, as calmly as she could, "as Elders, we have a responsibility to take care of the Triad and the Originals they care for. We also have a responsibility to each other. Which means no lies between us. Whatever it is you did, wherever it is you went, we'll figure it out. And if anything happened, we'll figure out a way to fix it."

"Nothing happened," Taka insisted.

"Then why won't you tell us where you went and what you did?"

"I already did."

Letting out a loud sigh of frustration, Arabella leaned farther into the table. "Okay, you want to play this game? Where on Canal did you stop? Did you happen to go into any shops or buildings when you were done there?"

Taka looked away, a sure sign she was hiding something. "I might have made a stop along Canal," she admitted, still not looking Arabella in the eye.

Arabella let a moment of silence pass before she finally said, "Just spit it out, Taka."

Taka let out a loud breath of frustration, slammed her purse down on the table and placed her hands on top of it. "Okay…okay. I went to Trey Cottle's apartment."

Arabella and Vanessa let out a collective gasp.

"Lights were out in the apartment windows above his office, so I threw a rock against one. You know, like they do in the movies. Just meant to tap it, hoping the noise would wake him up. Only I must've thrown too hard because the window broke. It woke him up, though."

"You did what?" Arabella asked in disbelief.

"Why—" Vanessa said, then seemed to lose whatever else she meant to say.

"I wanted to find out where Gunner Stern lived," Taka said.

"Why on earth would you do that?" Arabella asked.

Taka looked at her with a dumbstruck expression. "You were the one who was always saying that Gunner might be able to help us. That you sort of trusted him." Her voice grew stronger, angrier. "We've been sitting around here with our fingers up our butts while everything's being destroyed around us. I thought you had a good idea about getting Gunner involved, and I wanted to act on it right away. The only problem was I didn't know where he lived. Trey's address was all I had to work with, since he lives above his law office."

"You broke his window?" Arabella said, mostly to herself.

"I didn't mean to break it," Taka said. "I'd planned on knocking on the door. The problem was the door to his apartment is up a flight of stairs down a short alleyway behind the law office. And the alleyway was closed off by a locked wrought-iron fence. That's when I thought of the rocks."

"Sweet Mother Earth," Vanessa said, slapping her hands over her face.

"What the hell were you thinking?" Arabella asked.

"Well, I figured if I could get Trey's attention, he would certainly know where Gunner lived. Once I had the address, I planned to go and talk to him about what's been going on, just like you suggested earlier, Arabella. This wasn't something I just pulled out of thin air. We've been talking and talking about this. I figured it was time to act on it. No disrespect, Arabella, but you always seem scared to do anything outside of the box. So I sorta took things into my own hands."

Arabella and Vanessa sat gaping at her, speechless.

Taka soon filled the void of silence. "Anyway, it wasn't so bad. Trey invited me inside, gave me Gunner's phone number and let me use his home office in private to call him."

Now it was Arabella's turn to slide her hands down her face, while Vanessa looked at Taka agape.

"You went into Trey's apartment?" Arabella asked.

"Yeah, I just told you that. Trey told me Gunner lived out by the Causeway, which was too far for me to walk, and I'd forgotten to bring money with me. Didn't think I'd need any. Anyway, Trey was the one who suggested I call Gunner if I really needed to speak to him that badly."

"You were in Trey Cottle's apartment…?" Vanessa said incredulously.

"Are you deaf?" Taka asked Vanessa. "I've already told the two of you a hundred times that I went there."

"You're an idiot, no question," Vanessa said.

"Oh, bite me," Taka said.

Arabella held up a finger, signaling for them to stop the quipping. "What happened while you were there?" she asked Taka.

"Had no problems at all…well, sort of. I didn't get Trey involved because I know how everyone hates him. He led me to his office, closed the door, and I waited to make sure I couldn't hear his footsteps anymore before I called Gunner."

"What did Gunner say?" Arabella asked.

"Told me not to go to Trey's anymore. Said not to talk about anything more over the phone, after I said we really needed to talk to him. Needed his help. He said he'd meet me at Bon Appétit Café to discuss anything we needed his help with."

"For the love of the elements," Arabella said. "Gunner tells you to meet him at Evee's café and you come back here?"

Taka shrugged. "Since the Causeway is some distance away, I figured I had time to come back here and fill you in so we could all meet with him."

"Then why the hell did you take so long playing word games with us?" Vanessa demanded. "Gunner does have a car, and if you asked for his help, I'm sure he jumped right into it and is probably waiting at the café for us now."

In the midst of Taka's news, Arabella found herself simply staring at the Elder. How could she have been so out of line? Taking it upon herself to track down a sorcerer without the consent or approval of her and Vanessa? That was so unlike Taka it boggled Arabella's mind.

Suddenly a cold chill of intuition ran down Arabella's spine. "Are you sure Trey didn't hear your conversation with Gunner?" she asked.

"I told you, I waited until I couldn't hear his footsteps walking down the hallway before I even called Gunner," Taka said. "Trey didn't hear anything. Couldn't have."

"Did you happen to notice if he had a second phone anywhere in the apartment when you went inside?" Arabella asked, suspecting the worst.

"I didn't see one," Taka said. "Why?"

"If someone has a phone in their home office, where they're not always located in their apartment, chances are there's another phone in the house. The living room or the kitchen maybe."

"Okay, so?" Taka said, looking at Arabella quizzically.

"If he has a second phone, and I'd bet my broom on it that he does, chances are that he was listening to your conversation with Gunner on the other line. Probably heard everything you said to him."

Taka frowned. "But I didn't hear anything but Gunner's voice on the phone. If Trey had picked up another line, wouldn't I have heard a click or at least heard him breathing?"

"Trey's slicker than oil on wet grass," Vanessa said. "And you're forgetting that he's a sorcerer. He could easily have muted any sound he made to make sure you didn't hear it. Basically, you just stuck your foot in the lion's den. No, make that all of our feet in the lion's den."

"You don't know that for sure," Taka said. "Besides, Gunner said he'd be glad to help any way he could. So despite what Trey did or didn't do, my vote is that we go over to Bon Appétit and see if Gunner's there. Find out what he may have to offer in order to help us."

"We may never know what he has to offer, because I guarantee you," Arabella said, "if you used a phone in Trey Cottle's apartment, he was listening to your conversation. He'll probably put a stop to Gunner showing up at the café."

"You screwed up big time, Taka," Vanessa said. "And we're in enough trouble as it is. We can't control what we have going on right now, and you've just turned up the heat a thousand degrees. And that fire is right under our feet. Now what are we supposed to do?"

"I don't think Trey can stop Gunner from helping if he really wants to," Taka said. "Gunner sounded really worried over the phone. I'm sure he'll show up and offer his support. I'm counting on it because you said you trusted him, Arabella, and that he was a nice guy."

"I also said that I needed time to think on it before we made a move."

"But you were taking too long," Taka said. "Something had to be done right away. So many Originals missing. We could lose more. Maybe even the Triad. I was only trying to help."

"I understand that," Arabella said. "But you can't just take things of such magnitude onto yourself. The three of us have to be in full agreement and understand what we're getting ourselves involved in."

"And because of your stupidity," Vanessa told Taka, "there's a good chance Trey Cottle has got his nose right in the middle of it all. He never has anything going on around him that he isn't aware of. That egomaniac has snitches around every corner."

"So why don't we just go talk to Gunner and let him know what's going on?" Taka said. "Even let him know we suspect that Trey may have overheard the conversation."

Vanessa shook her head. "Don't you get it, oh brainless one? If Trey overheard your conversation with Gunner, chances are high that he's going to be snooping around the café to overhear our conversation."

"I don't know about you," Arabella said to Taka, "but I don't have keys to Evee's café. Do you?"

Taka chewed her upper lip for a second. "No. I figured I'd meet Gunner in front of the café and talk to him there."

Vanessa groaned. "What were you thinking? Talking to Gunner out in the open? We might as well call Trey up and have him come right over and join in the party."

Arabella's frown deepened and she shook her head. "Oh, Taka, what were you thinking?"

Taka began to tear up. "But…but I was only trying to help."

"And I said I was going to take some time to think about it," Arabella said. "You blatantly went against my orders."

"Yeah, yeah, I know," Taka said, looking forlorn.

"Arabella may take some time to think things through," Vanessa said, "but once she has, her advice is always sound. You take off on your own, and you've completely tilted this wagon over, and now shit will spill out all the way down the street to Cottle."

"You've got to get this in your head, Taka," Arabella said. "Trey Cottle is not to be trusted in any way. If he finds out what's going on with us, he's going to take advantage of us in a time of weakness and make our lives more miserable than they are now. You know how he's always had his nose stuck in the Triad's business. Sneaking around, watching everything they did. Not out of curiosity's sake. It almost felt like he was trying to learn something from them."

"Why would he do that?" Taka asked.

"Because he's a damn sorcerer," Vanessa said. "And he has his own agenda. Most sorcerers feel they're above witches anyway. Trey's never wanted anything to do with witches, yet he keeps an eye on the Triad. The only reason I can figure he'd do that is to learn more spells."

Taka nodded. "I know the sorcerers have always felt they were above us."

"Then why did you go to him?" Vanessa said. "Why on earth did you go to Trey Cottle's?"

"I've already answered that a dozen times," Taka said. "Have you ever considered getting a hearing aid? You might need one. Now I'm going to bed. I'm extremely tired. I've done my good deed for the day. If you two don't want to meet Gunner, then I'd suggest calling him, so the poor man won't be standing out by the café wondering what the hell has happened to us."

"Do you still have Gunner's phone number?" Arabella asked.

Taka nodded, dug into her purse and pulled out the piece of paper Trey had given her with Gunner's number on it.

Arabella took the paper from her and got up from the table. "I'll give him a call now. Try to straighten this out."

"What if he's already at the café?" Taka asked.

Shoulders slumping, Arabella said, "If he doesn't answer the phone, then I'll have little choice but to go to the café. But I won't discuss anything with him there. I'll set up another place and time to meet. I only hope this ridiculous faux pas doesn't cause him to get angry with us. Then he might refuse to help."

"No way he'd get mad at you," Taka said. "He's sweet on you."

"That's true," Vanessa agreed.

"Why is it so hard for you to admit?" Taka said. "I think it's cute."

"He is not, so stop saying it," Arabella insisted.

"The fact that you won't admit it doesn't make it not so," Vanessa said.

"Right," Taka said. "At our age, you can't just throw that kind of man interest away."

Arabella scowled. "You march yourself on up to bed. I don't want you out of this house again until morning. I'll get in touch with Gunner one way or the other. Set up a meeting for tomorrow, at a more decent time and place. Maybe. I'm still not sure about getting any of the sorcerers involved."

"Why won't you give Gunner a chance to help?" Taka asked.

Arabella blew out an exasperated breath. "When I talk to him or see him and feel he has something legitimate to offer, I'll consider it. Until then, keep your behind in your bedroom. If I have to put a lock on the outside of your door, I will."

Taka lowered her head, trying to hide a look of disappointment, which Arabella caught.

"And one more thing, Ms. Taka Burnside, don't you ever leave this house like that again without letting us know. You could've gotten killed out there."

Vanessa snorted. "Killed? You might as well chalk her up for it. Because if Trey Cottle is involved with this in anyway, we might as well be dead."

"That's not true!" Taka said loudly, then looked at Arabella. "Is it?"

Arabella gave her a weary look. "I have no idea. All I can say is that you've really done it this time, Taka. You've put all three of us, the Triad and the Originals in more danger than you know. Trey is a force to be reckoned with, and I don't know if we have the wherewithal to deal with everything that sorcerer might decide to dish out."

Chapter 19

Something inside his chest pounded so hard he thought it was going to explode from his body at any moment. He didn't know if he had a heart, but that was what he associated the sensation with.

Everything was building up to such heights that he had to force himself to calm down.

He sent a legion of Cartesians, which were always at his side, away for a moment so that he'd have time to establish a direct plan.

He didn't want any mistakes.

Nothing going off half-cocked.

Everything was nearing a conclusion, and he had to make sure it went as smoothly as possible.

No mistakes. He had to get it right, if this was going to work.

He'd never used pen or paper before because he'd never had a need for them, as he kept mental notes. His memory held on to every form of minutia. Everything that had happened to him since it all began centuries ago. He made a checklist in his mind, which seemed apropos, for he knew how to check ideas off mentally, without missing one. Not even the nuance of one.

He planned on killing off the rest of the Originals very soon. Possibly as soon as tomorrow. From there, his ultimate goal would begin. He'd take the Originals, and before the Triad even had a moment to mourn their loss, he'd grab them, as well.

The Triad carried the most power in the city, which was why he craved them so. Third on his list were the Elders. Although they recently seemed to have become ineffective as witches, much less Elders, he believed they still had some measure of power despite their advancing years, because they were in charge of the Triad. Not only were they responsible for the Triad but they kept control over the entire clan of the Circle of Sisters as well. That had to count for something. Certainly, with that much responsibility, regardless of age, had to come great power.

Once the Originals, Triads and Elders were taken care of, he intended to sweep the city for all netherworld creatures—the vampires and werewolves, fae, leprechauns, anything that claimed a stake in the netherworld.

And then would come the humans, in order of power. Out with the voodoo priests and priestesses, for what minuscule powers they possessed. Then he'd go for the humans who controlled other humans. Not that they possessed supernatural powers of any kind, but their control and power over other humans carried its own weight.

The mayor of the city of New Orleans was definitely on his list. Then the police chief of every district in the city. He'd have his Cartesians destroy them all. Every councilman, judge, police officer, everyone in pecking order of power, all the way down to the principals of schools.

Then his plan was to take the rest of the population by economic order. The richest, the rich, the heads of companies, down to the blue-collar worker, housewives. Then, of course, the children.

He'd leave the city barren. Cleaned of all netherworld and human debris before he sent thousands of his Cartesians to reinhabit the city and restructure it to his specifications. New Orleans would be his flagship, then all other cities around the world part of his fleet.

Once he had proven what his army was capable of under his command, which he considered far beyond genius, all else would easily unfold.

After conquering this city, he'd no longer have to take baby steps. He'd race from city to city, country to country, as he had done for the past few decades, striking a clan of vampires in New Zealand, a horde of werewolves in New York City. Only this time, he'd have thousands more Cartesians at his disposal, and his own powers would be infinite.

As quickly as he planned to move, he wanted to save the very top of the human heap for last. A coup de grâce, so to speak.

He'd finish off the United States first, of course, for in and of itself, the country carried great power. His next directive would send his Cartesians to Washington, DC. First the netherworld creatures that inhabited the city, and then, of course, for any additional boost of power, he'd send them directly to the president of the US. Followed by the vice president, all of congress, the senate, even NASA. Every source of power that held up and led the entire country.

Once these entities were destroyed, he anticipated the entire world to go into shock. Country after country, and all the powers who controlled them, would be shaking in their boots. Never having heard of such an enemy. And even better, not knowing how to destroy it.

He knew if he kept his wits about him, he'd soon be moving onto England, Japan, then country to country, continent to continent. All of it. Everything. Until he stood supreme.

And from the looks of things, he was well on his way to great success. Who would've thought it would come so easily?

A couple weeks ago, it had taken only one of the Triads to utter a handful of words to begin their demise. The oldest Triad, Vivienne François, in a moment of weakness, had made claim to her Originals that she'd quit. No longer wanted anything to do with them. Although those words might have been spoken in anger or frustration, it didn't matter. The words had been uttered, sent out into the universe and had called his name.

He'd heard it quite clearly, and sent his Cartesians racing in her direction before they lost compass of her. Wherever that Triad was, so were her Originals.

Prior to that, they had seemingly searched for the Originals, as well as the Triad, for what felt like forever. Then in one swoop of good fortune, the Triad had uttered her words of denying her brood, which opened the door for him so widely it allowed him to pursue his ultimate dreams.

Words indeed were powerful things. The Triad had

simply been too naive to realize just how powerful. Now all was in his favor.

As much as he hungered to accomplish his goal, he couldn't help feeling a twinge of understanding for the wayward Triad. It had to be difficult, keeping track of the Originals day after day. Feeding them, maintaining them under the radar of the humans. It most certainly was a full-time job. It didn't allow them lives of their own.

Now that he thought about it, wasn't that in fact his case? He had spent centuries going after the subspecies, attacking wherever and whenever he could find them, gaining power so he might grow more Cartesians. His dream had always been to find the Originals and Triad, so wasn't his world, his so-called life, just as singular and linear as the Triad?

Their job was to protect, his was to destroy. Same singular lifestyle, only serving different purposes.

For now, while the Triad and their rogue companions, the Benders, attempted to protect the Originals they still had in their possession, he'd made sure to throw chaos their way to keep the ball in his court. In the meantime— and without the Triad's knowledge, he suspected—he'd had his Cartesians picking off subspecies in the city as often as possible.

He needed whatever power he could get right now. His army now counted well into the thousands, but to accomplish his ultimate goal of world and universal domination, it would take an army of millions.

Each netherworld creature gave him the power to create one new Cartesian. But an Original, the ones his Cartesians had tasted in what the Triad called the North Compound a couple of weeks ago, had allowed him to create a hundred in an instant. How could anyone blame him for wanting them all? They would produce an army beyond any number he might hope for.

And promised a far, far greater reward.

Chapter 20

Leaving the Hotel Monteleone in the clothes Gilly had lent her, Evee headed for the docks.

It was past time to get the family's ferry ready to cross her Nosferatu and Gilly's Chenilles over to the North Compound for the feeding. She imagined her sister Viv, pacing and cursing, wondering where the hell they were. On a regular day, her Nosferatu would already be in the compound by now.

But for the last hour, she'd been otherwise detained. Fully and completely and happily detained.

Although Evee and Viv had both been warned by the Elders to stay away from the Benders, Evee had been unable to do that with Lucien. She'd known from the get-go that going to his hotel room to shower was tempting fate. Asking him for shampoo, then instead of allowing him to place it outside the bathroom door for her to fetch, she'd all but coaxed him inside. She'd acted like a wounded female, not wanting to step out of the shower and face the cold. For Pete's sake, how pathetic.

The last person she had any nerve to lie to was herself. She'd wanted him to come into the bathroom, wanted him inside the shower with her…wanted him inside her. The Elders' warning had been the furthest thing from her mind. She was determined to hold on to her concrete belief that the curse attached to all Triads had been literal. They weren't to marry or live intimately with a human. She'd done neither. So what the hell?

It had been difficult leaving Lucien. She'd felt like a pool of melted butter, unable and unwilling to solidify to anything reasonably worthwhile. Evee had never felt so satiated, so…so complete. And, if truth be told, she needed, wanted more. In a way, it frightened her because she didn't think she'd ever have enough of Lucien.

Forced to bend to obligation, Evee walked toward the dock to ready the family ferry to cross the river to Algiers, where the cattle were kept at the North Compound. The compound was the standard feeding area, and the feeding order had been established for years.

Viv had three ranch hands, Charlie Zerangue, Bootstrap and Kale. Their primary job was to keep the front forty acres filled with cattle, sheep, pigs, etc., then send a designated number of animals down a chute that led them past the ranch to the feeding area, which had always been off-limits to the ranchers. As far as she knew, from what Viv had told her and Gilly, not once had the ranch hands ever asked about why the animals were sent through the chutes nightly but never returned. They simply did what they were told. Such a rarity in today's world.

Once the cattle were in place, the Nosferatu were sent in to feed first, since they drained the animals of blood. Once they had their fill, they were ferried back to the city, and then Viv allowed her Loup Garous in, to feed on the meat. When the Loups were sated, Viv moved them to a different area of the compound, then signaled for Gilly to ferry over her Chenilles. They completed the feeding by draining the bones of the animals of every drop of marrow.

Evee had warned Lucien to stay behind the back of the cathedral when the Nosferatu were led to the ferry. He was human, after all, and at this time of morning, the Nosferatu were beyond starving. Once they were on the ferry and on their way to the compound, it would be safe for him to come to the docks.

And Evee would be with him again. Because of her absolute fear of water—the fear had been bad enough before her near drowning earlier, but now she was positively petrified—she never rode the ferry with her Nosferatu. She had no idea where or when her phobia of water had come from. It was possibly from drowning in a former life, but regardless, the fear was as real as the nose on her face.

Even prepping the ferry made her nervous. It made her think of when she'd run into the river to escape the Cartesian. Had it not been for Lucien, she would surely have drowned.

The family ferry was moored near the east of the riverwalk, where it was dark and there was rarely any foot traffic. This morning, predawn, it lit the riverwalk like a thousand Christmas trees. Viv, her Loup, and Nikoli had accomplished what they'd promised to do. The ferry now had an electric dome on top of it to protect the Originals riding to or from a feeding. The relief that sent through Evee was huge and physical.

Evee checked the engine, then checked the gates along the sides of the ferry as well as the one in the back that closed the ferry, forming a sort of pen. This was to make sure the Nosferatu, no matter how rowdy they became, stayed safely aboard.

Once the Nosferatu were stacked onto the ferry, she usually started the engine and, by incantation, sent the ferry across river to the compound, where Pierre, Evee's lead Nosferatu, made sure they were off-loaded into yet another chute to keep them from running wild in the five-hundred-acre compound. Their chute led directly into the feeding area.

After the Nosferatu were fed, Viv invariably sent out a loud whistle and cawing sound, which let Evee know they were done feeding.

Pierre, having fed himself, usually brought the Nosferatu back onto the ferry and then signaled to Evee with a howl that the loaded ferry was ready to head back.

At Pierre's call, Evee usually issued an incantation to restart the ferry motor and lead it back to the city. When they returned, she would lead them back to the catacombs.

This time, however, she was concerned. With her incantations seemingly choosing when or whether to work, she feared things might not go so smoothly today.

Forcing herself to think more positively, Evee tried to limit her concerns to one issue. The Nosferatu had been cooped up for too long because of the Cartesian attacks. When things had been normal, many of them had worked jobs in the Quarter, in handsome or beautiful human form, serving as bartenders, dancers, street performers or hotel clerks. All of them, however, returned to the catacombs for feeding time, where they quickly transformed to their natural state. Tall, lanky, with a large white, bald head that had a large vein across their forehead. The vein led to the top of their heads, where it branched off to smaller yet still prominent veins. Their eyes bulged out, large and black and red-rimmed. Every one of them lashless. Their noses were long, the hooked end nearly meeting their upper lip. The fangs, the tools they used to puncture and feed with, were their two front teeth, both long, crooked and yellow. Their fingers were twice the length of an average man's, and their fingernails, yellow and twisted, extended at least three or four inches past their fingertips. They remained in their natural state after the feeding, when daylight shortly followed, and it was their time to sleep.

Lately, because of the Cartesians, Evee had kept all her Nosferatu in the catacombs even after dark, allowing them out only for feedings. This had caused them to become extremely restless. More than once, Evee or Pierre had had to break up territorial fights. She couldn't blame the Nosferatu. With nothing else to do, it was only natural that they got on each other's nerves.

She'd have to be hypervigilant in moving them from the catacombs to the ferry. The fact that they'd been stuck in the catacombs for too long might cause some of them to bolt. The lure of freedom might be too irresistible for some. That could mean more missing Nosferatu. More danger for the humans in the city. If any did bolt, the chances that she'd be able to call them back into tow would probably be slim to none. She hadn't been successful calling to the ones who were already missing. Although she'd tried more times than she could count, not one of them had responded and returned to her.

Finally, after triple-checking the ferry and starting its motor, Evee left the ferry and went to the catacombs, where she signaled Pierre it was time to bring them out.

With a simple nod, Pierre called to the Nosferatu, lining them up near the catacomb gates.

Before she opened the gates, Evee said a calming spell, hoping it would keep her Originals in tow, at least enough to get all of them onto the ferry.

"Quiet thee, oh creatures mine.
Let these words turn thy rage to soothing wine.
Angst and boredom, fear and pain.
Bring to thy mind now that 'tis all in vain.
So it is said.
So shall it be."

Once she was done, she peered through the gate and saw that the Nosferatu were still fidgeting nervously, refusing to follow Pierre's orders. Some had started yanking on the catacomb gates as if wanting to rip them open. Some snarled, others whimpered.

Evee glanced at Pierre, who appeared at a loss and just as concerned about opening the gates as she was.

"Once more," Pierre said. "The calming spell. Louder. More forceful maybe."

Nodding, Evee held her hands against the gate of the catacombs, ignoring those who were still pulling on them. She overlooked her brood. Staring each one in the eye, she hardened her expression. And this time she shouted, allowing fury to carry her voice.

"Quiet thee, oh creatures mine.
Let these words turn thy rage to soothing wine.
Angst and boredom, fear and pain.
Bring to thy mind now that 'tis all in vain.
So it is said.
SO SHALL IT BE!"

Evee spoke the last line of the spell so loudly her throat hurt.

Surprisingly, loud worked. The Nosferatu gathered as directed without another whimper or snarl.

Evee gave Pierre a nod, then opened the gate and led

the Nosferatu out of the catacombs. She walked quickly, with Pierre bringing up the rear, and steered her Originals to the ferry, where they boarded without hesitation.

Once Pierre stepped aboard, Evee closed the back gate of the ferry, latched it, then with a wave of her hand, sent it chugging across the water.

As she watched it creep along the muddy Mississippi, Evee thought about Viv. Viv always stayed on the feeding grounds until all the Originals had been fed. Although she knew to make herself scarce while the Nosferatu and Chenilles were off-loaded from the ferry to the chute that took them to the feeding area, Evee couldn't help worrying.

The calming spell had worked, but only after she'd used it twice. Evee hoped it would hold. She had no control over the Loup Garous or the Chenilles. Her brood consisted solely of the Nosferatu. If her Nosferatu suddenly decided to go rogue while on the compound, that would put Viv in danger. Not only her personally, but it would screw up the entire feeding process for the other Originals.

Evee tried desperately not to think that way, but the thought kept niggling at her brain. That and the thought of Viv and Nikoli.

When they'd met with the Elders, Viv had confessed, just as Evee had, to having been intimate with one of the Benders. Evee couldn't help wondering if her sister fought with the same constant desire for Nikoli that she did for Lucien.

Evee knew Nikoli was with Viv now, and wondered if Viv had gotten distracted like she had with Lucien. Not that Viv would shirk her responsibilities when it came to getting her ranchers to send food through the feeding chute. But as Viv waited for the Nosferatu to arrive, was she kissing Nikoli? Was he touching her? Did Nikoli touch Viv in the same way Lucien touched her? Did her sister crave being near her Bender?

Or had she listened to the Elders and, even at this moment, was keeping an arm's length away from Nikoli? Out of the three of them, Evee had to admit that Viv was the most levelheaded. But that didn't mean she was the strongest emotionally. Maybe Gilly was. She'd claimed nothing had yet happened between her and Gavril, which was hard to believe. Gilly was so out there. She always said what she meant and meant what she said. How on earth had she not slept with Gavril yet? His looks were exquisite, and Evee had seen the way he looked at Gilly, like she was a walking goddess. Evee had seen them laugh easily together, noticed how they always stood near each other. A team. A couple. Who'd yet to have sex? It was mind-boggling.

From birth the Triad had been taught that they had one and only one crucial task to tend to in their lifetime. To take care of their Originals. No one, not their mother before she died or the Elders as they trained them, had taught them to stay emotionless in the face of an impossible attraction. No matter how firmly the Elders' order had been hammered into them about staying away from the Benders, it seemed to Evee that the directive had slid off her like water off a duck's back.

She could no more deny what she needed or wanted from Lucien than she could deny she was one of the Triad. And, knowing her sister Viv, she seriously doubted she could deny what she felt for Nikoli.

What the hell were they supposed to do? What kind of Triad were they? Purposely defying their Elders' commands. Hearing that their attraction to the Benders might be causing the trauma happening with the Originals and

Cartesians just didn't seem to stave off their desire. If what the Elders had said was true, how could she simply not care? Why didn't she feel one ounce of guilt?

Evee figured, as the Elders had mentioned when they reamed them out, that it was all in the interpretation.

A member of the Triad wasn't to marry or live intimately with a human. And they weren't doing so.

All Evee had to do was keep repeating that to herself, and like a magic spell from some unknown source, guilt never stood a chance in her brain.

She wondered if the same was true with Viv.

Logic. It all had to do with logic.

The only problem Evee had with that bit of logic was the roller coaster she rode with Lucien. Would she ever be able to get off it?

What was she supposed to do once their mission was complete, and the Benders moved on to their next mission? How would she survive?

Would she survive?

No one and nothing had ever touched her, satisfied her in the way Lucien had. He'd not only touched her body as if he read her mind but he had grabbed her heart, her soul, without her permission and before she knew it was happening.

And although Evee wasn't sure what that exactly meant, she feared she wouldn't be able to do without it ever.

Which meant she'd truly have to break the rules of the Triad curse, and her Originals, all of them, would be lost to her forever.

Could she—would she…ever let it go that far?

Chapter 21

"Don't you ever ride the ferry with them?"

At the sound of a man's voice, Evee spun on her heels, terror in her eyes.

Lucien quickly walked up to her and put his hands on her shoulder. "I'm so sorry I frightened you. You're always so alert. I figured you'd seen me walking over to you."

Evee let out a shaky breath. "No problem. I was daydreaming while watching the ferry. Guess I was lost in thought."

"Good thoughts?"

She gave him an easy smile. "Started with some worrisome. Ended with very good ones."

Lucien returned her smile, still holding her shoulder. He'd been watching Evee at work from around the corner of St. John's Cathedral. Although she'd warned him to stay out of sight until the Nosferatu had been loaded onto the ferry, he'd already known to do so. Since he was human, it was far from wise to be within view of a group of hungry Nosferatu heading out to be fed. The last thing Lucien intended to be was a snack before they reached the compound.

So he'd stayed behind the far column of the cathedral, watching Evee at work. He'd been very impressed watching her control her Nosferatu. How she'd sent the ferry on its way with a wave of her hand. The moment Lucien had seen the ferry start puttering slowly across the river, he'd headed in her direction. Along the way, he'd noticed only one or two people at the far end of the riverwalk. He'd spotted a couple holding on to each other, kissing under the moonlight, in the fog that slowly settled over the city, and it made him yearn for Evee. Made him think about how she tasted when he kissed her.

He'd watched her for a while before approaching her. Taking in the beauty of her standing there, hands at her side, as she watched the ferry start across the river with her Nosferatu, watching the lights from the makeshift dome on the ferry get swallowed by fog as it moved slowly north. Some of the Nosferatu were grunting, grumbling, shifting about on the ferry so that it tilted from side to side. At one point Lucien had thought the ferry might tip over on its side, and had it not been for the buoys beneath it, it very well might have.

Lucien had seen for himself how anxious the Nosferatu had been, locked up in the catacombs. How they'd fought, bitten and grabbled for the smallest of territory below the cathedral. He didn't know how Evee'd done it, but he had to admire how calmly and methodically she had loaded them onto the ferry. And now they were on their way to be fed. Finally.

He trusted Nikoli was on the lookout over the North Compound for any Cartesians as the feeding transfers were made. With the dome now protecting the ferry, the only worry spots they had for the Cartesians were the transfers to the ferry and feeding area, then back again.

Evee blew out a breath, and Lucien released her shoulder.

"I didn't know what to expect here or on the feeding grounds. Things have been so crazy lately. I don't know what to look out for first anymore. Cartesians, more Nosferatu going missing because I'm keeping them caged up, or some stupid sorcerer who's decided he wants in on our territory. It's like you never know who'll show up or not, when or where. It's confusing as hell, don't you think?"

Lucien nodded. "A good way to put it. I don't know much about the sorcerers here, but judging by what you've told me, we certainly don't need any one of them, much less all three, involved in this."

Evee stood silently studying his face, the smile on her face soft.

Without giving it a second thought, Lucien took hold of her shoulders, gently turned her around, then wrapped his arms around her. They watched the ferry in silence as it chugged its way to its destination.

Lucien felt Evee lean back against him, pressing her back against his body. He leaned over and kissed the top of her head. She smelled of chamomile and freshly cut roses. His arms, encircling her waist, felt like they belonged there. Had always belonged there.

He ran his hands through her ponytail, then moved it aside and gently kissed the back of her neck. He felt her stiffen slightly, so Lucien reluctantly released her.

She turned to face him, a look of longing mixed with confusion on her face. "I... I..."

"It's all right," Lucien said. "No need to explain anything. I know that you feel guilty about us and think that everything that's going on is because of our intimate relationship. But what the curse mentions…that damn curse that was issued down from so many generations ago, is not what we're doing."

The very next thing that came to Lucien's mind, he didn't verbalize. *Not yet anyway.*

"This…" Evee touched her chest, then pressed a hand to his chest "…is difficult for me to process. I was given a direct order by my Elders to not be intimate again with you, even if that meant staying away for you altogether. My head heard and understood, but the rest of me doesn't seem to give a damn. I always want to be close to you."

Lucien breathed a silent sigh of relief. For a moment, he'd thought she'd turn from him and never look back. "Evee," he said, touching her right cheek lightly with his fingers, "I feel the same way. I want to be near you, help you, protect you, always."

"That's what scares me," Evee said. "The always part."

Lucien leaned over and kissed her cheek. "We're adults. We can slow the tempo to whatever pace makes you more comfortable. Make sure we…well, stay in compliance with the curse's rule. We truly can do whatever it is we need to do."

Evee nodded slowly, but she didn't look convinced. "As if now I can even turn this conversation back to business."

Closing his eyes, and drawing in a deep, exaggerated breath, Lucien held out his arms, crooked them at the elbow and forced his biceps to bulge significantly. "See?" he said. "I am man. Hear me roar."

That drew a large smile from Evee, which he treasured.

"Okay, so business…right now all we have to do is wait for the Nosferatu to get back and corral them back into the catacombs safely. When you know the ferry is heading back with them, I'll check the catacombs to make certain the dome doesn't need recharging. Then we'll tuck your brood under it, and they'll be safe and sound. Then maybe you can get some much-needed rest before we start another search. That sound like a plan?"

Evee touched one of his bulging biceps, and Lucien saw something hungry cross her face. She looked up at him. "Lucien, I don't know what I'd have done without you through all this. You saved me from drowning... you've been such a calming influence amid all the chaos. I—I just really want to thank you."

Lucien smiled and ran his fingers over her cheek, brushing stray strands of hair away from it. As he touched her, gently, slowly, Evee said, "You know, I have to confess something."

"What's that?" Lucien asked.

"When you and your cousins first got here, to be honest, I didn't trust you."

Lucien chuckled. "You don't think I knew that? I wouldn't have trusted me, either, if I had been you. Four men, showing up out of nowhere, claiming to be Benders, and that we're here to help you. All because some wacko creature you'd never even seen before was hell-bent on attacking you and your Originals. Taking possession of you. I would've considered myself facing four loonies."

Evee grinned. "Yeah, it was sort of like that." She glanced over the water, and Lucien watched it with her. Dark with a fecund scent, the sound of it lapping against the shore. All of it held an odd, calming effect.

Looking back up at Lucien, Evee finally broke the silence. "You know, I really don't know what to think and make of us. Just like I don't know what to think and make out of all that's going on with the Cartesians, our Originals, now the sorcerers."

Instead of letting Evee attempt to tie a knot between what they'd experienced together and what they fought outside their intimate circle, Lucien once again smoothed hair from her face and said, "As for what's happened between us, I don't know about you, but it felt as natural as breathing to me. The rest of it connected on its own. Like a hurricane during hurricane season. The Cartesians simply found a way to the Originals."

"I think that happened because of what Viv said to her Loup Garous," Evee said sadly. "When she told them she quit and didn't want anything more to do with them."

"You and I both know your sister didn't mean that in the truest sense of the word. Frustration does that to a person. Makes us say and do things we wouldn't do otherwise. We can't keep pressing that button, though. You know, pointing to Viv as the reason the Cartesians are here. The simple fact is that they're here. The Cartesians got a taste of an Original, who they'd been searching for for what seems like forever. Too many years, centuries even. When they finally realized where they were located, the Cartesians' entire focus turned here. That's not your fault. It isn't even Viv's."

Evee looked at him, listening intently, her copper eyes large and bright even in the darkness.

"The fact is that there's a leader of these Cartesians, and its agenda is to take over the entire netherworld, to take over the Triad, to take your power and that of the Originals and make it its own."

"So you've said."

"It's a fact, Evee. When he's done with you, the Originals, the others from the netherworld in this city, it'll go after the humans here. Then it'll move on to another city, another country, another continent, taking every ounce of power from any netherworld creature and living being so it can ultimately control the world, then the universe. That's its ultimate goal."

"But why?" Evee asked. "What purpose would that serve this so-called leader? No one would be left then, but the Cartesians."

"That's the point and what it wants. Think of every crazy leader from history," Lucien said.

"History has shown us that such insane leaders do appear from time to time, for whatever reason, as if to test our wherewithal as human beings. Take Hitler for instance. His goal was to rid the world of what he considered to be inferior humans and produce a super race that would be under his control. Who can make sense of such insanity? From Hitler to this Cartesian leader, they have their own sense of purpose. And that purpose makes no sense to anyone except the creatures or people who blindly follow them."

"Scary analogy," Evee said.

"Yes, but true," Lucien said. "The biggest difference between the two is that the leader of the Cartesians has a special ability. Every time one of its Cartesians makes a kill and brings the essence of that kill to its leader, that leader is able to create another Cartesian. That's how it's been able to grow its army over all these years."

"So, are you saying that this leader was at one time the only Cartesian alive? Then grew its own army by killing?"

"That about sums it up," Lucien said. "The original Cartesian was created many generations ago. It's had plenty of time to build its army with every kill of a netherworld creature. Unfortunately, the Benders only came onto the scene ten generations ago. By that time, the first

Cartesian had plenty of time to grow its army. We followed them for ten generations but have only managed to get its minions. The leader stays well hidden."

"Do you even know what the leader looks like?" Evee asked.

"All I know is what we learned during our training as Benders. Supposedly, the leader is larger than any Cartesian any Bender has yet to face. And I'm not sure if it's rumor or not, since no Bender has admitted to actually seeing the leader, but supposedly its head is not covered with fur and scales, unlike its minions. I've heard that its head is humanlike. Only its body is covered in scales and matted fur."

"It almost sounds like you're chasing a shadow. A bogeyman," Evee said.

"Feels like that sometimes," Lucien admitted.

"Shadows or not, I'm in this with you," Evee said. "Remember, we're supposed to be a team."

Lucien gave her a long, tender look and even in the dark, he saw determination and longing in her eyes. It made his heart swell. No one, besides his cousin, had ever purposely chosen to stand by him during the midst of a fight with the Cartesians. Yet here was this beautiful, intelligent woman, offering herself to him. Offering to stand by his side when she just as easily could have left the bulk of the work to him.

Before Evee even realized what she was doing, she stood on tiptoe and kissed Lucien softly. His full, luscious lips set a fire to her own as they always did. The kiss was supposed to be one of gratitude. Gratitude for Lucien's help. For him being there for her. For standing by her side to protect her.

If truth be told, thinking a kiss of gratitude would be

just that, a kiss of gratitude, was ridiculous. She'd only been fooling herself. All she had to do was be near him, and her body was immediately ablaze with need.

Lucien, obviously feeling her, sensing her need, took her into his arms and kissed her. He held her tight, putting a hand behind her head and pulling her closer. Their kiss deepened to a maddening dance of lips and tongues. Their tongues seemed to battle with a hunger neither could control. Sucking, longing, reaching for the farthest corner of their mouths.

Evee found herself breathing harder, faster. With her body pressed so close to Lucien's, she felt his heart galloping beneath his chest, and she was certain he could feel hers doing the same.

The need she felt for Lucien was so great she likened it to a pot of boiling water. The heat grew so great and so fast it overflowed its container, popping, splashing, sizzling.

She broke their kiss for only a moment, looked about, saw nothing but darkness. Not one person in sight. And it would be a while before the ferry would return with the Nosferatu.

Knowing they were alone, she reached for Lucien, wrapping her arms around him. Kissing him with a scalding fervor she didn't know she possessed. She moved her hands over his chest, wanting him, needing him. Wishing she could strip him naked. But being in a public area, although seemingly empty, she didn't think naked was a good idea.

She felt like she'd die of thirst if she didn't have him here and now, no matter where they were. Her body overtook her mind. Logic felt like nothing more than a nuisance. She grabbed hold of the front of his shirt with both hands and pulled him along with her to the nearest pier poles, where they moored the ferry.

Lucien followed her lead, silent, eyes smoldering with desire.

Evee leaned her back against one of the pier posts and pulled Lucien close, her hands fisting in his hair. She kissed him harder, deeper.

Suddenly, Lucien took both of Evee's arms in one of his hands and held them over her head, against the post. His mouth moved down to her cheek, her neck, licked the lobe of her right ear.

Evee felt her breathing grow ragged, and the rest of the world seemed blind to her, save for Lucien.

"Take me," she whispered as he nipped the nape of her neck with his teeth. "N-now. Take me. Here. Now."

Lucien pulled away from Evee slowly, looking deeply into her eyes, his hand still locking her arms over her head against the pole. He glanced left and right so quickly it was barely noticeable. Evee was sure he was double-checking to make sure they didn't have an audience.

Evidently confident that they were alone, Lucien turned his full attention to her. He unbuttoned her slacks with his free hand and yanked them down and off without preamble.

No words were needed as Lucien released her arms, placed them around his neck, then lifted her into his arms as easy as if he were cradling a baby. He lifted her up, and her legs automatically wrapped around his waist. She heard the sound of the zipper on his jeans, and then before she knew it, Evee felt the hardness of him pressing between her legs. She was already wet and swollen, so ready for him. She wanted to cry out, scream, "Now! Now!" but there'd been no need.

As though reading her mind, Lucien entered her,

slowly at first, then evidently feeling how wet and ready she was, drove his entire length into her deep and fast. He held on to her legs, lifting her higher, pushing into her deeper, pulling her legs up even higher so she felt every inch of him, so he reached that spot deep within her that caused her to lose control and flood him with her juices.

As he dived into her again and again, Evee bit her bottom lip, holding back a cry of pleasure, as she erupted with an orgasm so powerful her vision blurred.

"More, damn it," Lucien said. "Give me more." He arched his back, giving her all he had. Hard and deep. "Give it all to me, baby. Everything."

Evee didn't know how or why, but the sound of Lucien's command sent her immediately over the edge again, her body erupting and soaking him.

Lucien continued to ram his hardness into her, refusing to stop until she was completely drained. Evee had no idea how he maintained such control over his own orgasm as he hammered himself into her again and again, making sure she gave him all she had.

Evee felt her body grip around his hardness, pulling him in deeper, contracting over his stiffness, her body sucking on his hardness, milking him.

Lucien met her stroke for stroke, and although Evee's back was pressed against a large wooden piling, all she felt was him.

As she felt another orgasm begin to roll through her, Lucien held her legs up a bit higher, shoved harder, and this time Evee couldn't hold back her cry as she exploded over him.

Only then did she feel him tense, his release so close. He drove harder, his eyes never leaving her face. A moan suddenly fell from his lips, and she felt him empty himself into her.

* * *

Lucien shivered with the intensity of his orgasm that seemed to last forever. This woman was nothing short of phenomenal in all ways. Never had he come across anyone with such depth, such sexuality, such commitment and daring. All of it was the wonder of Evette François.

Reluctantly, slowly, Lucien pulled out of her, lowered her legs to the ground and tugged her trousers up. With deft fingers, he zipped and buttoned them into place.

Evee still leaned against the piling, seemingly spent. Lucien held on to her with one hand while zipping up his pants with the other.

Once they were fully clothed Lucien took Evee into his arms and held her close. He pressed her head against his chest, hoping she heard the thudding of his heart.

And she rested there so comfortably, as if leaning against a familiar place, a comforting place.

Lucien held her close, smoothing her hair with a hand, kissed the top of her head. In that moment, he felt a twinge of pain hit his heart.

Where were they to go from here?

Lucien knew deep in his soul that he could never be without this woman. Yet the curse that held the Triad captive had now become his curse.

He needed more than one-night stands and an occasional sexual encounter with Evee.

He knew deep in his soul that they were meant to be together…always. Lucien wondered if there was a way to break the curse that refused to let a Triad marry or live intimately with a human. He wondered if the Triad had even explored the option.

As he kissed the top of Evee's head again, he made a mental note to himself. Besides completing the mission he and his cousins had been sent here to accomplish, Lucien would do everything in his power to find out if there was a way around the Triad curse. Someway to break it.

For in his heart of hearts, Lucien knew he could not live without Evee beside him...ever.

Chapter 22

Evee didn't quite know what to think. She felt slightly embarrassed, like some wanton slut. Not in a million years would she ever have considered having sex outside in the middle of a public venue, where anyone might happen by.

Even though it was dark, and she'd not seen any other person even close to the docks, she could have, should have shown a bit more decorum. A little discretion at least.

The simple fact was that the moment Lucien had put his arms around her, her body took over her brain. In that moment, there could have been a circus act going on ten feet away with twenty thousand spectators, and she still would have craved him, wanted him…taken him.

Fortunately, there'd been no one around to see when she willingly gave up her privacy standards just to have Lucien inside her.

With clothes straightened, she looked out onto the

water, afraid to face him. She wondered if he thought her to be too loose, too needy. She felt Lucien's hand rest on her shoulder and squeeze lightly. As if reading her mind, he leaned over and whispered in her ear.

"It's all right. No one saw us." He turned her to face him. "Evee, you're one of the most glorious women I've ever known. So open and honest in what you feel and the way you express it. Don't feel bad about any of this, please."

Evee gave him a half smile. "I'm trying."

She smoothed some wrinkles in his shirt with a hand. At least nothing on either of them looked out of the ordinary. As if nothing had occurred at all. It wasn't that she didn't want to think about the fact that they'd just had sex, but she'd be facing her sisters soon. The less they knew or suspected, the better.

In silence, Lucien and Evee stood side by side, looking over the water. Evee was waiting for Viv's special signal, the loud howl and squawk, that the Nosferatu were ready to return city side.

Evee stood with her arms folded against her chest. A cool night breeze washed over her, sending goose bumps up and down her arms. It might have been the breeze that sent a shiver through her or the fact that Lucien was still standing beside her.

Where he was concerned, Evee always felt like she was dying of thirst and no amount of having him seemed to fully quench it. Even if he stayed inside her for a month, Evee felt it still wouldn't be enough. In all her life, She had never needed anyone so desperately as she needed Lucien. And it wasn't all about the sex, which frightened and excited her at the same time.

Suddenly, Evee heard someone clear their throat behind them. She whirled about, her heart pounding in her chest. Lucien simply glanced over his shoulder.

Gavril had made it to the docks and was walking toward them.

When Evee saw him, she felt a slight flash of guilt. She'd just had sex with Lucien...again. Gavril's appearance reminded her of Ronan. She'd known by the way Ronan had looked at her from time to time that he'd been interested in her, wanted a relationship with her. They'd never have the dinner she'd promised. But that had been all she'd promised. She would never have led Ronan down a deceptive path. Her interest was in Lucien, and that was all there was to it. Although Ronan had been as handsome as the rest of his cousins, he had a seriousness and quietness about him that didn't quite call to Evee the way Lucien did.

"What's up?" Lucien asked Gavril.

"Wanted to check out the ferry before we brought out the Chenilles. How'd it work for the Nosferatu?" Gavil asked.

"So far so good, but we'll have a better handle on how it worked as soon as the ferry returns," Lucien said.

"Why aren't you with Gilly?" Evee asked, feeling her mood shift to angry and anxious.

"She's fine," Gavril assured her. "I triple-checked the dome over the cemetery before we left, but I didn't want to chance her getting hurt if the dome we set up over the ferry wasn't working. That's why I came to check on it."

Lucien narrowed his eyes. "What aren't you telling me?"

"Huh?" Gavril said.

"You know if anything had gone wrong with the dome on the ferry, we would've reached out to you with a warning."

Gavril shifted his eyes to Evee, then back to Lucien. "I hate when you're right, you know that?"

"What happened?" Evee asked. "Is Gilly really okay? You need to be back with her, watch over her."

"I will," Gavril said. "I just wanted to warn the both of you that we had a Cartesian attack right off Rampart Street. It was only one, nothing I couldn't handle, but there was something different about the way the Cartesian came through it."

"Different how?" Lucien asked.

"One second it wasn't there and the next, boom, there it was, hanging out of a rift by the waist. No warning at all. No scent of clove until the bastard shot out of the rift. Then it stank to high heaven with clove and sulfur. Their pattern is changing, and I don't like it one damn bit. No preamble. Just BAM and there they are, rift already open."

"I noticed the changes," Lucien said. "It happened the same way when Ronan...when Ronan and me fought them riverside."

"Hang on a minute, guys," Evee said, and cocked an ear toward the river. Clear yet faint, she heard Viv's whistle and caw, signaling that the Nosferatu had been fed and were heading back on the ferry.

"The Nosferatu are heading back," she told Lucien and Gavril. "The two of you need to leave before they get here."

"But we can't leave you and your Originals alone," Lucien said. "It's too dangerous. The Cartesians have become unpredictable, even more than usual."

"Then what the hell is Gavril doing here?" Evee demanded.

"He's here to warn us," Lucien said, his tone hardening.

Evee turned to Gavril. "Appreciate the heads-up on

the Cartesian, but please go to my sister and don't leave her again."

"Ten-four," Gavril said, then took off for the cemetery and Gilly.

As soon as Gavril was out of sight, Lucien said, "He knows what he's doing, Evee. I'd trust Gavril with my life. He won't let anything happen to Gilly."

Evee wanted to say, *Right, like Ronan knew what he was doing?* But she didn't say it. It would have been unnecessary and harsh.

"There's the ferry," Evee said, pointing straight ahead at the calliope of lights floating in their direction.

She turned to Lucien. "Why don't you go and give Gavril a hand while I put the Nosferatu away?"

"I'm not leaving you," Lucien said firmly.

"But there really isn't much for you to do. They get off the ferry, and I've got only a couple hundred feet before I can stash them away. Gavril and Gilly have to lead the Chenilles much farther."

"I'll gladly give them a hand," Lucien said.

Evee blew out a breath of relief. She didn't know what to expect from the Nosferatu when they were off-loaded from the ferry. All she knew was she didn't want danger to smack Lucien in the face.

"I'll give them a hand as soon as you've put the Nosferatu back in their hidey-hole," Lucien said.

Evee threw him a scowl. "I don't have time to fight with you about this now. The ferry's mooring. You need to be in the back of the cathedral. Not the side of it like last time when I loaded them onto the ferry. The back."

"But weren't they just fed?" Lucien asked. "Shouldn't they be satiated now?"

"That's the point of me sending them to the feeding ground, so they can drink until they've had their fill,"

Evee said. "But you never can tell with a Nosferatu. One can see a human, and it might decide to make a pig of itself and go for more."

"We have a little time before they get here, don't we?" Lucien asked.

"A minute," Evee said. "They're already mooring."

In that moment, a crack of thunder sounded overhead. Since the night had been foggy, they'd had no warning of impending bad weather. Lucien and Evee immediately focused their attention on the sky.

"Smell it?" Lucien asked.

"Yeah, just the clove, though," Evee said, her voice trembling. Nothing good ever followed the scent of clove.

Evee looked out at the ferry. Pierre had already killed the motor and was headed for the back gate of the ferry.

"Don't let them out!" Evee shouted at Pierre. "Stay there. Stay!"

Pierre looked over at her, cocked his head as if unsure of what she'd said.

Evee ran halfway to the ferry and shouted again, "Don't let them out yet! Looks like we've got problems." She pointed up at the sky, in the same direction Lucien was focused.

Pierre frowned and nodded, his expression one of extreme worry.

Evee ran back to Lucien. "Where—"

"Oh, Christ on a cracker," Lucien said, pointing overhead and a bit to the left. "There."

Evee looked in the direction where Lucien pointed. She didn't see anything out of the ordinary, but suddenly smelled the rot of sulfur. Gagging, she covered her nose and mouth with a hand. "What the hell is that—"

Another crack of thunder, and in that moment, Lucien pulled his scabior out of its sheath.

That was when Evee saw it. A huge rift appeared seemingly out of nowhere. Its maw was blacker than any black Evee had ever seen. The sky could have been painted white for the contrast it created overhead. The rift couldn't have been more obvious. It seemed to slice through the stars and part of the moon, and from it dangled three monstrous Cartesians. One actually had a leg sticking out of the rift, as if it planned to jump from the gap.

With scabior in hand, Lucien gave a quick twist of his wrist, twirled the scabior between his fingers and took aim.

He blasted the Cartesian who had the leg out of the rift, sending it tumbling back with a high-pitched screech.

Then he took aim at the one next to it, a Cartesian with arms that seemed long enough to reach the ground from the rift it hung from.

"Go to the catacombs!" Lucien shouted at Evee.

"No way."

"Goddamn it, stop being so hardheaded and go!"

"No fucking way."

And with that Evee held her hands out, palms up, aiming for the sky.

"Double, thrice, by tens ye shall see.

No longer one to be seen by thee.

Thine eyes shall fully confuse thy mind.

Making all evil intentions blind.

Blunder thee, blunder now.

I call upon Poseidon, Tiamat and Apsu, bring strength to my command.

So it is said.

So shall it be."

Just like the first time Evee had used that incantation for Lucien and Ronan, this time, too, her words produced the same results. The Cartesians started swinging blindly in all directions. Their snorts of fury sounded like thunder blasts.

"I'm at three," Lucien shouted, still aiming at one of the Cartesians.

"Three what?" Evee asked, terrified by what hung overhead. She wanted to take the question back. She felt stupid for having asked it while Lucien was in the middle of fighting for their lives. Her life. The Originals' lives.

"Dimensions," Lucien said. "We push them back to the farthest dimension before the rift closes. The farther we send them, the longer it takes for them to make it back to our dimension."

"I'm at six," Lucien said. "Rift's closed."

He aimed at the second Cartesian, whose arms seemed to do nothing more than dangle from the rift, as if it were tired of aiming for ghosts. "Four on this one," Lucien said. "Rift's still open."

Evee watched in wonder as the brightest lightning bolts she'd ever witnessed shot from the scabior. She suddenly bumped into something and turned to see she had stumbled over the first step in front of St. John's Cathedral. She'd never noticed she'd been moving backward as Lucien fought the Cartesians.

"Five," Lucien said. "Rift closed." He took aim at the last Cartesian, got two good shots to the head before the rift closed.

"Evee?"

The sound of Lucien's voice broke through Evee's numbness. She looked over at him, slowly, as if nothing out of the ordinary had just happened.

Lucien shoved his scabior in his sheath, then put an arm around her shoulder. Looked deep into her eyes.

"You did it again," Lucien said quietly.

"What?"

"Saved my life with your incantation." He leaned down to kiss her, but Evee put a hand to his chest to hold him back.

"Not with the Nosferatu watching. They might not understand and view you as a threat."

"But—"

"No buts," Evee said. "Let's just call it even. You saved me from a Cartesian and from drowning. I confused a few so you could work your magic. I'd say we're about even, don't you think?"

"Not even close," Lucien said with a grin. "But I'll leave that discussion for another time. You've got Nosferatu to get back into the catacombs. I'll be behind the cathedral if you need me. Just yell."

"Oh, don't worry, I will. Seems like I've become quite vocal these days." With that, Evee turned away from Lucien and headed for the ferry.

Even with the task ahead so uncertain, she couldn't help smiling.

Vocal indeed.

Chapter 23

This time Lucien did as he was told and remained behind the cathedral until all the Nosferatu were settled into the catacombs. He leaned against the massive building, chewed on a blade of grass and pondered all that had happened in the past few hours.

Without question, this was one of the most unusual missions he'd ever been involved in. He tried keeping his mind from settling on two of the most frightening experiences he'd had to date. The first being Ronan's death, and the second discovering Evee and how she affected him.

If he was a philosophical man, it'd be easy to see a new life beginning as one ended. The beginning being Evee and the ending Ronan, of course. But a new life interpretation involving a Triad was questionable at best.

So much for being philosophical.

Keeping one ear tuned to the grumbling and shuffling of the Nosferatu as they made their way into the catacombs, he heard Evee's soothing, lolling voice encouraging them inside. The sound of it made Lucien's heart feel bigger, and he also felt guilt creeping in.

So far the only thing they'd expressed between each other had to do with sex. Although Evee was sexually beyond any man's dream, she had captured more of him than just an erection. But what he felt for her went way beyond sex. The sound of her voice enamored him, as did the different expressions on her face. Whether she wore no makeup and a haphazard ponytail or dressed for a ball, it didn't matter. Lucien thought her to be the most beautiful woman he'd ever laid eyes on.

As hard as he tried, he couldn't help thinking of Ronan, how he had been interested in Evee. Lucien had honestly wanted to give him the opportunity to try to win her over despite what he felt for her himself. But that chance was gone forever. This left Lucien with two choices. Run as far away from Evee as possible and try to forget her, just out of courtesy to Ronan, or pursue her, hoping to fill her heart the way she filled his.

If he chose the first option, it meant building a steel cage inside himself that she couldn't get through, then leave as soon as the mission was completed, or possibly change partners with Gavril. As far as he knew, nothing physical had happened between his cousin and Gilly, so switching shouldn't make a difference.

As logical a man as Lucien was, just the thought of switching Triad made his stomach roil. He had to stay true to himself, which meant being with her and some-how doing so while keeping it a secret from everyone else but Evee. He had to tell her how he felt so she would not start thinking that he only wanted her for sex.

Even if he did run and hide behind one mission or an-other, how did a person reverse love? It wasn't like he'd meant for it to turn out that way. It had simply happened,

Triad curse or not. And falling in love was like falling into a deep hole. You couldn't just fall out of love, like you couldn't fall out of a deep hole. You had to be pushed or pulled out, and Evee had done neither.

Lucien was in the middle of that thought when Evee appeared behind the cathedral. She gave him a soft smile.

"I think that instead of just having Viv call Gilly and let her know it's time for her Chenilles to go to the feeding ground, we go and meet with her and Gavril. That way if there are any problems with the Cartesians between the cemetery and the ferry, Gavril will have you for backup."

"Great idea," Lucien said.

Evee nodded. "Now that we have a dome over the ferry, the switchover at feeding time will be less stressful. But it doesn't change anything where the missing Originals are concerned. We have to really put our heads together and come up with a plan on how to find them. That's the only way we're going to be able to protect the humans in this city."

"Another good point," Lucien said.

Evee cocked her head to one side and grinned at him. "Are you always this easy, Mr. Hyland?"

Lucien started heading for the Louis I Cemetery and said in a stage whisper, "Far from it, Ms. François. Far, far from it."

By the time they reached Gilly and Gavril, the Chenilles were all gathered tightly together, piled up next to their mistress, who stood by the electric canopy at the front gate of the cemetery. The Chenilles wanted out, and now.

Judging from the frenzy on the Chenilles' faces, Lucien worried that once the cemetery gates opened, Gilly might be faced with a stampede. He hoped Gilly knew the same calming spells that Evee used on her Nosferatu.

No sooner had Lucien completed that thought than he saw Gilly hold out her hands, palm up, and begin to chant.

"Quiet thee, oh creatures mine.
Let these words soothe thy rage to wine.
Angst and boredom, fear and pain.
Lead thy mind to see now that 'tis all in vain.
So it is said.
So shall it be."

Lucien watched in amazement as the Chenilles that had been twitching, nipping, whining, shoving only seconds earlier now stood in an orderly line, knowing they were going to be fed.

Of all the Originals, the Chenilles could easily have passed for human, even in their natural state. Male and female alike stood between six feet five inches and seven feet tall. They all appeared to be around the same age, somewhere in their midtwenties. Some had beautiful long blond hair, some short and black—handsome men, exotic women. He supposed they used their beauty as bait to lure in a victim. If victims paid close attention, however, they'd be able to see the most telling sign on a Chenille. Its skin. It was more yellow than white, like each carried a different stage of liver failure. What the victims didn't know until it was too late was that a Chenille's incisors were long and threaded, like a screw, yet hollow in the center.

Once a Chenille latched on to bone, it drilled small holes through it to reach the marrow, and then used the same incisors to suck the marrow from the bone. Like sucking through a thick milk shake with a straw. Although they preferred the blood and meat to be neatly discarded, as they were used to in the North Compound, an overly hungry Chenille could certainly forgo that formality. It would use its incisors to rip through skin and flesh until it reached its prize. Bone. Lots of bone.

Just before Gilly opened the cemetery gates, she motioned to Gavril that it was time for him, Evee and Lucien to move out of sight.

Peering around the corner of the cathedral, Lucien was relieved to see the Chenilles following Gilly's orders to the letter. Gavril chose to follow behind the Chenille parade by at least two hundred feet. Lucien and Evee thought it best to watch over Gilly and Gavril, but do so by way of alleyways and around dark corners of buildings. The last thing Lucien wanted was to draw attention to himself. What if one of the witnesses who'd seen him and Ronan fighting the Nosferatu showed up and fingered him? It'd wind up being a circus show.

So, sticking to that plan, Lucien and Evee ducked and swerved through alleyways as they watched Gilly and Gavril make their way to the docks. With every step they took toward the docks, Lucien felt like it was one too many. He kept one eye on Gavril and kept watch over the sky.

It was eerily quiet when they arrived. Which made Lucien's and Evee's sneakers sound like hammers on concrete.

Gavril swiveled about on his heels. "Damn, cuz, give a guy a heads-up, will ya? Why are the two of you here, anyway?"

"Since the Nosferatu are put away," Lucien said, "and you and Gilly have the farthest to walk without protection over to the docks, we thought it might be a good idea to follow the two of you in case you needed backup."

Gavril pulled his long gingerbread-colored hair behind his head, reached into the front pocket of his jeans with his free hand and pulled out a rubber band, which he quickly wrapped around his hair. With that done, he moved his head from shoulder to shoulder, and Lucien heard vertebrae misalignments pop back into place.

"I appreciate your having our backs," Gavril said. He aimed his chin down Rampart toward a section of run-down shops. "Let's wait out there until Gilly has them off-loaded onto the ferry. Don't want them picking up our scents."

Now that they were at the docks, Lucien took Evee's hand and motioned for Gavril to follow them. He planned on positioning everyone along the side of the cathedral, just as he'd done earlier with Evee and the Nosferatu.

They watched as Gilly led the Chenilles onto the ferry, stepped in behind them, then closed the ferry's back gate. The look Gilly gave Gavril as she untied the ferry made Lucien wonder if there was more to their relationship than either was letting on.

Before the ferry took off, two men suddenly appeared out of the shadows and walked toward the ferry.

"What the hell?" Lucien said.

"Son of a bitch," Evee said. "That's Trey Cottle and Shandor Black, two of the sorcerers I told you about."

Now that the back gate of the ferry had been secured and the electric dome activated, Lucien all but jogged over to the men to see what they wanted. Evee was right at his heels and Gavril only two steps behind Evee.

As they drew even closer, Evee suddenly skidded to a stop. She signaled for Gilly to get the ferry moving as she confronted their unwanted company.

"What are you doing here?" Lucien asked.

"No," Evee said. "What the fuck are you two bastards doing here?" she demanded.

Lucien raised an eyebrow, quite impressed with Evee's

extensive, spur-of-the-moment vocabulary. "I'm assuming I'm having the pleasure of meeting Shandor Black and Trey Cottle?"

"Oh, yeah," Evee said. "I don't know about pleasure, but the short, fat, sweaty one is Cottle, and the one with the hooked nose and two-foot jowls is Black."

"Miss François," Trey Cottle said, "there is no reason for you to be so condescending, so harsh with your friends."

"You're no friends of mine," she retorted.

Almost as if she hadn't spoken, Cottle said, "Concerning us being here, our purpose is only to help."

"Yeah, I know how you're here to help. Shandor has already confronted me about it. What did he do? Go whining to you that I wouldn't let him anywhere near us?"

Trey harrumphed. "I knew before he did. I'm the one who sent him to you."

"So just tell me what the fuck it is you want with me," Evee said. Lucien placed a hand on the small of her back, which oddly enough calmed her considerably.

"We want to help," Trey said. "I think you're missing a very important element where the Originals are concerned. Why some of them have gone missing and those missing have already started to kill humans. Now you're having to take extra measures just to get your Originals from their holding areas to the ferry. I'm sure all of that is quite inconvenient."

Evee swiped a hand over her mouth. "Just what the hell do you think you can do that we haven't done? Are you standing here telling me that you have some special spell or potion that can make everything right again? That you can bring back every missing Original and return things to normal?"

Trey shrugged. "I don't know about back to normal.

You do have some Nosferatu who've died. That I can't undo." He turned slightly to face Lucien. "Death can have an odd effect on people. Some can move on as if nothing's changed in their lives. Others exist knowing their lives will never be the same."

Lucien felt fury raging in his head, thundering in his temples. He didn't know Trey Cottle from any other stranger who walked the street. But instinct told him that Cottle was a greasy weasel that they weren't to trust.

"We don't need you here," Lucien said. "We don't want you here. I don't know how word is getting about. I don't know who your sources are or who's been feeding you this ridiculous information. And even if you did have an info source, I'm certain you're not going to spill the beans on his or her identity."

"Au contraire," Cottle said. "I'd be happy to give you that information."

Evee's and Gavril's heads jerked back in surprise.

"Then who's contacted you and given you all this information about the Triad, about the Originals?" Lucien asked.

A long moment of silence passed between them.

"Just as I suspected," Evee said with a smirk. "You're not going to tell us shit. You're nothing but a lump of fat, sweaty clay that needs to be removed from here pronto."

Trey tapped a finger against his chin. "Now, owing to your inhospitableness, and your determination to go through this fiasco alone, I won't give you the whole picture. Just another piece of the puzzle. Let you figure it out for yourself. The source you are so anxious to know about is someone you know. Someone close to you." Cottle let out a nasally snort, his eyes darkening. "Chew on that for a while and see where it gets you."

Lucien fought hard to keep his hands balled into fists

at his side. What he wanted to do was pummel Sweat Head and give Hook Nose a nose job.

With an odd bow, Cottle signaled for Black to follow him, and they quickly disappeared into the shadows from which they had come.

"What was that all about?" Gilly asked. "How did they know to come here? How do they know we're in trouble?"

"I'm not sure," Evee said. "Shandor met up with me earlier, here near the docks, whining about the same thing. Wanting to help, wanting to help. Same song and dance Cottle just gave us. Shandor wouldn't tell me shit about who'd told him."

"We'll figure it out," Lucien said, his mind already whirring with ideas. He turned to Gavril. "Once Gilly has her Chenilles back in the cemetery, meet us at Evee's café. We've got a lot to talk about. We've got to figure out who the snitch is. Chances are they snitched because they had something to do with the chaos we're experiencing."

"And the missing Originals?" Evee asked. "They have to be our priority."

"Oh, they are," Lucien assured her. "And we *will* find a way to get the missing Originals back here as quickly as possible. Come hell or high water, we'll make it happen."

Chapter 24

Somehow Gilly had managed to take the Chenilles to be fed and returned to the cemetery without any Cartesian incidents, which made Lucien and Gavril a bit nervous.

"We can always be grateful for small things," Evee said.

"Yes," Lucien said. "But things have been ramping up too quickly for the Cartesians to let that opportunity slide by."

They had all gathered at Evee's café—Evee, Lucien, Gavril, Gilly, Nikoli and Viv. As they relaxed in chairs, Evee had told everyone to make themselves at home with food and drink.

Nikoli and Gavril slammed down two ham sandwiches each, along with a Coke, while Viv and Gilly ate from a fresh fruit bowl they'd found in Evee's industrial-size fridge.

When everyone sat in the dining area again, Lucien

said, "I have an idea. I don't know if it's going to work, but it might be worth a try."

"What is it?" Evee asked, edging her chair closer to his so as not to miss a word.

Lucien frowned as if considering his words carefully before he allowed them out of his mouth. "Instead of us running all over the city, we've got to remember that some of the Originals have moved outside the city proper to places like Chalmette. The last thing we want is for them to head off to other states."

"We already know that," Gilly said. "So what's your idea?"

"Are we okay, being here in your café?" Lucien asked Evee. "Are you expecting anyone to come in early to open and get things ready for your morning business?"

"Not for a few hours," she said. "I called Margaret, my manager, and told her I'd be running late today. She normally doesn't get here until six a.m."

Lucien checked his watch. "That gives us three hours. We'll keep the lights off in here just in case someone walks by and assumes you've opened early."

"And we're doing this why?" Evee asked.

"Here is safe from the Cartesians and the Originals. Here is where we might have a chance for you to channel Chank, the Nosferatu you lost when Pierre had to take him out."

"I see where you're going with this," Evee said. "Since I knew Chank well, and we know for sure he's dead, I can get a clearer picture of him in my mind's eye, address him directly and hopefully get some answers about the missing Originals. Maybe he can see something from the other side that we can't here."

"Exactly," Lucien said.

"Many of my Nosferatu are missing, but I might have

a better chance of reaching Chank because I know he's dead and I knew him like a mother knows a child. I just might be able to connect."

"Great," Gilly said. "What do we have to do?"

Evee started pulling chairs and tables to the corners of the room. When the others caught on to what she was doing, they quickly lent a hand.

When the center of the dining area was vacant, Evee said, "Everybody sit on the floor, please, in a circle."

Lucien, Nikoli, Gilly, Gavril, and Viv complied without hesitation. Everyone sat cross-legged.

With everyone seated, Evee said, "Now put your hand on the knee of the person sitting beside you. For example, since Lucien is sitting to my right, I'll put my right hand on his left knee. Gilly's sitting on my left, so I'll put my left hand on her right knee. Like this…" Evee demonstrated what she'd tried to explain.

Everybody did as they were told. Not one funny quirk from anyone about how weird this seemed, which was usually a relief valve for someone feeling awkward in the moment. Instead, everyone kept their eyes on Evee, their expression absolutely serious.

Evee should have been the one cracking jokes because she felt nervous as hell. The last time she'd tried to channel hadn't worked out so well. But now she hoped Chank, whom she knew from cauliflower ear to cauliflower ear, might just be able to come through.

"Everyone please close your eyes and concentrate," Evee instructed.

They all closed their eyes tightly.

Evee began to rock her body slightly from side to side. "Chank, oh Nosferatu of mine, I call upon you to come to me. Without harm or foul, use my body so that we might learn from you. So that we might see through your eyes, hear with your ears, and find the Originals who've left this place. Be our guide, not our distraction, and keep all who'd mean us harm to remain beyond the veil. It is only you I invite to use my body. Heed my words."

She continued to call for him, focusing on his face, his body in her mind's eye. She felt the grip on both of her knees tighten.

"Tell me, Chank, what you see, what you know from the other side. Certainly you see more than we see here."

"…big head."

Evee heard the voice, but as always it seemed to be coming from some distance away and belonging to someone else. In this case that someone else sounded no older than seven or eight years old.

Evee felt herself falling deeper into a trance.

"Big head…big house," the childlike voice said. "Not house, but like house. High, almost to the sky."

"Are the missing Originals there?" Evee heard Gilly ask.

"Yeah, but they can't leave. If they leave, they get dead."

Gavril asked, "Where is this big building? Is it close or is it far?"

"Far away. Yep, far away."

"Do you know the name of the building?" Lucien asked.

"Big building. Big head. Big body. They try to leave. But if they leave they get dead."

"We've heard that some Originals have left the city," Gavril said. "Are there more who've left here?"

"Yep, left city. Call back. All back or they dead. They don't stay still in big house, in big building. They fight the big man but him is stronger. Him is their boss. Him won't let them go. Him wants them to die."

Evee felt a cold sensation run down her throat, like cold milk sliding down her gullet. She opened her eyes, knowing the connection was gone.

"Well?" Evee asked.

"He showed up through you all right, but I couldn't understand a goddamn thing he said," Gavril said.

"He didn't give us direct answers. Not like we would have liked them to be. But maybe he's given us enough to give us clues."

"What did he say?" Evee asked.

"Something about a big head and a big house," Nikoli said. "From what he said, it sounded like they were trapped in this house because he said a big man was their leader, and he didn't want them to leave. He wanted them to die."

"It was like trying to communicate with a child," Viv said. "It was hard to understand him. To make sense out of anything he said." She repeated nearly verbatim all that had come through Evee from Chank.

Evee dropped her head in her hands. "What the hell? I can't make any more sense out of that than any of you. A big house and big head... I have no damn clue as to what that means." She grew so frustrated she pounded a fist on the floor. "Damn it. Even when our spells work, they don't. Chank didn't give us any information that we can work with here."

"Wait a sec," Lucien said. "He did give us one clue. He said there was one big man, and that man was their leader and refused to let them go."

"So there is one person responsible for all this..." Evee said thoughtfully. "I wonder if he's human, a sorcerer or netherworld."

"I should have asked," Gilly said. "My bad."

"We can always try channeling him again later," Evee said.

"Why not now?" Lucien asked.

"Because it takes a lot of energy for them to come through that veil and speak through me. We have to give them time to build up energy so we can call them back."

"How much time?" Gavril asked.

"At least four to five hours."

"Damn."

"Yeah."

"But I'll tell you this much," Evee said. "Whatever time it takes and whoever this 'him' is, he may not be as big as Chank claims he is. But I swear on every living soul I know I will punch that son of a bitch in the face so hard he'll be sniffing his ass for the rest of his life."

Chapter 25

After everyone, including Lucien, left the café, Evee wasn't quite sure what to do with herself. She could have spent some time readying the café for its morning business, but Margaret would be in soon enough to take care of that for her. Besides, she didn't want to be in the café, not right now anyway. She had to check one more time.

Evee went back to the cathedral to make certain her Nosferatu were still tucked away safely in the catacombs.

When she finally arrived at St. John's and sneaked into the crypts, she saw all was well. Most of her Nosferatu were sleeping, some on top of crypts, others inside grave shelves, along with the bones of some former priests, bishops or deacons.

After seeing her brood was collected and sound, Evee felt better and headed back to the café to complete her duties.

Once there she made certain the appropriate amount of

cash was in the register to provide change for early morning customers. Then she went into the kitchen area of the café to make sure they had all the ingredients needed for the day's morning and noon rush.

As Evee ticked off eggs, bacon, rice, sausage, tasso and biscuit mix from her mental list, Lucien kept weaving in and out of her thoughts. She'd never seen him that way before. Quiet, seemingly actionless. Like a man unsure of what to feel. Not that she blamed him. Had she been faced with the same situations they'd gone through in one day, she'd probably have crawled into a hole and walled off the rest of the world.

Still, she had been surprised when Lucien, who appeared so absolutely empty, had simply walked away when they were done with the channeling session. Pride had kept her from calling out to him.

As Evee worked to finish off her to-do list at the café, she recalled how Ronan had died. The scene kept playing over and over in her head. The long, crooked claws of the Cartesian jammed into Ronan's head. How he hadn't so much as whimpered when the Cartesian took him.

Ronan had saved her life, and now she had no way of repaying him for his kindness, his heroism, his sacrifice. Evee knew she'd carry the nightmare of Ronan's death until her own came to claim her. She'd also remember the last words she'd said to Lucien. How they couldn't be together anymore. Although she'd said it for his own safety and the safety of the other Benders and the Triad, her heart nearly collapsed in on itself. She never wanted to be without Lucien, but Ronan's death had caused her to think way past what she wanted.

There was no denying that karma meant to kick her ass, using everyone she cared about and loved. It was then she'd come to the heartbreaking conclusion that her sexual liaisons with Lucien had to stop. If adding one horror to another was how the universe planned on breaking her down, it had succeeded.

It was nearly 6:00 a.m. when Evee finished her chores in the café. Before heading home, she called Margaret, the café's hostess and general manager, to let her know she wouldn't be getting back to the café until much later. She told Margaret that all the supplies for today's meals had been accounted for, which meant Margaret wouldn't be starting her day at ground zero.

Once Margaret agreed to hold down the fort until Evee returned, she locked up the café and headed home.

By the time Evee made it home, she was so exhausted that she all she wanted to do was collapse in her bed. Which she did, telling herself she'd shower whenever she woke.

No sooner had her head hit the pillow than she felt sleep capture her. It refused to remain a constant, however.

She kept seeing visions of Ronan being slaughtered by the Cartesian, the sadness that radiated from Lucien as he witnessed his cousin's death, the heartache of loss swelling up from Nikoli and Gavril. With so many horrid memories rolling across her mind, piercing into her dreams, she found herself jolting awake every thirty minutes or so.

Evee finally gave up on any form of deep sleep around noon. She got out of bed, feeling more fatigued than she had when she'd gotten into bed.

After showering and taking care of her other bathroom duties, Evee went down to the kitchen for something to eat. Evidently, Viv and Gilly had already left, either to check on their businesses or brood, because they were nowhere to be found in the house.

Oddly enough, Hoot wasn't home, either. He always did a flyby when Evee was preparing something to eat. She assumed he was out on one of his recon missions.

After making herself a grilled cheese sandwich, she ate it while standing near the stove. The house was quiet. Too quiet. The silence made her mind go abuzz with all that had happened over the last twenty-four hours.

The last thing Evee needed was to sulk around the house, reliving the nightmares that had stolen her sleep.

Having washed her grilled cheese sandwich down with a bottle of water, Eve left the house and went to a trolley stop about a block away.

The trolley jerked and shimmied as it stopped to pick up passengers or let some off along its ancient tracks. When it finally reached Canal, Evee signaled for a stop.

Exiting the trolley, she walked the seven or eight blocks to St. John's Cathedral. She wanted to check in on her Nosferatu once more before heading to the café and relieving Margaret.

She and Pierre had discussed how antsy the Nosferatu had been when they were off-loaded from the ferry. Fortunately, they'd been able to keep them under control. Antsy was never good when it came to a Nosferatu. One could never tell what it'd do next.

Inside the cathedral, Evee made her way to the side door that led to the catacombs. The door to the catacombs always stayed locked, which kept parishioners from snooping inside. Fortunately, the one small spell she used to open the lock on that door never seemed to fail.

Evee felt she might be getting a little OCD over her Originals. She'd checked on them only a few hours ago, and the majority of them had been asleep, which was usual for them after a feeding. They didn't start waking and grumbling until nightfall.

But worry was worry, and it would only be appeased when she laid eyes on her brood.

When Evee finally reached the catacombs, the first thing she noticed was the absolute darkness in the cavernous space. She froze when she walked into the dank, cool space below the church. The electric dome that had once lit up the catacombs like it held a thousand flashlights no longer existed.

The darkness was so complete she could barely see her hand in front of her face. Fortunately, she remembered that at the entrance to the catacombs, on a small table to the left of the door, stood two MagLite lights. These were used by the groundskeeper and by priests laying one of their own to rest.

Evee walked back a few steps, collected a MagLite from the table, then made her way back into the underground cemetery.

Her hands shook as she turned on the flashlight. And for good reason. Except for the decaying crypts and the wrapped corpses lying on burial shelves, the catacombs were empty.

She walked deeper into the belly of the catacombs, all the while calling out for Pierre and her other Originals. Her come-hither call was a high-pitched whistle that ended in a screech, much like the sounds Hoot made when he sensed danger. Her calls echoed back in the cavernous space until they overlapped.

No one appeared. No response to her calls. Not even from Pierre.

When Evee called out again and received no reply, her hands shook so badly that the light bounced around the catacombs in nonsensical patterns, turning it into a macabre funhouse.

Still seeing nothing of her Originals, Evee ran out

of the catacombs, out of the church and down Chartres Street. She felt tears burn her eyes and slide down her cheeks as she ran faster, as fast as her feet would allow. She had to reach her sisters to let them know.

Just as she turned a corner, heading for Snaps and Gilly, she ran into someone... She was so blind with worry she pushed away from him and was about to take off again when he grabbed her arm.

She looked down at the hand grasping her arm, then up at the face it belonged to. Lucien.

"What's wrong?" he asked, evidently seeing her tears, her wild eyes.

Evee didn't give a second thought about throwing her arms around him and sobbing.

Lucien held her tight. "Tell me," he said. "What is it? What has you so upset?"

"They're all gone," Evee wailed.

"Who's gone?"

"All of my Nosferatu! I just left the catacombs. It's empty. I don't know what happened. I went a few hours ago to check on them, and all was fine. Most of them asleep."

"There's no one down there?" Lucien asked. "Not even Pierre?"

She shook her head frantically. "No one. Not one Nosferatu. Nothing."

Without saying a word, Lucien grabbed Evee's hand and led her back toward the catacombs.

When they made their way inside, the only thing illuminated was the MagLite light that Evee had dropped when she ran from the catacombs. It lay on the ground, still burning brightly.

Lucien picked up the flashlight and walked through the catacombs, shaking his head. "I can't believe the electric dome is completely out. Do you have any idea where the Nosferatu might have gone?"

"N-no," Evee whimpered. "I haven't a clue. I called and called for them, but not one responded."

"Aside from the special call you give when you summon them, do you have any other way of contacting them?"

Evee sniffled, thinking hard, but her brain felt like it had clicked a pause button. She couldn't think of anything besides the fact that her entire brood was missing.

Suddenly, a thought hit Evee. "If any are dead, I might be able to channel one or more, like I did Chank earlier. See if they know anything."

"You feel comfortable channeling with only me here with you?" Lucien asked.

Evee sniffled again. "Of course. Channeling is no big secret society game. It's more like I open myself up to them so they can talk through me."

"Then let's try it," Lucien said.

"It's not as easy as that," Evee said. "I have to have a picture of the deceased in my mind's eye."

"Start somewhere, like maybe Pierre. He was responsible for watching over the Nosferatu when you weren't around, right?"

"Yes."

"Then logically, if Pierre was in charge of that group and now all of them are gone, chances are someone or something took him out."

"I can start there, but if he isn't dead, I don't know that I'll be able to find out anything. I can't attempt to summon every Nosferatu that's died. It would take forever."

"Understandable. But let's try Pierre. What can it hurt? If you can't summon him that way, it probably means he's still alive, which is a good thing."

Lucien held the flashlight so its beam pointed at Evee's feet. "It's at least worth a try."

Evee nodded, then quickly lowered herself to the concrete floor. She sat cross-legged and placed her palms up on her knees and closed her eyes. She tried visualizing Pierre, in human form and in his natural state.

Once her mind's eye was filled with the image of Pierre, Evee began to call for him.

"Pierre, oh leader of mine, I call upon you to come to me. Without harm or foul, use my body so that we might learn from you. So that we might see through your eyes, hear with your ears, and find the Originals who've left this place."

Suddenly, Evee felt a shiver run through her, always an indication that somebody or something wanted to come through and reside within her, if only for a moment.

She let her mind go blank, then felt her mouth drop open.

Evee heard a male voice from somewhere that seemed far way.

"They are all lost and near death," the voice said. "You stupid, archaic bitch. You and your spells are worthless. Completely asinine. Soon there will be no Originals for you to watch over. Very soon!"

Evee didn't recognize the voice and couldn't tell where it was coming from. It confused her, made her body shiver. She opened her eyes and looked over at Lucien. The expression on his face was nothing short of shock.

"I heard a voice," Evee said, "but it didn't sound like it was coming through me."

"Oh, it came through you all right, but I don't think it was Pierre."

"Who, then?"

"Possibly a Cartesian. Called you a stupid archaic bitch, and said your Nosferatu would soon all be dead."

Evee unfurled her legs, then pulled her knees up to her chest. She put her forehead against her knees and began sobbing uncontrollably.

Lucien leaned over and gathered Evee up into his arms.

She clung tightly to his neck, still sobbing.

Lucien rocked her gently in his arms. "Shh. I'm here. We'll find them. I promise to stay at your side. Now that all of your Nosfertu are missing, we have to prepare for a great war. We'll find them and bring them home."

"But don't you see?" Evee said between sobs. "This is my fault. It's my fault they're missing."

Lucien took hold of Evee's chin and turned her so she faced him. His emerald eyes were fierce, piercing.

"For the last time, none of this is your fault, Evette François. The fault lies in the leader of the Cartesians. It has an agenda and will do whatever it has to do to accomplish it."

She looked down for a moment, slightly embarrassed.

Lucien lifted her chin once more, made sure Evee was looking directly into his eyes.

"And one other thing," Lucien said, his eyes softening. "In case you haven't noticed… I'm falling in love with you, Evette François, whether you like it or not. Despite the missing Nosferatu, Cartesian deaths and the curse that haunts you, I will always be by your side."

He pressed her head to his chest and whispered, "Evee."

Evee felt herself go limp in his arms and with her face pressed against his shoulder, she whispered with great trepidation, "And I love you, Lucien Hyland. Come hell or be damned, I do." She hoped her whisper had been too low for him to hear, but judging by how tightly he held her, how he kissed her forehead, her lips, he'd heard.

And in that moment, Evee knew in her heart of hearts that with Lucien by her side, they'd win this war, despite the odds.

Evee had no idea about the how, when and where of it all. She simply knew they'd win. Lucien gave her strength.

She was a Triad, not a wimp. She had generations of powerful witches flowing through her blood. It was time to buck up and take control over what was hers. No more Miss Wimpy, which meant no more tears. The Triad was at war, and she concentrated on drawing the strength from her ancestors and from Lucien. The Benders were already warriors of great magnitude, not afraid to stare death in the eye. Ronan had proved that.

Now, Lucien deserved a partner just as strong, just as fierce and determined as he was. They'd set the Triad's world back on its axis and annihilate the enemy. Not only the Cartesians, but their goddamn leader.

Cut the head off the dog and the rest of the animal dies. Evee planted that goal deep in her heart, held tightly to Lucien. She and this man would find and destroy the enemy who'd taken so much from them. And with its death, she'd take Lucien as her own. Curse or no curse. There was no more to take from her, except Lucien, and she would fight at his side and protect him with her life.

She meant to spend the rest of her life with this man. If the curse stood true, Evee would lose all her powers.

So be it.

Better to lose every power she'd ever known than lose the one man who treasured her and made her feel whole.

* * * * *